# REBELLION

ALSO BY STEPHANIE DIAZ

*Extraction*

# REBELLION

## STEPHANIE DIAZ

St. Martin's Griffin
New York

REBELLION. Copyright © 2015 by Stephanie Diaz. All rights reserved. Printed in the United States of America. For information, address St. Martin's Press, 175 Fifth Avenue, New York, N.Y. 10010.

www.stmartins.com

Library of Congress Cataloging-in-Publication Data

Diaz, Stephanie, 1992–
    Rebellion / Stephanie Diaz.—First edition.
        pages cm
    ISBN 978-1-250-04125-8 (hardcover)
    ISBN 978-1-4668-3736-2 (e-book)
    1. Science Fiction.    2. Survival.—Fiction.    3. Love—Fiction.
4. Youths' writings.    I. Title.
    PZ7.D5453Reb 2015
    [Fic]—dc23

                                                            2014034014

St. Martin's Griffin books may be purchased for educational, business, or promotional use. For information on bulk purchases, please contact the Macmillan Corporate and Premium Sales Department at 1-800-221-7945, extension 5442, or write to specialmarkets@macmillan.com.

First Edition: February 2015

10  9  8  7  6  5  4  3  2  1

*For Mom and Dad,*

*for not kicking me out of the house yet*

# REBELLION

# 1

When I close my eyes, I see the explosion.

Fire consumes the acid generator on the moon, like a sun swallowing it whole. The escape pod that carried the bomb to the generator tower rips into a billion pieces. The burning bits of metal get sucked out into the vacuum of space.

Oliver dies.

The explosion happens over and over, like a CorpoBot broadcast on repeat. Every time, I try to stop it. I bang my fists on the window of the escape pod, begging Oliver to let me take his place.

He refuses to listen. He grabs the flight levers and turns the pod in the direction of the moon's surface.

I scramble back to the main cockpit and turn the spaceship around as the bomb timer ticks down to zero. I try to save him.

But I am always too late.

✳

I wake drenched in sweat in the darkness, choking back tears.

It takes me several moments to remember I am not on the spaceship anymore. I'm in a bed in a secret military base, buried deep in the mountains on the Surface. Beechy brought me here to join the others who were part of his undercover rebellion in the Core, after he and I escaped the explosion and returned from the moon without Oliver.

The only light in the room comes from the pale glow of the space heater above the door. It shows me the outline of the bunk bed across from mine, the storage lockers built into the wall, and the safety suits hanging on hooks in case the deadly acid in the world outside seeps into the KIMO facility. In case our safety is compromised.

I've woken up in this room almost every morning for the past seven days, but every day I still wake thinking I am somewhere else. On the spaceship with Oliver, in a cold prison cell, in a death simulation in the Core. Lost in one of my nightmares.

It doesn't help that Logan sleeps in a different room. We were apart all those days I was in the Core, after I was picked for Extraction and had to leave him behind on the Surface. But I never really got used to sleeping without him. I still miss the warmth of his body near mine, the comfort of his strong arms bracing me against the world outside.

As it is, I have to handle the night terrors on my own. I untangle myself from my bedsheets and take in a slow, deep breath through my nose, counting to five, then exhale at the same rate. My muscles are tight, but the tension should ease if I keep breathing like this.

Oliver's death is not your fault, I remind myself.

Commander Charlie put the bomb on that ship and forced Oliver to guard it. He took down the protective shield surrounding Kiel's atmosphere, letting the deadly acid seep in, forcing us to fly to the moon to destroy the generator. He didn't care how many innocent lives were lost that day, so long as he got what he wanted.

*Oliver's death is not your fault.*

I try to believe it.

Wiping my watery eyes, I shove away my covers and slide off my top bunk. My bare feet thump as they hit the floor.

The bunk below mine is empty, thank the stars. My roommate, Skylar, caught me thrashing in my sleep during a nightmare I had two days ago. She didn't say anything about it after I assured her I was all right, but I couldn't stand the way she looked at me afterwards. Like I was a krail with a broken wing or something.

The other two bunks in our small, cramped sleeping quarters are also empty. The twins who are a few years older than me, Fiona and Paley, are probably busy in the flight port, refueling pods or refurbishing the old jets Beechy and the other rebel leaders found when they discovered the base.

They'd happened upon the compound on a mission to the Surface a little over a year ago. The facility proved useful when two of their friends needed somewhere to hide to escape imprisonment. When the rest of us showed up a week ago, after the Core rebels made their first real strike against Commander Charlie, there was still work to be done to make the base fully operational. The security systems were up and running, but many of the other systems needed repair.

According to the computer logs, the base was out of use for nearly three centuries before the Core rebels made it their headquarters. The last inhabitants were members of KIMO—Kiel's Intelligence Military Operative—the special military corps that led the war strikes against the humanoids on the distant planet, Marden, when our leaders sought to reclaim the home Kiel's people originated from. KIMO abandoned the facility, fleeing underground along with the rest of the Surface population, after Marden's army placed a weapon on our moon powerful enough to pump acid into our sky and poison our cities. But the KIMO members left behind military equipment and nonperishable food in their old base, perhaps meaning to return.

Thus far, we've had no sighting of Core ships anywhere nearby. But that doesn't mean Commander Charlie and the other four Developers—the scientists who rule Kiel—don't know this place exists. All it means is they haven't realized we found it, or they're preoccupied with bigger things. Maybe Charlie is holed up in the Core, uncertain whether his plan to reignite the war with Marden is such a good idea after all. But I don't believe we could be so lucky. He has probably already begun construction on a new bomb, or a stronger tool that will succeed in launching his Core battleship into space, abandoning the rest of us to die. Likely, he believes those of us who know what he's doing and oppose him are too disorganized to threaten him any longer.

But he is wrong.

I switch on the ceiling light and grab my clothes from my locker: a crumpled tank top, a jacket, and a pair of old gray army pants.

After I strip off my sweaty nightshirt, I pull on the clothes. I hate this outfit—the gray pants, especially. They remind me of the suit Lieutenant Sam used to wear, when he wasn't dressed in his uniform to impress Commander Charlie. They remind me of him slamming me into a wall and trapping me with his hands all over me in a Core elevator.

*His lips molding against mine, his tongue in my mouth.*

I slam my locker shut, shoving down the memory. I will not think of Sam. He is far away, and I won't let him scare me any longer.

Someone raps twice on my door.

I check the small mirror beside my locker, hoping I don't look like I've been crying. My cheeks are slightly flushed, but there's nothing I can do about that.

"Come in," I say.

The door opens, and Logan walks in. The sight of him sends a flood of warmth and relief into my body.

His hair is slick and wet from the showers. His pants hang a bit low on his waist, made for someone who wasn't starving in a work camp a little over a week ago. He's been showering every day, but there are still remnants of field grime on his face and under his fingernails.

"Good, you're awake," he says with a smile. "You ready? Skylar wants to take us out for a flight drill in a couple minutes. We should hurry and get breakfast."

For the past few days, my roommate has been training us and a couple other newbies how to fly. Everyone part of the Alliance is supposed to have experience in both ground and flight combat. We're preparing not only for the possibility of enemy ships finding our headquarters, but also for the attack we plan to launch against the Core as soon as we know what's happening out there—as soon as the scouts we sent outside the compound return with news.

"Almost ready," I say, closing the door behind us. I'm glad Skylar's taking us out for a flight drill. I could use the distraction. "Did you just wake up?"

"No, about an hour ago. Went in the training room for a while. I thought you were going to meet me there."

"Sorry, I slept later than usual." I grab my boots from the floor and sit on Skylar's bunk to pull them on. There's a dull pounding in my temple, an undercurrent that remains of the panic I woke up with. But Logan's presence soothes me.

"You missed me hitting all the targets with those old blasters we found in the storage room," he says, leaning against the bunk post.

"Oh, really?"

He mimes firing a gun in the air. "Hit the bull's eye, four in twenty."

I snort. "That's terrible."

"True. But I hit the target almost every time, so I'm getting better. I might actually have a chance of hitting an official when we infiltrate the Core."

An image flashes through my head of Logan in the Core under attack, facing men who've been turned into mindless soldiers by their monthly injections. I picture them firing at him again and again until he falls limp with blood spilling from his chest.

A knot of panic twists in my stomach. I can't lose him; I won't let that happen. I'll make sure he isn't on the front lines when we start the invasion. I'll make sure he is safe, no matter what.

"You all right?" Logan asks. A crease of concern forms between his eyes. The bluish glow of the wall heater brings out the color in their stormy gray.

"I'm fine," I say.

I haven't told him about my recurring nightmares. He doesn't need to know I've been waking up in terror, afraid I haven't escaped the danger yet. I don't want him to worry any more than he already does.

I finish knotting the laces of my boots and push off the bed.

Logan shifts toward me, reaching for the small of my back. I slide my arms into their familiar hold around his waist, pulling him close until I can feel all of him against me. The hard outline of his hip bones; the warmth of his skin through his shirt.

He is comfort and quiet and everything I need. I'd give anything for the world outside to pause and let us be happy here, instead of dragging us apart again.

"You're safe here," Logan says softly. "You know that, right? You're safe with me."

I want to believe him. I want him to be right.

But every time I've been sure I was out of danger, I was wrong. I thought I'd won freedom when the Developers picked me for Extraction, but they only wanted to control me. They picked me for my intelligence, but they wanted to turn me into a soldier who would kill for them without question. And they would've succeeded if I hadn't been allergic to their serum that turns strong citizens into mindless bots—if I hadn't found the will to fight.

If I'm lucky, Commander Charlie thinks I died in the explosion. Once he finds out I'm alive, he will want to punish me for how I screwed up his plans. He will make me watch as he destroys everyone I care about—Logan and the rebels in the compound and the thousands of innocents in the work camps—to save his precious, elite followers in the Core.

I don't know if I can kill him before he succeeds. But I have to try.

"Forget everything else," Logan says. "You don't have to worry right now."

He pulls away a little, moving his hand to caress my cheekbone. His thumb trails in a slow line along the curve of my jaw, drawing close to the tender spot where Charlie slammed a gun into my face a week ago. The scar hurts like vrux every time I accidentally bump it.

Leaning in, Logan brushes his lips against the sore spot. I brace myself to flinch away, but the pain doesn't come. There's only a light flutter of nerves in my stomach.

Logan's hands trail back to my waist, drawing me closer. "I won't let anyone hurt you again," he whispers against my skin. "I promise."

He presses his mouth to mine, and I believe him.

# 2

The mess hall is crowded when we arrive. Men and women wearing faded army clothing sit at the round tables with their breakfast trays, some of them playing cards or dice, laughing as they eat, as if this life is normal to them.

I didn't know what to expect when Beechy told me about this place, when he said the base housed a group of people who'd been working undercover to overthrow the Developers and liberate the work camps. I had no idea the operation was so complex. But I didn't know a lot of things until a few days ago.

"Clementine, over here!" My roommate, Skylar, waves at me from a table by the wall. She has two open seats beside her.

"I'll grab you a tray," Logan says, dropping my hand.

"Thanks," I say.

As he heads for the counter at the back of the room, I slip between the tables, avoiding people who are trying to scoot their chairs out or stand up. But I bump into a woman on accident, nearly knocking her tray over.

"Sorry," I mumble.

She gives me a small smile, edging out of my way. I can't help staring at her. Her face and arms and neck are covered with more bruises than I've seen on anyone, all of them horrible shades of purple. Like she was cut up with knives or stuck with too many needles.

I've seen another woman with scars like these. She was strung up inside a glass cage when I arrived in the Core after I was picked for Extraction, and Commander Charlie made me shoot her to prove I would do anything to stay alive. He was disappointed when my shot didn't kill her and someone had to finish the job for me.

Quickly averting my eyes, I hurry past the woman. There's only one place she could've gotten those bruises: Karum. The prison on a cliff above the sea, where Charlie and the other Developers send those they can't control with their monthly injections. They study them and do everything in their power to break them, and mostly they succeed.

I try to avoid the others who came from there. I know it's stupid. I was one of them; I was Unstable too. But whenever their eyes catch mine, I see the cell bars reflected in them. I see the doctors leaning over me, and the needles that left marks on my arms.

I see bodies in the sea.

The memories cause my hands to tremble, my throat to clog up, and my chest to feel like it's about to explode. If I told Logan or Beechy I keep having panic attacks and nightmares, they'd probably tell me to go to the sick bay and have the nurses give me something to help me feel better. Maybe medicine could make all of it go away.

But I don't trust injections or pills, not even here. What I need more than anything is a distraction. I need to *do* something. It's taking too long for us to gather the information we need to form a suitable attack plan.

"You all right?" Skylar asks when I reach her. My expression must not be as composed as I thought it was.

"I'm great," I say, dropping into the seat beside her.

Her eyebrow raises slightly, but she shrugs. "Shiny," she says, snatching up the set of dice on her tray. Today her shoulder-length blond hair is twisted into a bun at the nape of her neck. Her pilot helmet sits on the table beside her tray. She carries it with her everywhere, so she'll always be ready to fly.

"Take your roll," the male pilot across the table says. I recognize him as one of the men who broke me and the other Unstables out of Karum prison.

"What, Buck, are you so eager to lose?" Skylar smirks, tossing her dice on the table. She rolls double sixes. With a hoot of excitement, she throws her hands in the air. The pilots at the table next to ours glance over, some of them laughing, others shaking their heads.

Buck groans and throws the rest of his rusty nails into the pot. "I swear, you're the vruxing luckiest winger I've ever laid eyes on."

"The *smartest*, Buck." Skylar scoops up the pot and moves it to her side of the table. She nudges my elbow. "I'm also the youngest person ever to make head pilot. Started flight training when I was ten and got promoted at fourteen."

Buck rolls his eyes and takes a swig of his drink. "Started bragging the day she was born."

"Oh, shut up." Skylar throws a die at Buck, and he fumbles to catch it. "You've done your share of bragging too, Mr. No-One-Can-Fly-the-Pipeline-as-Fast-as-I-Can."

"They sure as moonshine can't." Buck curls the edges of his thick mustache. Skylar laughs.

Chewing my lip, I snatch up the other die from her tray and turn it over in my fingers. I want to challenge Skylar, but I need more practice against easier opponents first. She's won every single game I've seen her play. She might be one of the youngest people in the Alliance, but she's certainly not the least experienced when it comes to gambling games or piloting ships.

"When did you two join the Alliance?" I ask.

Beechy told me he and his wife, Sandy—Commander Charlie's only daughter—founded the Alliance a little over a year ago, with a few of their closest friends. It took months and months for the insurrection group to grow to the size it is today. Now they have about two hundred people working to overthrow the Developers. Most of them aren't here; they are still undercover in the Surface settlement or in the lower sectors.

"Sandy recruited me about two months ago," Buck says.

"I joined a couple weeks ago, after Commander Charlie made his announcement," Skylar says. "If Beechy or Buck here had trusted me more, I would've joined a hell of a lot sooner." She snorts, but a subtle hardness seeps into her expression.

"Yeah, I know how you feel," I say, setting the dice back on the table.

Beechy didn't use to trust me either. He was my friend in the Core, but he didn't confide in me about his plan for an uprising until after he rescued me from Karum. Until I'd already been captured.

Instead of being part of something, I thought I was alone. I thought everyone in the Core was a mindless soldier and I had to stop Charlie with absolutely no help.

Logan takes the seat beside me and hands me a food tray. Today's breakfast offering: yellow hash beans and dried shir bread.

"Thanks," I say.

"Sorry, they were all out of the stew," Logan says, unscrewing his water canteen.

Bansa stew is my favorite. But all the food we've had in the compound has been better than the food I used to eat in the Surface work camp, so I'm not about to complain.

"This looks good too." I spoon a bite of hash beans into my mouth. There are hardly any in my bowl, but at least they're sweet and aren't too watery.

We've been rationing the nonperishable food from the storage rooms, since there are thirty-five of us to feed. We don't know how long we'll be holed up in here, nor when we'll be able to find fresh food. There used to be herds of animals roaming the snowy mountains outside, but it seems many perished when the deadly acid seeped into Kiel's atmosphere. Even though the protective shield was down for only an hour, the acid had plenty of time to contaminate the air and everything on the Surface that wasn't indoors. Even vegetation in the ground probably isn't safe to eat.

Beside me, Skylar stands up and dumps the remaining contents of her tray in the trash receptacle. Taking her seat again, she pulls a rag out of her pocket, spits on it, and rubs her helmet to make it shiny. "So, you two ready to fly today?" she asks.

"Definitely," Logan says through a mouthful of bread. He swallows before he continues, "Are we going out in the tunnels again?"

"We are, presuming Beechy gives us the go-ahead."

"Have you seen him today yet?" I ask before taking a sip from my water canteen.

"He's been in the command center all morning, keeping an eye out for the scout ships to give his wife and the other techs a break."

Of course that's where he's been. Beechy's been spending all his time overseeing repairs, plotting strategy with the heads of our flight and ground specialist teams, and keeping all systems in the command center running. I've hardly spoken to him these past few days, not since he helped me return from the moon and brought me here to safety.

"There's been no word from the scouts yet, has there?" Logan asks.

"None," Skylar says.

It's not a good sign. We sent two scouts outside the compound to bring back news of Charlie's movements since our battle with his men one week ago. Cady—an Alliance leader who helped Beechy break into Karum—and her copilot were supposed to make their way to the Surface city and attempt contact with some Alliance members working as officials. The mission shouldn't have taken more than a few days, unless Cady and the other scout ran into trouble.

Skylar rubs her helmet harder with the shining rag. "I'm not sure it's smart to keep waiting for them. We need to make a move before Commander Charlie does."

Buck takes another swig of his drink. "Problem is we don't know what to expect out there. Could be everyone's dead on the Surface 'cept for us. Moonshine could'a killed everyone in the work camp."

An image of my old friend Grady crumpled up on the ground outside his shack, his face charred away by the moon's deadly acid, flits through my head.

I set down my spoon, not sure I can eat another bite of food. I want to believe he's alive and okay. But Buck is right. Grady and the others in the camp might not be.

"The people in the city could've survived," Skylar says. "They have well-fortified buildings. They have safety suits to wear if they need them."

Buck gulps more of his drink, which I'm beginning to suspect might be something stronger than water. He wipes his mouth and mustache with the back of his hand. "The point is, we don't know what we're up against. We can't make smart tactical decisions until we do."

"The scouts will come back," Logan says firmly. "I'm sure the mission just took longer than they expected."

"It's been six days. They could be lying in a ditch somewhere. They could'a deserted."

"Cady wouldn't desert," Skylar says. "She helped found the Alliance—"

"Could'a changed her mind."

Frustration makes me ball up my hands into fists under the table. "Then what do you think we should do, if you don't want us to wait for them and you don't want us to start fighting?"

Buck gestures to the room, to the people chatting at the other tables. "To be honest, I'm happy sitting right here. I'm pretty comfortable."

If he thinks this place will protect us forever, he's an idiot.

"We can't abandon the people outside," Logan says, his nostrils flaring in annoyance.

"Besides, Charlie knows some of us survived," I say. "If we sit here and do nothing, he'll come looking for us, or he'll build another bomb that'll blow up the entire Surface—including our headquarters."

"That's just it, we ain't safe anywhere." Buck's voice grows louder and gruffer than before. "We don't have the numbers to launch a full-scale attack against the Core. Maybe if we had all the kids from the camps on our side, maybe then, but that ain't gonna happen. We'll die before we get there, if we don't die in here. Maybe today, maybe tomorrow. Don't make a difference to me." He scoots his chair back and stands, grabbing his tray.

"Buck, come on, relax," Skylar says.

He doesn't turn around. He nearly walks into several people as he heads for the door, making me wonder how much of his non-water he's had to drink.

"Is he serious?" Logan asks.

Skylar rolls her eyes, but her knuckles whiten as she balls up her shining rag. "I doubt it. He can be a real pain in the ass sometimes, but I know he believes in what we're trying to do here. He wants to overthrow the Developers. He just gets scared we're going to lose."

I stare at the door to the mess hall, swinging shut behind Buck's angry figure. He might be right; our fight might be hopeless. But even if it is, we can't give it up. We can't forget those who are still imprisoned in the work camps, especially now that there's acid descending on them from the sky. They already lived in fear of death, and now they have one more way to die.

They deserve freedom. But even if the scouts return and bring us news so we can launch an attack, it will take a lot more than a single battle to liberate everyone in the camps.

Our uprising has barely begun.

—✕—

After breakfast, Logan and I go to the flight port with Skylar. The port lies at the center of the KIMO facility, spanning a width of about thirty yards, filled with ships of varying sizes and models. The port separates the mess hall and bunk rooms on one side of the compound from the training rooms and medical ward on the other.

The buzz of drills grows louder as we walk through the doors. Sparks fly to my left, where a man wearing a mask over his eyes drills underneath a flight pod. The rebels brought six pods with them from the Core, and two bigger hovercraft. One is the hovercraft Beechy and I flew back from the moon—the one that used to carry the bomb that would've destroyed us all. We landed the ship out in the valley, but we couldn't leave it there, in case Charlie's people found it.

I hate that it's here, reminding me of what happened aboard it every time I walk into the port. But we didn't have a better place to hide it.

The only other ships in the compound are the four old Davara jets left behind from KIMO corporation. They sit front and center in the hangar, in varying states of repair. My other roommates, Fiona and Paley, feed an oil line into the fuel tank of one of the jets. With both of them in matching mechanic uniforms and their dark hair tied up in ponytails, it's difficult to tell the twins apart.

Skylar whistles. "Beauty, isn't she?"

Logan casts an amused look in her direction. "Don't you mean 'they'? They're identical, aren't they?"

"Oh, come on, I meant the ship. I took her out for a test drive yesterday and got pretty attached. Though the girls aren't half bad either." Moving closer, Skylar calls to the twins: "How's she coming?"

Fiona looks over at us and waves. Her smile stretches the dark mole on her upper lip. "She's ready to fly, if you want to take her out again."

"Maybe later," Skylar says. "Got some newbies to teach first."

There's the clang of a door opening and closing to my right. Beechy appears at the top of the spiral staircase leading to the command center—the room housing the main security computers and power generators, which sits above the flight port.

"Perfect timing," Skylar says, adjusting her helmet under her arm and moving toward the staircase. "Commander!"

"I'd prefer if you wouldn't call me that," Beechy says as he walks down. He sounds tired, and there are dark circles underneath his eyes, even darker than mine. "Did you need something?"

"I need your permission to take these newbies out in one of the pods," Skylar says.

Beechy glances at me and Logan. "Go ahead. I'll let Sandy know so she can open the security doors. Just don't take them out too far."

"Copy that, sir." Skylar pulls on her helmet. "Newbies, suit up. We leave in five."

Beechy's eyes stray back to me with a question as Skylar hurries away from us to prep one of the flight pods.

"We have names, don't we?" Logan mutters. He turns toward the locker room on the right side of the port, but pauses when he notices I'm not following him.

"Can you grab me a suit?" I ask. "I'll be right there."

"Sure," he says, understanding I want to talk to Beechy alone. I give him a grateful smile before he turns to go.

When I look back at Beechy, he smiles too, but it's weary. "How've you been?" he asks.

I hesitate, trying to figure out how to answer. I remember how I woke up in a cold sweat, how I got dressed and went to breakfast with Logan as if nothing had happened, because I didn't want him to worry about me.

Part of me wants to tell Beechy I'm not entirely okay. He was with me in the Core and on the spaceship. He would understand my nightmares better than anyone. But now isn't the time to lay my burdens on him.

"Okay," I say. "You?"

"I've been better. I could use an extra twenty-four hours to catch up on sleep." He rubs a spot between his eyebrows. "Didn't get to bed until four last night, thanks to a situation in the command center."

"What happened?"

"One of the main circuits shorted and the security computers went offline."

I gape at him. The security computers control all the compound's defenses; they let us keep an eye out for unidentified ships in the entrance tunnels. If the circuit shorted and the computers shut off, our radar screens went dark. Anyone could've broken in without us knowing.

"It wasn't difficult to fix," Beechy says, since I'm still staring at him. "A couple wires came loose. Nothing to worry about."

He smiles to reassure me. But I can't help thinking of the things Buck said earlier. How he doesn't think it matters whether or not we leave the compound; how he doesn't think we can overthrow the Developers. Would he go so far as to screw up things here at headquarters, so we'd have no choice but to stay where we are?

"You're sure no one loosened the wires, right?" I ask.

I hate to think someone in the compound would betray us like that, but I have to consider the possibility. Maybe Buck had nothing to do with this. But there could be someone else here who's only pretending to be on our side, who really wants to lower our defenses. Someone who is still allegiant to Commander Charlie.

"There were no signs of foul play," Beechy says. He sets a hand on my shoulder. "I have things under control. Trust me."

I take a deep breath. I trust him, don't I? Of course I do.

I keep forgetting: I am safe here. I am with people who are on my side.

"Clementine!" Logan waves at me from over by one of the flight pods. He changed into his safety suit, and he's holding the one he grabbed for me. "We're almost ready to go."

"Have fun," Beechy says, dropping his hand from my shoulder.

"Thanks," I say.

I get my safety suit from Logan and pull it on over my clothes, letting him help me zip up the back. The suit is big and bulky, but I'm not stupid enough to go without it. If anything happened while we were flying out in the tunnels, moonshine could leak inside the flight pod and fry me alive. I had to experience what that felt like during a simulation for my Extraction test, and I don't need to go through it again.

Skylar calls for us to board the pod we'll be flying today as I'm snapping my helmet into place. Logan and I follow her up the ramp.

"Who wants to pilot first?" she asks.

I'm eager for something that will keep my hands and my thoughts busy, so I volunteer. Logan doesn't argue.

"Buckle in," Skylar says. "Make sure your helmet comm is on, and remember the preflight checklist."

I slip into the seat in front of the control panel, pull the strap over my waist, and flip the switch on my helmet to turn on the speaker. Skylar takes the copilot chair, and Logan buckles into a passenger seat behind us.

I focus my thoughts on what I've learned in the training sessions I've had these past few days. The checklist comes back easily.

I turn on the master power switch. The panel screens flicker on.

"Fuel levels are high," I say, glancing at the gauges. "The cooling fans sound normal. All exterior hatches are shut."

"Good," Skylar says. "What next?"

"Fire up the engines."

I press a button and flip three switches in succession. The engines roar to life.

"Engines are a go."

"Take the bird out," Skylar says, her eyes shining in anticipation.

I slide my fingers around the control clutch and ease it back. We lift off the ground, hovering higher and higher until we're above the other pods.

Without hesitation, I turn us in the direction of the tunnels leading out of the compound. I push the clutch forward and we speed up.

It's an exhilarating feeling, being in control of something. It makes me feel like I can do anything.

⋇

Flight practice lasts almost an hour. Logan and I take turns maneuvering through the tunnels at various speeds, and then we practice using the ship guns—not firing real ammunition, just going through the motions. Afterwards, I am exhausted, so I nap until lunchtime.

When I get to the mess hall, Logan isn't there, and I'm not really hungry yet anyway. So I look for him instead. I find him in one of the training rooms, soaked with sweat and smacking punching bags.

"Hey," he says, pushing some stray hairs out of his eyes.

"Did you even take a break?" I ask, walking across the mat.

"A short one." He shrugs and smiles. "But I got bored, and you were still asleep."

"So naturally you decided to hit things."

"I figured it wouldn't hurt to practice."

He steps around to the other side of the punching bag, fixing his stance. But he winces with the movement, drawing my attention to the limp in his bad leg. He's had a deformity since birth, but his leg has seemed to cause him more pain ever since we were reunited in Karum. I don't know whether to blame the officials who transported him to the prison under Commander Charlie's orders, or the prison doctors who tortured Logan so I would finally stop fighting them.

I tease my lower lip with my teeth, wondering if I should ask him about something I've been waiting for him to bring up.

He smacks the punching bag with his knuckles.

"You never told me how it happened," I say.

"How what happened?"

"How the officials captured you in the work camp, to take you to Karum."

Logan falters in his next punch, and doesn't hit the bag as hard as before. He pauses and rubs the cuts that are forming on his knuckles. "They did it the usual way. Dragged me into a hov-pod on my way home, knocked me out when I tried to fight them." He rubs his nose with the back of his hand and reassumes his punching stance. "I figured they were taking me to quarantine, replacing me early. Though waking up on an electrocution table wasn't much better."

A shiver crawls across my skin at the memory of him on that table, his body convulsing every time the nurse pressed the red button on the wall. No, it couldn't have been much better than waking up in a gas chamber.

But at least the nurse stopped before she killed him. No one ever escapes quarantine alive.

"I'm sorry," I say softly. "I know it was my fault they took you there."

"Of course it wasn't your fault. Nothing bad that's ever happened to me was your fault. It was the Developers'. Don't you forget that."

Dropping my eyes, I rub my arm. "I know. But I did leave you behind."

"I don't blame you, so you don't need to blame yourself. I'm the one who couldn't pass the stupid test. Couldn't save you from Charlie or anyone, either." Logan hits the bag again. He barely recovers before going in for another punch, but he stops halfway, his face contorting in pain. He leans over and puts both hands on his knees. His leg must be giving him trouble.

"You okay?" I ask, moving closer and touching his back to steady him.

"Yeah," Logan says. He closes his eyes and inhales, exhales slowly.

Straightening, he turns to me. The slight creases around his eyes make me think he must still be in pain, and he could use a distraction.

I rise onto my tiptoes and press my lips against his. Taking my face in his hands, he kisses me back harder. I put my palm against his chest, feeling his fast heartbeat through his tank top as his hands move into my hair. His lips coax the worries out of me until all of them slip from my fingers.

I hope I am making him less afraid too.

We're still pressed together when the alarm blares from the ceiling. A loud *whir-oooom whir-oooom whir-oooom* that grates at my eardrums.

I pull away from Logan, my body flooding with tension. There's a red light flashing above the door. The emergency light that's supposed to go off only if we need to evacuate the base because the air has become contaminated with moonshine.

"What's going on?" Logan yells.

"We need to get our safety suits on," I say, grasping at the threads of what I remember Beechy telling us we should do if this happened. "We need to get to the flight port."

I turn to run for the door, but as suddenly as it started, the alarm shuts off. The emergency light stops flashing.

This can't have been an accident. Something is wrong.

Logan opens his mouth to speak, but he's cut off by Beechy's voice erupting through the ceiling speaker: "I need everyone's attention. This is not a drill. An unidentified ship has been sighted near the entrance tunnel."

Oh, vrux.

"All hands, report to the flight deck with safety gear. Head pilots, prep weapons and ships. There may be a full-fledged attack at hand. I repeat: *This is not a drill.*"

An unidentified ship. Core officials might be here.

I can't move at first. My body refuses to function normally until Logan grabs my hand.

"Come on," he says. "We have to go."

There's no time.

I force my feet to move.

# 3

The flight port stinks of exhaust fumes, and there are red lights flashing everywhere. People race up ramps into the flight pods.

Logan helps me zip up my safety suit as quickly as he can, but we're not moving fast enough. Every second we don't get our ships in the air, the likelier we won't be able to hold off an attack. We could get trapped in here if enemy ships overtake the entrance tunnels; there's not another way out.

Beechy shouts flight assignments from the center of the port. But I can't hear him call my name over the roar of the engines already turning on.

But Skylar grabs my arm as she runs past. "You're with me," she says. "Logan, get on Buck's pod."

"Be careful," I tell him.

"You too," he says.

"Let's move out!" Beechy yells to my left, boarding his own ship.

I pull my helmet on as I run after Skylar. It takes me a couple of seconds to realize she's leading me to one of the Davara jets.

I can't help panicking. I might feel comfortable using the flight controls in the pods, but I've only been practicing for a week. This is a two-person fighter jet, which I've never flown in before. And she expects me to be her copilot?

"We're taking this one?" I ask.

"Sure are," Skylar says, scurrying up the ladder. She climbs into the pilot seat. Her cheeks are bright red from excitement. "My bird will get us back safe and sound, don't worry."

The golden paint is peeling off the wings of the rusty red jet. The ship creaks loudly as I climb up into the seat behind her.

I'm not sure I believe her.

"I hardly think I'm the most qualified copilot you could've picked," I say.

"You're a natural at flying the pods," Skylar says. "Anyway, all you need to do right now is control the ship guns. I have complete faith you can handle it."

I'd argue with her, but that wouldn't do me any good. We might be under attack. I need to pull myself together and do what I can to defend our headquarters.

I strap myself in and make sure oxygen is flowing through my helmet, then skim the gauges before me to familiarize myself with the mechanics. The control panel is rearranged differently from the one in the flight pod I practiced in earlier, but I can still tell where all the gauges are. Hopefully I can still work the gun controls.

On the ground below, Fiona moves the ladder away. "Good luck!" she calls.

The jet cover lowers over us and seals, drowning out the deck noise. Skylar initiates the launch sequence.

"This is Skylar," she says. "Engines are go."

The comm inside my helmet isn't turned on yet, so I flip the switch. The voice of Sandy, Beechy's wife, crackles through the speaker inside my helmet. She must be in charge in the command center. Beechy doesn't want her out on any attack missions unless it's absolutely necessary, since she's pregnant.

"There's still just the one ship on the radar," Sandy says. "It's entering the tunnel from the south side. We've identified the signal. It's definitely a Core ship, not one of ours. Slight damage to the hull, by the look of it."

Damage? Did the ship crash on its way here?

"We'll have to capture it," Beechy says. "Can't risk it getting away and coming back with friends. Buck, Harriet, and Jensen, I want you coming at the ship from behind in case it tries to get away. Exit via the north tunnel entrance. Circle back around to the south side. Watch for more incoming ships on your radar."

"Copy that."

"Yessir."

"Right away."

Through the window, one flight pod lifts off the ground and makes for the tunnel leading out of the facility. A second ship follows, and a third. Logan's on one of those ships. If there are other enemy ships out there, he will be the first to face them.

*Please don't die on me, Logan.*

"Derrick and Sloan, hang back and await further orders," Beechy says. "Skylar, follow me. We'll intercept the ship in the southern tunnel."

"Got it, Captain," Skylar says. "Hang tight, Clementine."

She pulls the control yoke back. I grip the edges of my seat as we lift into the air. My palms are already sweaty. I'm not used to how cramped a two-person jet feels compared to a flight pod.

The jet rumbles beneath me as we speed after Beechy's pod into the entrance tunnel. I stare at the blue lights dotting the ceiling until they blur.

I know I practiced this earlier, but I don't feel ready. I feel like I'm right back on the spaceship with Beechy, fumbling for the controls and praying we'll make it to the moon before the bomb explodes.

There will be no innocent deaths this time, no repeats of the past. I won't let what happened to Oliver happen again.

Straight ahead, the tunnel branches in two directions: one heading north, one heading south. North is the side of the mountain I entered the first time I came here, when I saw the barrier with the words KIMO FACILITY written across it in faded paint.

We head in the opposite direction, south. A set of double security doors zips open as we approach, controlled by Sandy in the command center. They close behind us once we're through. The dark steel walls on either side of us blur as we zoom past them.

"The ship's not on radar yet," Skylar says. "Must be going slow."

The only ship on my control panel's radar screen is the one careening through the tunnel ahead of us—Beechy's pod.

"Make sure your guns are prepped," he says over comm.

"Copy that."

Turning my attention back to the control panel, I flip the red switch that should initiate the sequence. A target monitor lowers from the ceiling.

I wrap my palms around the control clutches. The *beep-beep-beep-beep-beep* of the system fills my ears. Circles appear on the green grid, showing me where the guns are aimed. Right now I could hit Beechy's pod if I wanted. If I accidentally pressed the clutch buttons, a stream of fire would hit his ship and knock him off course.

I'm not sure I trust myself with these controls. But I need to calm down. I know how to do this.

"Weapons system engaged."

"Good job," Skylar says, glancing sideways so I can catch the small smile on her lips through her helmet. "You've got this, Clementine."

The radar on my dashboard still shows only our jet and Beechy's pod. Where's the other ship? This tunnel is long, but it can't be far ahead.

I pray there's only one ship. Charlie's full force could pummel us with gunfire and rip apart our hulls, along with the walls of our facility. His ships could destroy us.

"Enemy contact," Skylar says.

My eyes flit to the radar once more, and my heartbeat quickens. There's a new dot on the radar. A new ship ahead of us in the tunnel, heading our way.

"If there's only one, it's likely to try to run," Beechy says.

*If* there's only one.

I grip the control clutches tighter as Skylar maneuvers to close the space between us and Beechy's ship. I stare at the moving dot on the radar, begging it to turn around.

"It's not running," Skylar says.

Beechy's pod veers to the left and the enemy ship comes into view at the far end of the tunnel. A sleek, silver hovercraft, small in our sights but growing bigger by the second. There are burn marks on its hull, as Sandy said.

It's not turning back.

"Buck, Harriet, Jensen, are there any enemy ships on your radar?" Beechy asks.

Buck's voice crackles into my helmet: "No, sir. We have zero enemy contacts."

"This is Jensen. I second that."

The symbol of the Core—a bronze full moon—is painted on the left wing of the enemy hovercraft. We have the same symbol on our hovercrafts in the flight port, but this one isn't ours. If the pilots on board were our men, they'd have the proper ID code to show up as friendlies on our radar and connect to our comm system.

But if this ship isn't ours and it didn't bring backup, why isn't it fleeing?

"What should I do?" I ask.

"We should question the pilots on board," Skylar says.

"Hold positions," Beechy says. "Clementine, fire past the ship when I give the command. Let's see if it surrenders."

I grip my control clutches tighter. We're well within firing range.

The green circles on my target grid move this way and that as Skylar maneuvers our jet. The circles keep passing over the nose of the hovercraft, but I'm not aiming for the nose. I don't want to injure those on board if they might surrender, if they might not be the enemy we expected.

"Fire past the ship," Beechy says again.

*Beep-beep-beep-beep-beep-beep-beep—*

The target circles keep jumping onto the hovercraft; I can't keep my hands steady. I'm afraid if I nudge the firing button, I'll hit the ship.

I feel like I'm suffocating inside my helmet. "I can't do this."

"You can," Skylar says. "Just aim and squeeze the clutch like you practiced."

My breaths are coming too fast. My vision blurs around the edges as I squeeze the clutch with sweaty palms.

*Beep-beep-beep-beep-beep-beep-beep—*

I blink and I'm not in the copilot seat anymore; I'm on a hard, metal table in Karum prison, my arms and legs chained so I can't move. Commander Charlie looms over me in the near darkness.

With a gleam in his eyes, he steps forward and wraps his fingers around my neck. I struggle against him, but he is too strong. He squeezes harder and harder. His fingers are knives and he's cutting into my throat.

*Stop,* I choke. *Stop, stop, stop—*

"Stop!" Skylar yells inside my helmet.

Her voice snaps me back to reality. My hand is frozen on the clutch, squeezing it hard.

Laser fire streams from our ship's guns, pummeling the hovercraft ahead of us. It shudders and tilts sideways. It's going to crash-land.

"Clementine, let go!" Skylar screams.

Panicked, I tear my fingers off the clutch, but it's too late.

The hovercraft crashes and skids across the steel floor of the tunnel. It takes centuries to stop.

When the screeching sound dies, the ship sits in silence, engulfed in smoke erupting from its damaged hull. My pounding heartbeat fills my ears like thunder endlessly roaring.

*What did I just do?*

# 4

Skylar puts us down on the ground near the rubble, beside Beechy's pod. The jet cover lifts above me.

"What the hell was that?" Skylar says, unbuckling.

She looks at me for an explanation. But how can I admit what happened? I lost control and let Commander Charlie intimidate me, though he is far, far away.

Shaking her head, Skylar climbs over the edge of her seat and hops out of the jet.

"Sandy, get a medic team here immediately," Beechy says over comm, his voice rough and angry as he and his copilot climb out of their pod. His eyes find mine and then move swiftly away. There's something sad in them. I've disappointed him.

*I'm sorry.* The words freeze on my lips and I don't know how to force them out.

*BOOM!*

Fire bursts from the hull of the damaged hovercraft. My hands fly up to cover my head, and I cry out instinctively.

Skylar and Beechy ducked too. They're okay, thank the stars.

When the smoke clears, the enemy ship is in flames. The engine must've exploded.

Beechy curses over comm. "We need to get the pilots out of there!" he shouts, running forward.

I need to get down there and help them. I need to unfreeze and face what I did.

I shot down a ship that didn't even threaten us. I might've killed everyone inside—people who might be innocent, not allies of Charlie. After all, why would he send someone here with orders not to shoot at us?

The whir of engines reaches my ears over the loud crackling of the flames among the wreckage. Three flight pods arrive from the direction of the tunnel's southern entrance. They must be the ones who circled around from the other side, as Beechy directed them.

A fourth ship—the medic team—arrives in a pod from the flight port. The team rushes onto the ground as soon as the ship lands.

If I don't move, everyone's going to wonder why I'm not helping. They're going to realize this was all my fault.

And they'll be right.

*Just do it.* I climb out of my seat and slide off the side of the jet. My feet hit the ground as Logan appears near the wreckage.

He barely looks at the flames; his worried eyes go straight to me. He limps past Skylar and Beechy and the medics, who are prying open the door of the hovercraft.

"What happened?" he asks. "I heard Skylar yelling your name over comm. Are you hurt?"

"No, I'm fine. Nothing happened. It . . . was an accident."

He stops before he reaches me, confused. "An accident?"

I use the first excuse that pops into my head: "Our weapons malfunctioned. They wouldn't stop firing."

The lie tastes like acid in my mouth.

Logan presses his lips together. He knows I'm not telling the whole story.

"Bring the stretcher closer!" Beechy shouts.

Over Logan's shoulder, Skylar and Beechy haul a passenger out of the hovercraft. The woman's clothes are all but shreds. There's something familiar about her, but I can't make out her face—she's covered in soot.

"Cady," Skylar says in a broken voice. "Oh, stars, no."

*Cady.* My hand flies to my mouth.

Cady, who helped me escape from Karum. Cady, who fought beside me the day I flew to the moon.

The medics lift her limp body onto the stretcher. Cady's eyes aren't open; she doesn't seem to be breathing. Her black hair has burned away. What skin is visible through the tatters of her uniform is charred, red and raw like meat meant for frying.

Skylar pushes one of the medics aside and tries to resuscitate her. "Come on, come on, come back!"

"She's gone," Beechy says, pulling her back. "Sky, it's too late."

*Gone.*

My fault.

I'm going to be sick. Turning away, I hurry around the Davara jet and throw up the hash beans from this morning.

When I'm finished, I wipe my mouth with the back of my hand. My hands tremble a little, and I ball them up to make them stop. I can't have a panic attack, not now.

"You okay?" Logan asks behind me.

I turn to see him standing a few feet away. "Fine."

He hesitates like he's going to ask me something more. I can guess well enough: *Did you shoot the ship down?*

"We should see if they need help," I say, pushing past him before he can speak. I'm not ready for him to force the truth out of me.

The medics cover Cady's body with a sheet and carry her back to their ship. Skylar calms down enough to help Beechy and his copilot pull another passenger out of the wreckage and lift him onto a second stretcher.

I don't recognize him. He's a young man not much older than me, his blond hair falling out of a ponytail. He's wearing the dark armor of Surface officials, but he is covered in blood. His chest rises and falls, so he must not be dead. But his eyes won't open, and his left arm seems broken.

I know there are a few Surface officials working undercover for the Alliance, but I have a hard time believing it. I've had too much experience with officials who taunt and hurt and kill children without remorse.

Beechy seems worried too; he must not recognize him either. But all he says to the medics is, "Take him to the sick bay."

Whoever the boy is, he's already incapacitated, and we need him to talk.

There's one more survivor amid the wreckage. The pilot.

Logan joins me again and slides his fingers between mine as the medics heave the pilot out onto another stretcher. He's awake but in shock and retching, his face stained with grease and tears. There's a deep gash in his abdomen where a piece of metal lodged inside him.

He is another member of the Alliance.

"Darren, stay with me," Beechy says.

He presses a cloth to Darren's wound to keep him from bleeding out while the medic secures a safety helmet around Darren's head in case there's any acid drifting through the tunnel.

"Where am I?" Darren asks, his voice small and cracking.

"You're back at headquarters," Beechy says. "Do you remember how you got here? Can you tell me what happened?"

"We did what you said. We found out Charlie's plan." The helmet muffles Darren's voice. "But everything got screwed up. Our ship broke down when we were trying to leave. Mal helped us steal another—"

"Who's Mal?"

"A good guy, an official. He saved us. Wants to fight the Developers too."

"The young man in the uniform," Logan says, more to himself than anyone.

I hope that's who Darren means. I hope that official isn't dangerous.

"He helped you steal a ship," Beechy says. "And then?"

"It had a tracker on it."

Jaw tensing, Beechy looks back at the wreckage of the hovercraft. There's no way the tracker survived the explosion; there's no part of the hull that isn't burning, though some of our fighter pilots are working to put the fire out. But the ship wasn't burning fifteen minutes ago. If Charlie's men were keeping an eye on the tracker's location, they know where the ship ended up.

They know where we're hiding.

"Did you notice anyone following you here?" Skylar asks, hovering close behind Beechy.

Darren shakes his head, but I can't tell if he's responding to Skylar's question or struggling against the pain. His eyes are streaming water.

Beechy stands, letting the medic take over pressing the cloth to Darren's wound. "We need to get everyone back to headquarters. We need to evacuate."

"Should I give the order?" Skylar asks, reaching to switch on her ear-comm.

"No, wait," Darren says, blinking fast like he's fighting to stay alert. "No one followed us—we got away. We got the tracker off. That's not what I needed to tell you."

"What did you need to tell us?" Beechy asks, his voice rising in frustration.

Darren struggles as he explains: "What we found out . . . what Charlie's doing can't be a good thing."

His voice trails off. He closes his eyes briefly, his face contorting.

"What did you find out?" Skylar asks, her eyes wide and alert. "What is he doing?"

Darren's eyes flutter open. "He's evacuating the Surface. The kids, the adults—everyone. He's moving them all belowground. Day after tomorrow."

Beechy stares at him. I wonder if his heart is racing as fast as mine.

Before, Charlie said he didn't need anyone in the outer sectors. He said the Core had become self-sufficient, so the kids in the camps didn't need to stay alive anymore. He could send them all to quarantine now, if he wanted.

Instead, he's saving them all. He's getting everyone off the Surface. *Why?*

"Do you mean he's transferring them to the Core?" Skylar asks.

"No, he's dispersing them throughout Crust, Mantle, and Lower. But not the Core."

"Are you sure?" Beechy asks.

"Positive."

Voices and engine sounds fade into the background, dull and pounding in my temple. My mind races, seeking an explanation for Charlie's move. Every move he has ever made was a selfish one, and this is no exception. He must need the Surface citizens for something. *But for what?*

"What does this mean?" Logan asks.

"I don't know," I say.

Darren starts coughing again. Hacking coughs that rack his whole body.

"We need to get him into surgery," one of the medics says.

"Right," Beechy says. He sounds distant, lost in his thoughts.

"What are your orders?" Skylar asks. "Are we still evacuating?"

"Not yet." Beechy clears his throat and grips one side of the stretcher to carry Darren over to the medical transport. "We'll return to the compound and talk things over."

"Yes, sir," Skylar says, and repeats his order to everyone over comm.

Logan lets go of my hand. "I'll see you back there."

All around me, people return to their ships. Only a few small flames crackle on the hull of the wrecked hovercraft, slowly dying. But they already did their damage. They already destroyed Cady's body, and wounded Darren and the young official.

The memory of what I did slams into me again like a knife through my chest.

I killed Cady.

"Clementine," Skylar says behind me.

I jump at the sound of her voice.

"Let's go," she says.

I'm scared to look at her face, but I do anyway. Her jaw is tense again; the disappointment is clear in her eyes.

I don't like it. But I know I deserve much worse.

# 5

When we return to the main facility, I want to talk to Beechy. I need to explain what happened earlier—how I lost control, how I didn't mean to fire the weapons—and I need to know what he thinks about Charlie's plan of action.

But I can't get his attention for even two seconds. He makes sure Darren and the wounded official, Mal, get to the sick bay, and then he goes straight into debrief meetings with members of the Alliance who have more say in strategy planning than I do, including Skylar and Sandy.

I can't sit still, waiting to hear what they decide we should do.

✕

At dinner, I can barely touch my food.

"You sure you're okay?" Logan asks, brushing my hand under the table.

"Yeah," I say. "I'm just tired."

"Go sleep," he says. "I'll come get you if anything happens."

I'm too restless to sleep, but getting out of the crowded mess hall would do me good. So I push my tray toward Logan and head out the door.

Instead of going to my bunk room, I slip inside the smallest training room and slam my fists against punching bags for a long time. Hours, maybe.

Sweat beads on my forehead, and my curls stick to the back of my neck. My knuckles redden and ache. The pain is a lot at first, but after a while my hands feel numb.

My head doesn't clear, though. My regrets slip away for a little bit, but soon they return with full force.

I shouldn't avoid Logan. I should tell him the truth about what happened earlier. But I'm terrified to explain everything because he'll probably think I'm losing it. He doesn't know I keep having nightmares about Oliver and Karum and Charlie. Telling him I hallucinated and thought Charlie was strangling me in the jet might be too much for him to handle.

I miss my next punch and lose my balance. My knees bang against the floor mat. I try to get back up, but pain shoots through my hands and I double over instead.

I should not be this weak. I was strong enough to fight the serum Charlie used to control me, and strong enough to survive torture in Karum for weeks.

Why can't I fight this? Why can't I stop being afraid of Charlie?

There's a crackle in the ceiling. The speakers turning on. I wipe my nose with the back of my hand and listen.

"Evening, everyone." Beechy sounds tired, like everything has finally caught up with him. "I know it's been a difficult day. But I have one more favor to ask of all of you: If you would please gather in the flight port in ten minutes, there are some things we need to discuss. And there is someone we need to honor."

He pauses. "Thank you. See you soon."

There's a click, and the speakers shut off.

Still breathing deeply, I struggle to my feet and remove my punching gloves. I'd rather keep hiding in here, but I should go to this meeting. Beechy might announce something about what he and the other leaders decided for our next move. And I might be able to talk to him afterwards.

Anyway, I owe it to Cady. She was brave enough to go out on a scouting mission when she knew she might be discovered. I can be brave enough to get through tonight.

*

When I walk into the flight port, almost everyone is here. They all wear the same gray slacks, tank top, and jacket as me. Standing side by side in the clear space to the right of the ships, they could almost pass for an army.

At the front of the group, Cady's body lies on a metal gurney, draped with a white sheet.

She isn't the first person I've killed. There was that Unstable my first day in the Core, and probably a Karum nurse or two. But Cady is different. She saved me. She fought beside me.

She would still be here if I wasn't losing it. If I were stronger.

*It was an accident*, I remind myself. *I didn't mean to kill her.*

But I'm not sure that's any better. It means I'm not in control of myself, and I should be.

I slip into the back of the crowd, where Logan is standing.

"Did you have a good sleep?" he asks.

"Yes, I did."

His eyes search my face for something. The truth, maybe.

I'm going to tell him. My lips will part and the words will flow, and he won't hate me because of them.

But as I start to open my mouth, Beechy steps out of the group's formation and walks toward Cady's body. Logan turns away to watch him. Another time, I will tell him. There is plenty of time.

Beechy turns to face us. "Thank you all for coming." His voice is soft, but the walls make it echo. "We lost a member of our company today. Cady was a brave fighter, a leader in the Alliance, especially in our most recent attack against Charlie. She volunteered to break into Karum. She volunteered to head a scouting mission, though she knew it would be dangerous. Cady never cared much about the risk. All she wanted was for her sacrifice to be worthwhile."

Logan slides his fingers into the open spaces between mine. I focus on the warmth of his hand, begging it to keep me steady.

Sandy joins Beechy and hands him a folded sheet. Beechy turns to Cady's body.

When he steps back, I see he placed the new sheet over the white one. But it's not a sheet—it's a Core flag. Black and blue stripes; a silver circle in the center inscribed with the words: IN-VENTION. PEACE. PROSPERITY.

The second word is such a lie.

"Tonight we remember Cady, warrior and friend," Beechy says.

A second voice arises from the room's near silence. Sandy sings a sweet, mournful melody while resting one hand on her stomach, where her baby is growing inside.

My throat chokes up from the beauty of her song. By the time she reaches the final verse, I can't hold back my tears anymore:

*Now the stars, they call you home*
*Now the days have passed*
*Sleep, my darling, don't lose hope*
*For you are safe at last*

Sandy's voice fades away, but the song echoes in my chest like an ache I'll never destroy. Logan wraps his arms around me, pulling me close. But it's not enough.

Beneath my sadness, I can feel something else building inside me: rage like gunfire, like cannons blasting over and over. Rage at myself, for not being able to deal with the things that have happened to me. But also rage at Charlie, for making me this way.

Again and again, he steals my friends from me. But I won't let him steal anyone else, or make me do anything against my will. I have to be stronger.

I have to defeat him.

"In the Core," Beechy says, "it's the tradition to burn bodies instead of burying them. Here, we must do the same, because we have no good place to bury our friends. But Cady won't burn alone."

He beckons, and Skylar emerges from the crowd to join him and Sandy beside the metal table. Skylar's back is to us, so I don't see her light the Core flag. But when she steps away, a flame leaps up from the silver circle, the color of exploding stars. It races across the fabric, eating away the black and blue stripes and the lies.

Cady's body burns like a brilliant beacon, and the Core burns with her. Commander Charlie burns.

"We've stayed here in hiding long enough," Beechy says, facing everyone. "Today we learned the Developers are transferring all civilians of the Surface settlement to the lower sectors the day after tomorrow, including those in the work camp."

I glance around to see people's reactions. Murmurs slide through the crowd. Logan already knew about this, but there's caution in his eyes. I pull away from him and find his hand again.

"This is the perfect opportunity for us to infiltrate my father's ranks and relocate closer to the Core," Sandy says. The metal stud in her nose gleams in the light. "Our goal is to sneak a few of our people into each sector, disguised as officials, teachers, or other positions that will put us in prime position to damage the infrastructure of the political system. We'll draw his attention away from whatever he's planning, and then we'll break into the Core and capture him and the other leaders."

Finally.

"We will overthrow the Developers, and we will liberate those in the work camps," Beechy says. "We will fight for freedom and for everyone we've lost. We will fight for Cady."

"We will fight for her!" Skylar yells, throwing her fist in the air.

"Charlie thinks we're hiding," Beechy says. "He thinks we're afraid to face him head-on. Now is the time for us to prove him wrong."

There are cheers and clapping hands, people shouting for joy.

But my excitement mingles with nerves. I don't know how Beechy intends to disguise me enough that I won't be recognized. I don't know how he plans to disguise himself, either. Charlie must have people looking for us, even if he doesn't know for sure we survived.

"We will fight for Cady!" Skylar yells again.

Others join in the cry: "We will fight for her! We will fight for her!"

The cry builds and builds until it seems like it's everywhere, in the walls and the floor, exploding through the mountain tunnels.

*We will fight for her.*

Almost everyone is smiling, but Beechy isn't. And I'm not.

Neither is Logan. The pressure he puts on my hand tells me he's thinking the same thing as me.

We will fight for Cady, for peace, for hope. Some of us will die for them too.

⚹

Logan and I don't speak as he walks me to my bunk room for the night.

Earlier, I was ready to tell him the truth about my part in Cady's death. But talking about it will make it real; I won't be able to deny that I need help to keep it from happening again. And what if nothing will help? What if I keep spiraling out of control, and everyone abandons me because they're afraid of what I'll do?

I don't know; I don't know.

When we reach my door, he lets go of my hand. He leans in and touches his mouth to mine. I clench the bottom of his shirt in my fist, reveling in the distraction from my worries.

He pulls away too soon. "You know you can tell me anything, right?" he says.

"I know," I say. But I don't quite meet his eyes.

He is silent, waiting for me to say something more.

When I don't, he sighs and rubs his forehead. "I'll see you in the morning."

He turns away to go to his room, three doors down from mine. Three walls sit between us when we sleep. But it feels like a hundred, especially now that I've shoved lies between us too.

A word claws its way up my throat and escapes before I can stop it: "Wait."

Logan pauses with his hand on the door handle.

I don't want things to be strained with him. I want them to be secure and right and comforting, the way they were before all of this, before I left him and nearly lost him forever.

But they will not get better unless I start being brave.

I don't think I can handle bringing up Cady right now, because I might start crying again and not be able to speak at all. But I can start somewhere.

"I keep being afraid." I fiddle with my hands, looking anywhere but at Logan. "I keep waking up in the middle of the night screaming because I think I'm back in Karum, or on the spaceship with Oliver. I'm afraid Charlie's going to steal more people away from me—especially you. And sometimes I'm walking around this place, doing normal things during the day, and all of a sudden I'm inside my nightmares again. And I freeze up and I feel like I'm spiraling out of control." My palms sweat, and I blink hard to keep my eyes from watering. "I don't know what's happening to me. I think I'm going crazy, and I don't know how to stop it."

Logan's in front of me again, though I didn't notice him come back to me. He places his palms on my face, one on each cheek. They are warm, steadying.

"You're not crazy. And I don't blame you for being afraid. But know this: I'm not going to leave you, no matter what. And I'm going to do everything I can to keep you out of harm's way." He gently wipes my tears away with his thumbs. "We'll get through whatever comes next, together."

"You promise?" I ask.

"I promise."

He kisses me once, on my forehead. I touch his arms to keep him close to me. "Would you stay with me tonight?"

A smile curves the edge of his mouth. "Don't have to ask me twice."

Lacing his fingers with mine, he pushes open my bedroom door. I follow him inside.

"You know, all those nights after you left for the Core, I kept catching myself heading toward your shack instead of mine," Logan says. "I never got used to you being gone."

I let go of his hand and lean down to tug off my boots. "I hope there wasn't some other girl my age staying in my shack, asking you to spend the night."

"Nah, a couple of younger kids moved into it."

"Good."

Logan's eyes twinkle with amusement. "Why? Were you worried about that?"

A touch of heat rises to my cheeks. I shrug. "Only a little."

"That was silly of you." His arm brushes mine as he removes his shoes. "You're the only girl I'd spend the night with."

My blush deepens as he straightens, leaving his boots next to mine on the floor.

"Really?" I ask.

"Really." He leans in and kisses me softly.

I climb up the ladder to my bunk, and he follows me. I let him take the space by the wall, the way we used to sleep back in my shack. He wraps his arms around me under the covers. When Skylar and my other roommates come to bed, they might see us and assume things. But I don't really care if they do.

I lean into Logan's chest and breathe him in, trying to let go of my fears. Trying to forget about my enemies and the people they've stolen from me.

Logan is with me and we are okay. I haven't lost him yet.

# 6

Sometime in the night, I wake up and can't fall back asleep. I don't think I had any nightmares, or if I did, I can't remember them. But once I'm awake, I'm too restless to close my eyes again.

Logan sleeps beside me with one arm tucked under his head, the other resting across my stomach in a loose embrace. He's snoring softly, like he always does when he sleeps on his back. It's a familiar sound, comforting even.

I brush his sweaty hair off his forehead. Part of me wants to wake him up to talk to him, but a bigger part knows I should let him sleep. I have no idea when he'll get a chance to rest in a comfortable bed again.

As for me, there's no use lying here for hours when I can't keep my eyes shut anyway. Trying to be quiet, I gently push his arm off me and climb down from the bunk. The whole bed creaks with my movement, and I pause to make sure I didn't wake him. But Logan doesn't stir and neither do Fiona and Paley, who are knocked out on the bunks across from mine. Skylar's bunk is empty.

My boots are tucked under her bed. I find them and pull them on. Once the laces are tied, I open the door and slip outside, working my hair into a bun at the same time.

Down the corridor, I turn a corner and nearly crash into Skylar.

"Whoa, there," she says.

"Sorry," I say.

I can feel my whole face heating up. Of course I'd run into her, of all people. Judging by the annoyance in her expression, her anger hasn't cooled off since our last interaction. I'm sure she still blames me for Cady's death.

Skylar rubs her eyes. "You do realize it's three in the morning?"

I hadn't checked my time-band yet, but sure enough it's eight minutes past three. "Well, I couldn't sleep." Before she can ask why—and bring up things I don't want to talk about—I say, "Anyway, looks like you've been wandering around too. Where were you?"

"In the flight port, checking flight equipment and whatnot." She yawns. "Beechy and Sandy should be over there still, if you were looking for them."

I do need to talk to Beechy, but not in front of Sandy. I suppose I'll go see what they're doing, at least.

"Okay. Thanks."

I start to move past her, but she stops my shoulder. "I hope you've found a solution."

"Excuse me?"

"I hope you've dealt with whatever it is you're going through, because we're launching an invasion in a couple of hours. And it won't do us any good if you lose control again and jeopardize the mission." She gives me a hard look.

"I know that," I say, as steadily as I can. Fighting the urge to pull away from her. "I have everything under control. Yesterday won't happen again."

"It better not," Skylar says, her voice almost brittle. "I sure wouldn't want someone who's actually Unstable screwing everything up for the rest of us."

Before I can argue, she releases me and stalks around the corner. A clang tells me when she's shut the door to our bunk room.

I spin around and head in the opposite direction, rubbing the sore spot where her hand pressed into my shoulder. She is wrong; I'm not really Unstable. I am perfectly in control.

Even as I think those words, I know they're a lie. Skylar has every reason to worry. Maybe I am in control right now, but in the midst of chaos and battle things will be different. The next time I'm controlling a weapon, I could lose control again and hurt people without even realizing.

Maybe this was part of Charlie's plan: to screw with my head until I kill all his enemies for him.

✳

The lights are dim in the flight port. The Davara jets and flight pods stand lonesome and silent like phantoms. I wonder how many of them have been privy to war, how many have been used by pilots to kill innocent people.

There's no sign of Beechy and Sandy. Maybe Skylar meant they're up in the command center. I could climb the staircase and check, but I'm not sure I want to talk to them anyway. They're not the real reason I came here.

My feet carry me with purpose across the flight port, past the other ships until I see what I'm looking for: the massive hovercraft on the far side of the port. It looks the same as it did when I last climbed down the ramp, with Beechy at my side as we returned to a world with no more acid seeping from the moon, but plenty of it in the atmosphere. A world I didn't expect to set foot on again.

A world part of me wished I could escape forever.

I haven't been inside the hovercraft since that day, a week ago. I've been avoiding the silent ship, along with the memories it carries. But it seems important for me to face them tonight. No matter how difficult it might be.

I need to prove to myself I am stronger than everyone thinks.

On the side of the hovercraft, I find the hidden compartment with the cargo lift controls. I tap the buttons in succession, and the ramp lowers to the ground with a creak.

After a quick check over my shoulder to make sure no one has come into the port and noticed what I'm doing, I hurry up the ramp before I can change my mind.

The smell of engine oil is strong inside the ship. I switch on the lights, so I can make out my surroundings. To my right are the wall compartments where I found the injection syringe I used to put Oliver to sleep because I couldn't stand seeing him as a mindless soldier. Straight ahead is the passage to the cockpit where I saw the universe through the window and dreamed of other worlds where I might be truly free.

Everything in here is all too familiar, almost the exact setting of the dreams that wake me screaming every night. But I'm standing here and I don't feel any panic. In fact, for the first time in a week, I am calmer than I've ever been.

I'm not sure the nightmares are what made me afraid to come here. I think it's something else—something I've been trying to forget.

I take the right-hand passageway, moving past the chair where I sedated Oliver. Past the corridor to the engine room. When I reach the ladder, I feel for the rungs and climb to the top.

In the passageway above, a window straight ahead shows me the steel wall of the flight port outside. I don't see any of the stars I saw a week ago. But I remember how beautiful they looked from beyond the acid shield. I remember sitting inside the escape pod, preparing to fly the bomb to the moon on my own. Accepting the fact I would die and never see Logan again.

That was the only part of death that scared me: the separation from him. I wanted a way out, a way to escape the Developers and all the pain they had caused me. In many ways, death would've been a relief.

But Oliver took my place, so I didn't die. I watched him fly away and had to come back to all this. Now I'm stuck on the brink of an uprising I might not survive, even if we win.

I'm not sure I want to survive it. I'm not sure this world will ever be worth living in. It feels good to admit to myself, like a weight has been lifted off my chest.

"Clementine?" a soft whisper from behind and below me in the darkness reaches my ears. I'm surprised it didn't startle me.

I turn and see a person at the foot of the ladder.

"Can I come up?" Beechy asks.

I wipe my eyes to make sure they aren't watering. "I'd rather come down. I wasn't planning on staying much longer."

"Oh. Okay." He steps back from the ladder. I glance at the window behind me one last time, then lower myself down the rungs.

"Were you in the command center?" I ask.

"No, I was in bed. Been trying to fall asleep for the past hour, but it's useless. I thought I'd give the nighttime tech some company, only I saw someone walking in the flight port. Wondered if it might be you when you came in here." He smiles.

I twist my lips. Why did Skylar tell me he and Sandy were still in the flight port? She must've been confused about the timing.

"You couldn't sleep?" I ask. "Couldn't stop thinking."

"We're like twins."

His mouth quirks into a half smirk. "If only I were three feet shorter."

I scoff. "I'm not even a foot shorter than you. Six inches, maybe."

"Eight inches, at least. You're tiny."

I glare at him, giving his shoulder a soft punch.

He doubles over, as if it hurt more than it really did. "Tiny, but strong," he says, laughing.

I start to smile, but stop because it feels weird. All of this feels weird. We've barely spoken at all the past week, since he's been so busy with his leadership duties. And we haven't said a word to each other since yesterday. Not since what happened with Cady.

Dropping my eyes, I feign interest in my bootlaces, hoping Beechy will break the silence and hoping he won't at the same time.

"Listen," he says. "We've figured out assignments for the mission, how we're going to sneak everyone into the lower sectors."

Good. This is a much easier subject.

"We're going to disguise most people as officials if we can." Beechy pauses, hesitating. "But I've been stuck on what I should do about you and Logan. You, especially, must be on Charlie's wanted list, and I'm afraid making you an official will put you in a situation where it's too easy for someone to recognize you. Your face is pretty distinct. And Logan's in a similar situation. He has the limp in his leg, which could draw attention to him."

I can't argue with him. "What assignments do you want to give us, then?"

"I came up with two options. The first is that I would assign both of you to the secondary team. A few people aren't leaving tomorrow; they're staying here to keep the facility running, including Sandy."

My calm evaporates as I realize where's he's going with this.

"They'll back us up once we're ready to break into the Core," Beechy says. "So you and Logan could stay here too—"

"No vruxing way. I can't keep sitting here, waiting for things to happen. I need to *do* something. Or what's the point of anything?"

"Okay, I know, I know," Beechy says quickly. "It was only a suggestion, and I assumed you'd shoot it down. So, I came up with one other option. In all honesty, I prefer this one myself, in terms of its strategic nature. My reservations come from the fact that I don't want to see you get hurt. But what I want is to put you in one of the work camps in the lower sectors, whichever one we can get you into with the least amount of trouble. I don't mean as an official or someone who sneaks into the camp—I mean as an actual worker, as a girl expecting to be replaced. Since there are so many people in the camps, you'd have a good chance of blending in. We need to rally those in the camps to our cause, and the best way I can see of accomplishing that is by giving them someone like them to lead them in rebellion. Someone like you. And Logan, if he'll agree to go with you."

He pauses, waiting for me to say something. Waiting for me to yell. But something holds me back.

Beechy's right: I couldn't pass as an official or an instructor. I look like someone who lives in one of the work camps, and that's the part I'm fit to play. It's a part we need someone to play, if we want those in the camps on our side. Most of them wouldn't trust any adults, even ones claiming to be trying to help them.

But if I agreed to this, I'd be trapped in one of the camps again. I'd have to worry about being beaten by officials, or dragged off to one of the kill chambers. I'd have to be prepared for the possibility of being captured and turned over to Commander Charlie at any moment.

"You okay?" Beechy asks.

"Fine." I've been saying that a lot lately.

But I force myself to stay calm. I will be calm about this.

This is exactly what I wanted: an important part in the mission. I will be in danger wherever I go once I leave our headquarters. But at least in a camp I might have a shot at rallying more people to help us overthrow the Developers.

"You don't have to agree if you don't want to," Beechy says. "And I didn't mean I'd send you in alone. There will be other rebels posing as officials, to keep an eye on you and step in if things get out of hand. This isn't a one-man mission."

And Charlie won't expect this. He'll expect me to holler and beg and plead before I let someone imprison me in another work camp. So, officials are less likely to look for me there.

I force the word out before I can change my mind again: "Okay."

"Okay?" Beechy says.

"I'll do it."

Even if I fail and end up captured, I will be one step closer to Charlie—one step closer to killing the man who has taken almost everything from me. I owe it to Oliver, to Cady, to avenge their deaths. I owe it to everyone Charlie has ever stolen from me.

"Good," Beechy says. "As I said, I'll do my best to protect you."

"How come you trust me, even after what I did to Cady?" I blurt out the words. I'm sick of not talking about this. I'm sick of pretending it's not my fault she's dead. "You saw what I did in the jet. You saw how I lost control. I . . . I killed her, Beechy."

In the silence, Beechy doesn't say anything, and his expression is impossible to read. I keep talking because I don't know what else to do.

"I didn't know what I was doing." The words come out hoarse, like I'm wrenching them from my lungs. "I started hallucinating and I thought I was back in Karum. I thought Charlie was strangling me, and I couldn't do anything to stop him. But I need to stop him. He needs to lose something, since he's stolen so many people from us."

"He will." Beechy moves closer to me. His palm touches my cheek, gently guiding my face to look at his.

My eyes water, but the warmth of his hand helps me focus. The emergency lights turn his normally brown eyes a shade of midnight blue, making me think of the sky I sometimes wish would swallow me whole.

"We'll beat him," Beechy says softly. "You and I. All of us, together. But only if we don't fall apart."

"It's hard not to."

"I know." He presses his fingertips into my cheek, then lets his hand fall away.

Silently, I promise myself I won't cry for a long time, maybe not ever again after we leave the KIMO facility. I need to shed my weak skin and put on armor, or there's no way I'll survive.

In my next breath, I make a decision. Wiping my eyes, I push past Beechy until I reach the wall of compartments. I open them until I find a medikit with a small pair of scissors inside. The blades seem a bit dull, but they'll have to do.

I put the medikit back where it goes and walk down the perpendicular corridor to the passenger bunk room. There's a mirror inside. The light is dim, as it is everywhere, but there's enough of it for me to make out my reflection. I pull the elastic band out of my hair and watch my curls fall down. They're longer than they used to be; the tips reach well past my shoulders.

I open the scissors and slide the blades between my hair, lining them up with the base of my neck and moving them higher. Shorter is best. Short like a boy, so hopefully I'll be harder to recognize.

I make the first cut to my hair, then the second. Again and again, keeping my hands as steady as I'm able. Beechy helps me cut the back straight.

When we're finished, my reflection stares back at me, unfamiliar. She looks uncertain at first, fingering the short ends of her hair.

Slowly, the edges of her lips curve upward. When she smiles like that, she looks braver than I feel, but maybe that's all that matters.

# 7

When I return to my bunk room around four thirty in the morning, the compound is starting to wake up. All my roommates' beds are empty; they're probably in the mess hall. Logan is rubbing his eyes and pulling on his boots in the dim light from the space heater.

He looks up after I walk in.

"Hey," I say.

He opens his mouth to reply, but freezes as soon as he notices what's different about me. My cheeks flush under his gaze.

My hair isn't just shorter; it's also blonder now. I spent the last half hour soaking my curls with bleaching chemicals Beechy helped me find in the storage room, to better my disguise. It's not foolproof, since the color won't last forever and there's not an easy way for me to bring chemicals with me on the mission. Once I'm in the camp, I'll have to improvise.

I have more pressing concerns at the moment though. Beechy

asked me to talk to Logan, to see if he'll come with me to the work camp. I have a feeling he's not going to be happy I agreed to it. He's going to try to talk me out of it.

But I've made up my mind, and I won't change it.

"We need to talk," I say.

Logan blinks once, twice, falling out of his stare. "When did you wake up?" he asks.

I bite my lip. "About an hour ago. Sorry I left. I just couldn't fall back asleep, and I didn't want to bother you."

"It's fine," he says, but the slight hitch in his voice makes me think it isn't. He rubs his eyes again, as if he isn't fully awake yet. Walking closer to me, he reaches out and touches my short curls. "This looks nice, by the way. Different, but it suits you."

"Thanks," I say, though I'm not sure I believe him. But I don't care if it looks nice or not, as long as it helps me survive a little longer. "I figured it might make me less easy to recognize, since we're going into enemy territory and all."

"I think it'll help." Logan gives me a sad smile. "Though I'll worry no matter what."

He'll worry even more once I tell him where I'm going.

"What did you want to talk about?" he asks.

I hesitate, searching for the right words. "I ran into Beechy. I talked to him about my assignment for the mission." I pause. *Just get it over with.* He's going to find out sooner or later. "I'm going to go undercover in one of the work camps in the lower sectors. Beechy wants me to spread talk of our rebellion among the workers and recruit their help."

Logan stares at me, his smile slowly fading.

"He thinks it will work best coming from someone like me, instead of someone disguised as an official," I continue.

"Beechy's sending you to a camp. And you agreed to it?" Logan's voice cracks on the words. "You didn't argue against it?"

"I said I would do it."

"Why?"

"I think I can do the most good there. We'll have the best chance of overthrowing the Developers if we work with the kids in the camps. You know what they're like, Logan. They'll want to fight if they know they're not alone."

"Yes, but you won't be safe there."

"Beechy said he'll send in rebels disguised as officials too—"

Logan presses his fists against his forehead in agitation. "But they can't stay with you every second. You could still end up hurt or captured. You could still end up in quarantine."

I run a hand down my arm. My chest hurts, but I ignore it. "I know."

Logan's silence stretches as if he's waiting for me to say something else, something that might convince him to stop worrying. If only I had words that would help him feel better.

"But you don't care," he says.

"There are more important things than what might happen to me," I say softly.

I'm more afraid of what will happen to Logan if he comes with me. I could handle getting captured or beaten or shoved into a kill chamber, but I don't know if I could handle that happening to him. It would be easier if he'd stay here in the compound, so I could do what I have to do without worrying about him.

"You're always trying to protect other people," he says. "Like you don't even care about yourself. Like you think no else cares about you, either, or would be affected if you were killed. But I would be. I want to protect you, if I can, but you have to let me."

*No one can protect me*, I want to tell him. As long as the Developers rule Kiel, I will always be facing capture and death.

"Beechy said you can go with me, if you want," I say, no longer meeting his eyes. "Or you can stay here with some of the others and join up with us when we attack the Core. It's your choice."

"Of course I'm going with you. If I'm not going to change your mind, there's no vruxing way I'm letting you go in there alone. I'm not losing you again." Logan's jaw hardens, and he balls his hands at his sides.

I can see there's no changing his mind, either.

"Okay," I say. "Together, then."

Logan nods stiffly. "I'll tell Beechy."

He limps past me and opens the door.

I stand alone in the bunk room after he's gone, releasing the panic I was bottling up so he wouldn't see it.

I hope I made the right decision when I agreed to this. I hope I haven't put Logan in a position where I will lose him forever.

But worrying about what's going to happen won't change a thing; it will only make me more vulnerable to losing control of myself again.

I will count to three, and then I will take control. I will stop being afraid.

*One*

*Two*

*Three*

I walk out the door.

—⋇—

"You're sure this will work?" I ask, watching the nurse, Uma, fill a thick syringe with black ink.

Machines beep around me in the medical bay, and the scent of antiseptic fills the air. Beechy brought me and Logan here so Uma could alter the citizenship numbers branded on our wrists, which officials could use to identify us with their special scanners in the work camp.

"Don't worry, she knows what she's doing," Beechy says, giving me a reassuring smile. Logan stands beside him, his arms folded, waiting for his turn in the chair.

Uma finishes filling the syringe and sets the half-empty tube of ink on a tray. She flicks the syringe. "The consistency should be right. But this may hurt, honey. Usually doctors use a special machine for branding."

"I'll manage," I say, trying not to squirm in my seat. I want her to hurry and get this over with. If I could remember my first branding, I'd know more what to expect. But new children in the work camps are tagged with their identification number within a few days of birth.

At least we're altering only two of my numbers, not giving me a brand-new set.

"So how will this work?" Logan asks. "You give us each a new tag and the officials won't be able to identify us in their system?"

"Yes," Beechy says. "Their scanners will pull up a new profile, a fake one. Sandy and one of our techs figured out how to hack into the Core citizen registrar through our computers. There's a file for every single citizen in both the cities and the work camps. We'll create a brand-new file for you connected to your new tag number. No one should notice it among all the other files, and then officials shouldn't have any reason to suspect who you really are. It'll be safer than tampering with your real file, since that could alert Charlie to the fact you're both still alive."

"Good," I say. I'd prefer if Charlie wasn't certain of that fact until I'm standing in front of him with a gun aimed at his forehead.

Beechy glances at his time-band. "I hate to leave, but I need to hand out mission assignments and check on how the prep is going. We're aiming to leave in about an hour."

"We'll be fine," I say. "You can go."

"Good luck," he says, and heads out of the room.

"Lay your wrist flat on the armrest," Uma says, setting the syringe down and picking up an antiseptic wipe.

I set my left arm on the rest and flex my hand. The harsh light directly overhead makes the inked characters on my wrist—S68477—paler than usual. I focus on the beeping of the monitors and the rustle of the curtains around the beds as Uma wipes my skin.

"Ready?" she asks, picking up the syringe.

"Ready." I do my best to keep still as she guides the needle under my skin and squeezes out a drop of ink.

"Is it bad?" Logan asks.

"Stings a little." It could be much worse.

The curtains stir around the cot across the aisle from my chair.

"I need some help," a male voice says. A short cough follows.

The other nurse on duty walks over. "Everything all right, Mal?"

The nurse pushes the curtain back enough for me to glimpse the young man in the bed. His blond hair is pulled back in a ponytail. His arm is in a sling, and there's a thick bandage on his forehead.

My body tenses. It's the young official on Cady's ship, who came from the Surface city.

The curtain shuts again, blocking him from view.

Uma continues guiding the needle under my skin, in and out,

but I barely feel it anymore. Mal was on a gurney yesterday, covered in blood after the medics pulled him from the recon mission wreckage. He was unconscious because of me.

The nurse draws the curtain open again a minute later, and Mal steps out from behind it, fixing the collar of his shirt with his unwounded arm. He's dressed in a tight gray suit and knee-high boots, like Sam and other Core officials used to wear. Mal must've had the outfit on underneath his armor.

"You sure you feel strong enough to walk?" the nurse asks.

"I feel strong enough to lift a mountain," Mal says. "Though I'm not sure my left arm agrees."

The nurse laughs. "If you say so. Make sure you let someone know if you change your mind. Feeling weak or dizzy after what you went through wouldn't be unusual."

"Understood." Mal's gaze falls on me as he heads for the door out of the sick bay. The softest frown creases his brow. I quickly return my focus to Uma's hand guiding the ink needle.

He was unconscious when he saw me last, so there's no way he'd recognize me from yesterday. But if he's worked in the Surface city for a long time, he might've seen me. He might've yelled at me a hundred times, or hurt me, even. I have no way of knowing. Most officials wore their helmets when they were on patrol.

Out of the corner of my eye, Mal disappears through the door. Thank goodness.

"You okay?" Logan asks, looking at me strangely. I wonder what my face looks like.

"Yeah." I grimace. "The needle's just hurting a bit much." It's not a complete lie.

"Almost finished," Uma says. "Keep holding still."

I shouldn't be afraid of Mal, since he's on our side, but it's hard to believe he's really different than all the other officials I've met. It's hard not to worry that he would do something to me if he discovered I'm the reason he almost died yesterday.

Hopefully he won't find out.

✳

Logan and I leave the medical bay half an hour later. Distant voices echo in the corridors, and a low rumble comes from the flight port ahead. People were just starting to load the ships with equipment when we passed through there earlier.

"We should get something to eat," Logan says, wincing as he flexes his wrist. "I bet everything's almost ready for departure."

"Hopefully," I say, rubbing my own wrist. The skin is raw and red around my new citizenship tag: S88472. The two changed numbers are slightly thicker and darker than the rest, but hopefully most officials won't look closely. The code just needs to fool their scanners.

As we approach the port entrance doors, an odd smell drifts into my nostrils. I sniff the air, unsure what it is or if I'm making it up. But it smells a lot worse than engine oil.

"Do you smell that?" I ask.

"I smell something," Logan says, picking up his pace.

We walk through the open doors into the port. I freeze in my tracks.

Thick, black smoke billows from the open engine cover of one of the Davara jets. Figures run through the hazy air around the ship, smacking at the smoke with dirty rags.

Logan curses, hurrying forward. I follow him, looking frantically around for something we can use to help.

But by the time we reach the ship, the people already helping seem to be stopping. It looks like they have it under control. There are no flames in sight, only smoke.

Paley and Fiona are here, both of them looking exhausted. But they can't have been working long to put out the fire, or one of them would've sounded an alarm and Beechy would be here.

Skylar steps around from the other side of the ship, her face and safety suit covered in grease. She throws her rag on the floor and screams in rage.

"What's with the smoke?" a voice says behind me. I turn as Buck walks through the doors leading to the mess hall, waving the air in front of his nose. He's holding a piece of bread in his hand.

Skylar storms at him. "You've got some nerve."

He throws up his hands in defense. "'Scuse me?"

"Did you think I wouldn't try another test run this morning? I knew you weren't exactly on board with the mission, but I can't believe you'd go this far."

He looks from her to the smoking jet and back again, then barks a laugh. "You think I did this?"

"I don't know anyone else who's been having reservations. The fuel lines on my jet are completely busted—hell of a job you did there, buddy. Did you do it to all the ships? If you wasted even half our fuel supply, I swear I'll carve your brains out with a knife."

Skylar circles around Buck, forcing him to take a step backwards in the direction of the smoking jet.

We need a solid fuel supply to reach the Surface city in time. And we need enough left to be able to get back here, in case something goes wrong. Otherwise, we could be stranded.

"Skylar, how can you be sure this was his fault?" Paley asks nervously.

"Listen to her," Buck says. "This wasn't my doing, I swear."

"It was your shift all night in the command center, wasn't it?" Skylar asks.

He stutters. "Y-yes."

"Show me the tapes from this morning, then. Show me who did this."

"Well, now, the cameras went off for about an hour overnight due to a slight malfunction—"

Skylar shoves Buck hard into a ladder leaning against one of the jets. "Do you think I'm an idiot?"

Fiona takes a step forward, her nostrils flaring. "Sky, I think you need to calm down."

"We should break them up," I say to Logan.

But before either of us can move, Skylar slams her fist into Buck's nose. His back hits the ladder again and he curses loudly, cupping a hand over his nose. She flexes the hand she used, wincing.

"What's going on?" someone says behind me. Beechy hurries into the flight port, Sandy with him. "There was a small fire due to a fuel leak, thanks to Buck here," Skylar says, her voice cool and her eyes narrowed, "but don't worry, we've got it under control. Though we do need to do a thorough check of all the ship engines for part damage."

"You've got no proof it was me," Buck says. He moves his hand a little, and I see his nose is bloody, if not broken.

Beechy walks forward to examine the jet engine, which is still producing a thin stream of black smoke. "How did the fire start?" he asks.

"I went to do a last-minute test flight and discovered all the fuel lines were fried, leaking all over the parts," Skylar says.

"They'd definitely been tampered with," Fiona says, cutting in.

"The engine sparked and the lines caught fire, but we helped her put it out."

"Our bigger problem is that the jet's fuel supply is less than half what it should be," Skylar says. "And whoever tampered with this ship might've messed with all the others."

"We need to examine them immediately," Beechy says, moving around to the other side of the jet. "Fiona, Paley, if any fuel lines can be fixed, fix them. Sandy, if any mechanics are in the mess hall or the storage rooms, please inform them they're needed here."

Sandy nods, tucks a strand of her short dark hair behind her ear, and hurries away.

"Skylar, lock Buck inside your bunk room."

"Captain, please, I swear I didn't do this—," Buck says.

Skylar grabs him roughly by the arm and hauls him across the floor, ignoring his protests.

Beechy reappears from the other side of the jet, frustration in his eyes.

"Is there anything we can do to help?" Logan asks.

He shakes his head, seeming distracted. "Did Uma finish fixing your ID tags?" he asks.

I hold out my wrist for him to see.

"Good. I already dealt with both your citizen files. And there's no need to worry about the fuel supply. We'll take care of it. Just get your safety suits on and be ready to leave."

He sounds calm enough, but I note the tension in his jaw as he walks past me.

"Well, we should probably get breakfast first," Logan says.

"We'd better," I say, "or we might not have time."

"Come on." He grabs my hand, and we head for the mess hall.

I can't shake off my uneasy feeling. Beechy is wrong; we should be worried. Not just because we might not have enough fuel to reach the Surface city, or make it back here if we need to, but also because whoever tampered with the equipment is still in this facility. Maybe Buck's a liar and it really was him, or maybe he's telling the truth and it wasn't.

But there is someone among us who wants us to lose.

# 8

By the time inspections are completed and we're ready to depart, there's a buzz of nervousness in the air. We don't know exactly when Charlie's officials are transporting everyone out of the Surface settlement. We're not sure we'll reach the city in time.

My safety suit crinkles with every step as Logan and I head for the hovercraft we're supposed to board. Underneath my suit, I'm wearing the clothes I wore when I first arrived at the compound: the dirty rags I was given in Karum. They smell like sweat and death, but they'll help me blend into the work camp better than the army tank top and jacket I was wearing earlier.

Ahead of us, Fiona and Paley are hugging at the hovercraft's cargo lift. One of them must be staying here. A third of the Alliance will remain behind to keep the headquarters running, but they'll meet up with us again once we're ready to infiltrate the Core. Beechy has arranged a method of contact with them.

"Do we know how much fuel leaked?" Logan asks. His arm brushes mine as he walks beside me.

"We can ask Beechy," I say. He's saying good-bye to Sandy under the wing of a Davara jet. Dropping to his knees, he plants a kiss on her belly, where their baby grows inside, still too small for a bump to be visible. It's a sweet gesture, but it makes me sad.

Sandy found out she was pregnant not long ago, the week I was in the Core. She still must have several more months until she'll give birth. I wonder where she'll be, and if Beechy will be with her. The uprising might be over by then. There's no way to know which side will have won, or who among us will come back here once we leave on the ships today.

Looking around at the steel walls, the ships, the lights, I wonder if I'll come back. I'm not even sure if I want to. I might be better off not getting through the mission in one piece, if worse things are still to come. But I hope it will be my choice when the time comes.

"We're all set for departure, sir," a pilot calls from one of the two flight pods we're taking.

"Good," Beechy says, pulling away from Sandy. "Let's get everyone on board."

I linger near the cargo lift, to intercept Beechy before he boards the hovercraft.

"You talk to him," Logan says, heading up the ramp. "I'll save us seats."

"Okay."

When Beechy reaches the lift, I ask, "What happened about the fuel? Do you know how much we lost?"

"We have enough to reach the city," he says, his voice oddly stiff. "It'll be fine. Go take your seat."

He didn't answer my question.

"Do we have enough in case we need to get back?" I ask. "And the people staying behind, do they have enough for their ships?"

"Clementine, please let me deal with this. It's not your concern."

"It's everyone's concern."

"We're not backing out of this," he says, almost snapping the words. "Is that what you want? Because it's the only other option."

I press my lips together. But he's right. This is still the best plan we have—the *only* plan. It was always going to be a risk, every step of the way. Whatever Darren thinks he found out about Charlie's plan could be false information. We might show up to an empty city, or one with ships poised and ready to blast our hulls with bullets. We might show up when everyone's leaving and slip in among them just fine, only to be recognized once we're on board their ships. We could be discovered any time.

But we have to take this chance. We have to try for an advantage.

"Fine," I say.

Beechy's expression softens. "Sorry, I didn't mean to snap at you. But I really am confident we'll be okay. If we run into problems, it won't be because of fuel."

"Yeah, you're right." I move past him to head up the cargo lift. "Let's get out of here and get this over with."

The clump of his boots tells me he's following.

At the top of the lift, I walk through the small cargo bay into the aisle between the passenger seats. There are eight on either side of me, in rows of two. All the seats are taken. Paley's sitting up front, looking a bit lost without her sister.

To my right, Mal's settling into the front seat, struggling to pull the straps over his shoulders with one hand. He's wearing his armor again.

"Let's get buckled in, everyone," Beechy says, moving past me in the aisle and through the door into the cockpit. He and Skylar are piloting the ship.

I slip into the window seat Logan was saving for me, in the row behind Mal.

"What did Beechy say?" Logan asks.

"He said not to worry," I say, pulling the belt straps over my shoulders and clicking them into place. "So, I'm trying not to."

There's a rumble as the ship engines start. Behind us, the cargo lift slides up into the hovercraft, sealing the exit.

Skylar's voice rings through the ship over the intercomm: "Hang tight, everyone. We are cleared for departure."

Logan slips his fingers through mine, tightly. Like he's afraid something could still separate us, making one of us leave while the other stayed behind.

Through the window, I see Sandy, Fiona, and the other rebels who aren't coming with us standing near the entrance to the port. A couple of them wave as we lift off the ground. But their faces are tense, worried.

For an instant, I wish whoever messed with the fuel supply had leaked all of it, so that we wouldn't be able to fly away. But staying here won't save us. Charlie and the other Developers won't stop killing for selfish motives, not until someone takes away their power, their voice, their weapons. As long as Charlie is still able to kill, I could lose friends again. I could lose Logan.

I might not care whether I survive, but I do care what happens to him.

—✳—

Morning sunlight streams over the snow-topped mountains when we emerge from the compound tunnels. I half expected the world changed entirely in the past week. But the valley is exactly as I remember it from before, with crooked, gnarled trees along the riverbank, and the river full of rapids.

The sky looks the same too. The acid shield a thousand miles above us is faint in the daylight, a shimmering, pink bubble enclosing Kiel. Commander Charlie put it back up after he realized Beechy and I wouldn't turn his ship around and bring back his bomb. But the shield can't do much for us anymore; enough acid got into the atmosphere in the short amount of time the shield was down. Still, I'm relieved to see it shimmering up there.

As Skylar guides our ship higher, we rise above the mountain peaks. I feel exposed in the open sky. Maybe Charlie's officials know where we've been hiding, and they've been waiting for us to emerge.

But no ships appear with guns firing. No one blasts our hull to bits, and Skylar makes no mention of contacts on our radar.

No one knows we're on the move yet.

⁂

The KIMO facility sits deeper in the mountains than I realized. By the time we reach the ocean, the sun has moved behind us.

There's a lot of turbulence; it must be windy outside. Some of the other passengers look nervous in their seats, gripping their armrests. Beside me, Logan dozes in his seat, his arm bumping against mine. I wish I could fall asleep as easily. The incessant rumbling of my seat makes me dizzy. I stare out the window so I won't be sick.

Below, the water looks peaceful. The waves roll and I picture the animals swimming beneath them. I've never been in the ocean, but when I was in the Core having difficulty with Extraction training, Beechy distracted me from my worries by showing me some of the sea creatures scientists had captured on expeditions to the Surface. My favorite was the vul, which looked almost human, but had skin like gel and only three fingers on each hand. Beechy said it was the last of its species; it's all alone in the universe. Unless there are creatures like it far, far away. If Marden's existence was a secret, maybe there are more worlds not so different from this one.

There is something strange about the ocean surface. Most of the water is bluish green and clear, but there are faint streaks that almost look like blood here and there. It takes a minute for me to realize what it must be: moonshine.

Back at headquarters, the scientists took a reading in the valley to see how much leaked into our air before Charlie put the shield back up. They said 5 percent of the air concentration was lethal acid—more than double the amount of carbon dioxide, and moonshine is far more potent.

The concentration is likely to go down. After all, it seeped into our atmosphere before the protective shield was built, and eventually neutralized. But we don't know how long that will take. It could be months, years, decades. Long enough for a lot of people to die, if they're exposed to it.

Charlie must've known this would happen. But when he shut off the shield, he didn't care about the loss of lives. All he cared about was recovering his precious bomb so he could rip our world into pieces, fly his Core battleship away, and destroy Marden's civilization. All this so he could build a new empire far away.

I tilt my head to the sky. There are no stars out yet, but I can picture them the way they were beyond the shield: brilliant and numerous. Like something out of a dream.

Marden is out there, orbiting a distant sun. It's been roughly four centuries since we sent our battleships there to wipe out the Mardenites, and three since they planted their acid generator on our moon in retaliation, if the stories Fred told me in Karum are true. We lost contact with them not long after that, during the Great Rebellion, and we haven't heard from them since. Most of the citizens of Kiel don't know Marden exists.

The Mardenites have either forgotten us too, or they believe their poisonous moon permanently removed us as a threat. In all likelihood, they have no idea our commander still wants to wipe them out and build his own regime on the ruins of their civilization.

Surely Charlie hasn't given up. He could've already started construction on another bomb. He has Fred, the original constructor, in his custody, and I'm sure he has the necessary supplies, so he has the means to re-create the one we used against the moon.

But he's clearly up to something else too. Instead of ignoring everyone in the outer sectors, he's moving them belowground. I bet the people in the work camp, especially, think he's saving them. They will be safer from moonshine, yes, but I don't believe they'll be safe from Charlie. He must've realized they'll be more useful alive; he needs them for something. But for what?

I need to understand his full motivation. Whatever his new plan is, we need to stop it.

※

Someone shakes my shoulder, and I open my eyes abruptly. My face is covered in a sheen of sweat. I had another nightmare, where I was back in Karum, and a nurse was shoving a tube down my throat. The tube had insects inside it—silver-and-blue bugs with sharp pincers. They crawled out of the tube into my esophagus and slowly chewed my insides while I screamed and screamed and the nurse whispered, "It's going to be okay," over and over.

"You okay?" Logan asks. His hand's still touching my shoulder. I give him a tight nod. That's easier than lying through my teeth.

The transport rumbles beneath me. It's still windy outside. I look out the window. The moon is half shadow tonight, and a thick layer of clouds hides the stars from view. The clouds are so dark, I wonder if it's going to rain.

One of the flight pods hovers into view through my window, traveling alongside us. Blue dots of light blink on its hull. I focus on the light until my eyes adjust and I can see the gray shapes of cacti and tumbleweeds below us. We've reached the desert. I don't remember leaving the ocean; I must've fallen asleep before we passed over Karum.

"Where are we?" I ask.

"We're almost there," Logan says.

Ahead of us, the force field shimmers in the distance. The barrier around the Surface settlement. It's faint at first, a thin band of emerald like an aurora, but it grows brighter as we near it.

I can almost see the city beyond: the high steel towers still a few miles away; the dot of light flying above it that must be a ship. The city must not be empty, at least not yet.

I dig my nails into the seat upholstery. In a few minutes, we will be in Charlie's territory.

The ship-comm crackles on, and Skylar's voice rings through the ship: "We're about to cross over the Surface settlement line."

In the row in front of me, Mal gets up from his seat and moves to the cockpit door.

"The security team in the city is likely to spot us immediately and send out patrol ships," Skylar continues. "But we have friends on the inside. We're hoping to contact them before the patrols reach us, so we can get clearance to the city. In case that falls apart . . . please stand by."

The comm link shuts off, and the compartment falls silent.

I stare at the closed cockpit door, which Mal just disappeared through. If he was working in the security hub two days ago, he has the proper communication codes. He must be the one helping us contact the patrols.

A bad feeling curls my insides. Mal helped Darren and Cady escape the city, yes, but he could've had an ulterior motive. He could've lied; he could still be working for Charlie. He could be leading us straight into a trap.

I need to be up in the cockpit when he helps us contact the patrols. I need to do something, if I can.

The ship is still shaking a lot, and it might not be smart to move around. But I don't care; I unbuckle and stand. I can't sit here and wait for something bad to happen.

"What are you doing?" Logan asks as I squeeze past him in his seat.

"Going to talk to Beechy."

He opens his mouth like he's going to say something, but shuts it, changing his mind.

I move down the center aisle and press the button to open the cockpit door. A gust of cold air washes over me as I step inside. The compartment seems small with three people crowded inside. Skylar sits in the pilot's seat with Beechy in the seat beside her and Mal standing to his right. The force field shimmers in the distance, drawing ever closer through the window.

"You're sure no one's changed the code since you left?" Beechy asks Mal, tapping a sequence of numbers into the comm box.

"They change it once a week, and they'd just changed it the day I flew away," Mal says.

"You'd better be telling the truth."

"I am. I swear."

I stare at the back of Mal's ponytail, wishing I could see his face. Then I might be able to tell if he's lying.

"Can I help you?" Skylar asks, swiveling in her chair.

I was hoping I'd be able to talk to Beechy instead of her. I'm pretty sure she still thinks I'm not entirely stable—and she's probably right.

"Um." I use the first excuse that pops into my head: "I was feeling a bit sick. I thought it might help to look out a bigger window."

The slight pinch in Skylar's cheeks tells me she's annoyed I came in here. But the flush in my cheeks must be passable as real sickness, because she presses her lips together and turns back to her controls. "Take a seat. Just don't throw up on any of the flight mechanisms."

"I'll try not to." I pull out the passenger seat from the back wall of the cockpit and sit and secure the safety straps. Out the window, the force field shimmers directly ahead of us. It's a bright and brilliant emerald from this close up.

For what feels like a hundred seconds, it floats before our transport.

We could still turn back. We could still try to find another way.

Then it's too late. We've passed over the force field, and the settlement line is behind us. Before us is an open stretch of sand, dust, and rock spanning at least a mile, maybe more. There's nothing to hide us. Three dots probably just popped up on the radar screen in the security hub. Whoever's on duty knows we're here now.

A beeping sound comes from the comm box.

"We have contact," Beechy says. The muscles of his arms and back form ridges beneath the fabric of his safety suit.

"You should let me talk to them," Mal says. "I covered all my bases when I left. They should give me clearance."

Slowly, Beechy hands the comm to Mal. "Be careful."

Mal twirls a blue knob, and there's a crackle.

A deep voice cuts in: "This is the Surface security hub. Pilot, we do not recognize your ship. Please identify."

"This is Cadet Malcolm, citizen H63587," Mal says without a pause. "I'm returning from a supply run in Sector B-7."

"Stand by while we confirm."

I fidget with my hands. I stare out the window, at the faint outline of trees in the distance. Drops of water speckle the window as the rain starts.

It was raining the last time I was here too, the morning I said good-bye to Logan.

I remember the officials dragging him away; I remember boarding the ship afterwards; I remember thinking I was safe.

There's another crackle through the speaker. "Cadet Malcolm," the voice says, "you are not authorized to go farther without an escort."

"Cadet Demetrius gave me authorization," Mal says. "As I said, I'm returning from a supply run. I assure you, I don't need an escort."

"Cadet Demetrius is not available to confirm," the voice says. "I repeat, you are not authorized to go any farther. Stay at your current position. Patrol ships are on their way."

Mal hisses through his teeth. Beechy cuts the comm link.

"I'm sorry," Mal says. "Demetrius always runs the night shift. He must've run into trouble."

"Or the operation's already under way, and most of the guards are at the departure station," Skylar says.

Tension runs through Beechy's jaw, but he doesn't say anything.

Half of me believes Mal is telling the truth and this isn't his fault. The other half feels like stringing him up and throwing him in my old Karum cell.

"What's our next move?" Skylar asks.

"We need some cover," Beechy says. "The patrols will be here soon. Head for those trees, and make it fast."

"Copy that." Skylar pushes the thrusters forward, speaking into her ear-comm: "Pilots, we're switching to Plan B. Stay close behind me."

I grip my armrests as we speed up, until we're going full throttle. Mal hurriedly takes the other passenger seat so he won't fall over.

The ground is a blur below us. Lightning flashes across the sky above the city, turning the clouds purple.

I hope Skylar is wrong and the operation isn't already under way. If the last transports leave for the lower sectors without us, our plan is ruined whether or not we evade the patrols.

The floodlights appear when we're almost to the forest. Three small pairs of white lights; three patrol ships rising from between the distant skyscrapers.

Skylar nose-dives our transport toward the trees. We're flying too fast. We're going to crash; we're going to hit the branches and spin out of control.

But Skylar pulls us up at the last second, easing off the thrusters. We glide above the trees. I stop gripping my armrests so tightly.

"Should I go lower?" Skylar asks.

"Put us down where the trees are thickest," Beechy says, unbuckling and moving toward the cockpit door. "Tell the other pilots to do the same, but leave their engines running. I think I have a plan."

# 9

Rain splashes on my safety helmet and turns the forest floor to mud. I crouch low, my spine pressed against a tree trunk, gripping a gun in my hands. The gun feels heavy, much too powerful. I don't know if I trust myself to use it, after what I did the last time I controlled a gun, but I have no other choice if I want to help the Alliance reach the lower sectors.

Logan crouches behind a tree a few feet away. Mal, Skylar, and another pilot, Jensen, are still on board our transports. The rest of us are hidden around the clearing.

The roar of the patrol ship engines is loud. They're almost here.

We have the advantage, I remind myself. We are the ones the patrols should fear, since my friends and I have outsmarted Charlie and his men on more than one occasion. We are the ones who can't be controlled by his serum.

He can't control me, either. As long as I don't panic; as long as I remember I am stronger.

I squint to see the clearing through the branches. The lights of our ships are still on, and the engines are humming.

Light floods the branches above me, and I look up. The ships hover low, sending wind rustling through the trees. A flash of lightning fills the clouds above them.

A loudspeaker comes on: *"Come outside your ships. Surrender your weapons."*

I snap my teeth together. We need them to land and come out of their ships. We need them to try to board us, but I'm afraid they'll shoot from the air.

*"I repeat, come outside your ships with your hands in the air, or we will shoot."*

I can't see the clearing well enough from where I'm standing. I need to get higher.

Clutching my gun in one hand, I straighten and reach for the lowest branch of the tree I'm under.

Logan notices too soon. "Clementine, please don't."

"I just want to see what's going on."

He looks like he wants to argue, but all he says is, "Be careful, okay?"

"I always am."

He mutters something in reply.

Ignoring him, I heave myself up onto the branch. It's difficult with only one hand, but at least the gun is smaller than the one I held the last time I climbed a tree, in Phantom, the war game I played in the Core. I had trouble shooting a gun then too, though it was only a simulation and my targets couldn't really die.

But that was a game. This is real life, and if I have to shoot someone to defend myself and those I care about, I will do it.

I can't see much until I'm a few branches higher. I balance on the one below and lean against the tree trunk so I won't fall. Brushing aside the leaves in front of me, I peer into the clearing. The back of the passenger hovercraft has opened and the ramp has lowered. Someone in full-body armor is walking down it with his hands over the helmet on his head, one arm slightly bent in injury.

Mal is surrendering.

The patrol ships hover lower. I don't take my eyes off them.

One by one, the ships land, surrounding ours. They are sleek silver hovercrafts, but they're not very big. My guess is they hold only two or three passengers each. I hope I'm right.

A door slides open at the back of each hovercraft, and officials in armor climb out. Seven of them. They all carry guns the size of my arm, and I glimpse smaller weapons in their holsters. I could shoot them from here, but there's a good chance I'd miss and give my position away. And I'm not supposed to yet. I'm supposed to wait for Beechy's signal.

The patrolmen march up to Mal. The leader says something, and Mal replies, but I can't make out his words.

The leader signals two of the men to check out the flight pods. A second pair heads up the ramp into the passenger hovercraft. Skylar and Jensen are still inside.

The minutes pass like days while I wait. I keep expecting to hear something—a shout, maybe. Or a gunshot. But except for the sound of thunder in the distance, there's only silence.

The patrols who were checking the flight pods come back out first. "No one's on board, sir," one of them says.

The other two patrols appear at the top of the hovercraft ramp. "This ship's empty too."

Their leader steps closer to Mal and grabs his arm, the injured one. I wince in his behalf.

"Where did they go?" the leader asks.

"I told you, I came here alone," says Mal. "I found these pods abandoned."

I don't hear how the patrol leader responds, because I'm staring at the two men who went into the hovercraft. Maybe I'm only imagining it, but one of them seems shorter than he was before. He's holding his weapon differently too, letting it dangle from his hand instead of cradling it to his chest.

"Sweep the area," the leader says.

"Yes, sir." The patrols move off into the trees, all heading in different directions.

One of them heads straight for me and Logan. *Vrux.*

I don't want to leave him alone on the ground, but there's no way I can get down without the patrol seeing me. I position my gun to fire from where I am. I won't wait for any signal if he gets too close to Logan; I will simply shoot. My hands might refuse, but I will force them to squeeze the trigger.

I'm half-distracted, though. The shorter patrol and his companion are heading into the trees more slowly than the rest, like they're waiting for something.

It happens in a split second: The shorter patrol lifts his gun and spins, shouting, "Now!" Mal twists away from the patrol leader. A shot rings out.

The leader falls, blood spilling from the hole in his shoulder. He lets out a strangled cry.

I recognized the shorter patrol's voice, even through the warping mechanics of his helmet. It's not a he; it's a she. It's Skylar.

The other patrols realize what's happening. But the rebels have already opened fire.

The roar of gunshots fills my ears, blasting again and again. People yell, and bodies stagger through the trees. I can't tell if anyone's down. The rain makes it hard to see.

The patrol below me was distracted by someone, but now he moves toward Logan again, firing as he runs. Logan fires back, but misses. I watch him turn and limp farther into the forest. The patrolman chases after him.

I have to bring him down. He is going to kill Logan.

*Don't think. Just do it.*

I wait for the first clear shot between the branches and squeeze the trigger hard. But my sweaty hand slips. I don't know where I hit, but I'm sure I missed the patrolman.

The recoil is worse than I expected; I nearly lose my balance. I hang on to the branch above me with everything I have.

Two more shots ring out. There's a thump as the patrol hits the ground. I can see blood pooling in the mud and grass even from a distance. Logan must've hit him.

But I can't see Logan. I don't know if the patrolman hit him too.

Panic makes my heart race.

"Logan!" I scream.

He doesn't answer.

I climb down as quickly as I can. I have to find him. He has to be okay.

I'm moving so fast, I don't get the proper footing on the lowest branch, slick from the rain. My foot slips and I fall with a cry. I throw myself into the jump as best I can, but my knees don't bend all the way.

I hit the ground hard. The pain in my legs is immediate and crippling, but I have to keep going. I need to find Logan.

"Logan!" I yell again.

There's a rustle in the trees ahead, and I lift my weapon, ready to shoot if it's one of the patrolmen.

"Don't shoot! It's me—it's Logan." He shoves aside the branches.

I lower my weapon, relief flooding my body. "Are you okay?" he asks.

"I'm fine," I say, walking toward him to prove it. My legs ache from the jump, but not so much I can't move. Nothing is broken.

My eyes fall on the reddish-black stain on Logan's crippled leg, above his knee. "You were shot." My voice sounds far away.

"Barely skimmed me. I'll be all right," Logan says, shifting his weight to his other foot. "Come on, let's go help the others."

He moves past me toward the clearing. I can see his pain in the way he holds his shoulders rigid with every limping step. I hurry forward and stop him, grabbing his arm and pulling it around my neck.

"Here, lean on me," I say.

"I'm fine," he says gruffly. But when I start to help him along, he doesn't pull away.

The gunshots have stopped, I realize. Still, I grip my weapon with my free hand as we step out of the trees, into the rain again.

There are three bodies on the ground. Three patrolmen. I can't tell if they're dead or unconscious, but all of them look wounded. Skylar is directing Paley and the other rebels to lug the bodies up the ramp into the hovercraft, probably to strip them of their armor so we can use it to disguise ourselves.

A fourth patrolman kneels, stony-faced, before Beechy, who has a gun raised to his head. Mal pulls the weapons out of the patrol-man's holsters.

Four patrolmen, plus the one Logan and I shot down in the forest. There were seven who stepped outside, and two of them were knocked out by Skylar and Jensen in the hovercraft. But they must've had at least one pilot with them.

My blood runs cold as the rain patters on my helmet and I real-ize what's missing from this picture: One of the patrol ships is gone.

Beechy lowers his gun and turns away from the kneeling pa-trolman. He spots me and Logan and stomps toward us through the mud, a hand over his head to shield his face, even though he's wearing a helmet.

"Are you two okay?" he asks.

"Yeah," Logan says, lifting his weight off me and pulling away. "What's going on?"

"I need you both to go with Skylar, Mal, and Jensen," Beechy says. "If the patrolman's telling the truth, most of the transports have already left for the work camps. The one headed for Crust is about to leave. We need to get you on it."

"What about everyone else?" I ask.

"There will still be a couple more transports headed to the lower sectors—they're just not going to the camps. So getting you two to the station is our first priority."

Skylar's already boarding one of the patrol ships left behind, and Mal's passing off the weapons he collected from the patrol-man to someone else. With their armor, they certainly pass as of-ficials. But it won't matter if the patrol ship that got away warns everyone we're here.

"Who's going to stop the patrol ship?" I ask.

"I'm going after it myself," Beechy says. "Mal blasted its transmitter before it got away, so whoever's on board can't tell anyone what happened until he reaches the security hub. Don't worry, I'll catch up to him."

*And if you don't?* I want to ask. He could run into more patrols. He could end up in real trouble. But the look in his eyes tells me there's no use arguing with him. He'd tell me not to worry. He'd tell me this is the only way.

"We'd better go," Logan says.

I hesitate. I don't know when I'll see Beechy again. If all goes well, we'll both be in Crust tomorrow, alive and ready to fight Charlie. But if everything goes wrong . . .

Beechy must be thinking the same thing. He steps forward and pulls me into a tight hug, as tight as he can make it with our helmets interfering.

"I'll see you soon," he says, releasing me.

"You'd better," I say.

He turns and hurries to one of the flight pods, grabbing a bigger gun from Paley on his way.

A bad taste seeps into my mouth, a bad feeling that he is wrong and I won't see him again. But I do my best to force it down. He'll be fine. He can take care of himself.

I turn and follow Logan. We climb through the open door at the side of the patrol ship. It zips shut behind us as soon as we're inside.

"Buckle in," Skylar says from the pilot seat. "We need to hurry."

Mal sits in the copilot chair, fiddling with the comm dial. Jensen is in one of the passenger seats. There are three in a single row, with cargo space behind them.

Logan and I slip into the empty seats. The ship lifts into the air as I buckle in. Through the cockpit window, I watch the forest glide past below us. Above us, lightning flashes across the sky. It leaves a thin streak in the clouds, a hole that lets me glimpse the stars.

A dot of light shoots across the sky—a meteor blazing to bits as it hits the protective shield at the outer rim of our atmosphere.

It fades away a second later. The clouds roll back over the stars again.

I'm left with a hollow feeling in my chest and a strong worry that Beechy won't intercept the patrol ship in time. And we will reach the transport too late.

# 10

I've been in the main departure station in the Surface city only once before, on the day I was picked for Extraction. That day, I entered on foot through the front entrance. This time, we enter through a tunnel in the side of the building.

The tunnel is almost as dark as the city outside, but white lights dot the walls, reminding me of the Pipeline. Skylar eases off our thrusters. We don't want to crash, and we need to figure out which way to go. The tunnel branches off in four directions a few hundred feet in, and giant letters painted on the ground tell us which way each branch leads. The first leads to Terminal A, the second to Terminal B, and so on.

"Do we know where the transports are loading?" Jensen asks. He has his helmet visor open, so I can glimpse the fierce green shade of his eyes, which look unusual against his dark skin.

"The patrolman said they're loading in dock ten," Mal says, re-loading the thick gun in his lap with bullets from a cartridge he stole from the patrolman. "That's in Terminal A."

"If he was telling the truth," Skylar says. Her new helmet gives her voice an odd, deep resonance. From behind, I can trick my mind into thinking it isn't really her, except she says things Skylar would say.

"We had him at gunpoint," Mal says.

"Guns don't stop people from lying," Skylar says. "It just makes them do a better job of it."

Still, she heads left, down the first tunnel branch. We don't have time to check the others first, and this is the only lead we have.

Skylar dims the lights in the cockpit until I can see only the faint outline of her and Mal. She looks over her shoulder, at me and Logan. "You two should change out of your safety suits," she says. "I doubt the kids from the work camp will be wearing those."

I have to agree with her, though I don't know how they've been surviving if they've had no protection from the moonshine. They would've been exposed to it in the camp.

But maybe Charlie's been letting them stay here in the city. Usually I wouldn't believe that, but he clearly has some motive for keeping them alive, if he's transferring them all belowground. He's going to use them for something bad—I'm sure of it.

Swallowing hard, I unbuckle and stand. I slip through the small space between my seat and Jensen's, into the cargo space at the back of the ship. Logan follows, ducking his head because the ceiling is almost too low for him.

There are a few empty compartments on both sides of the walls, as well as a storage space below our feet. I take off my helmet and shove it into one of the compartments. Logan helps me unzip the back of my suit. His fingers brush my skin through my shirt, and I shiver involuntarily.

When he's finished, I work the sleeves over my arms to my torso, and push the suit down so I can step out of it. I remove my boots too. They would look out of place in a work camp; I will have to go barefoot. I lean against the wall to steady myself as the ship rumbles.

Logan pulled his boots and helmet off already, and he's removing his suit. His undershirt has worked its way up his body, exposing his stomach and a hint of muscle that wasn't there before. It must be from all the time he spent in the training rooms back at headquarters. The sight makes my breath hitch, which makes my face warm. We aren't alone, after all.

He notices me watching him pull his shirt back down, and I shift my eyes away. But not before I see the amusement in his eyes. He leans down to tie a strip of fabric around the bloody cut above his knee.

"I'm putting us down in dock fourteen," Skylar says up in the cockpit. "We'll enter dock ten on foot. Seems like it'll make people ask fewer questions."

"Just follow my lead," Mal says. "We look like officials, so they won't question us unless we give ourselves away."

Through the cockpit window, I watch us turn into another tunnel branch, the one leading to docks eleven through fourteen.

Mal, Skylar, and Jensen look like officials, but Logan and I look like ourselves. Blending in will be a lot harder for us. I reach up and touch the short strands of hair on my head, wishing I could dye my skin a different color too, or grow taller. Anything to keep me from looking so much like the girl who screwed up Charlie's plans and escaped him one too many times. I feel like a walking target.

But I *have* escaped him. Every time he's tried to break me, I've fought and I've won. I have to remember that.

Logan takes a step closer to me and touches my hand. "You okay?" he asks.

"Yes," I say, but my voice is tight.

"It's okay to be scared, you know," he says softly. "It doesn't make you weak. It means you care about surviving."

He's wrong, but he's also right. If I were truly at peace with sacrificing myself to secure a better future for the world, I wouldn't be afraid of Charlie or anything he might do to me.

I focus on the tiny mole on Logan's cheek to avoid meeting his eyes. "Maybe it would be easier if I stopped caring. Sometimes I wish I could just . . ."

*Give up.*

The unspoken words hang in the air between me and Logan.

Instead of arguing with me or making me promise I won't, he presses his mouth against mine. I bet he hopes his kiss will do what his words can't: convince me to stay alive.

His tongue coaxes my lips apart. I lose all track of where we are and slip my hand under his shirt, trailing my fingers across his back. He is warm and strong and I want to stay with him.

I'm glad he's coming with me.

The jolt of the ship landing makes the two of us bump into the wall, and snaps us back to reality. Logan pulls his mouth away from mine with a sigh.

The door at the side of the ship slides open. Skylar shuts the engine down as Mal and Jensen unbuckle. Logan and I move back up to the cockpit.

"Ready?" Skylar asks, removing her gun from its holster.

My own gun is lying abandoned. I'd feel better with it in my boot, but I can't risk a real official noticing it in my possession.

"Let's go," Logan says.

Skylar closes her helmet visor. "Follow me," she says, and steps through the open door.

Jensen follows after her, and Logan and I move after him, with Mal bringing up the rear.

Loading dock fourteen is silent. The only lights on are emergency lights, and there are no other transports. There's no sign that anyone knows we're here.

I hope Beechy managed to intercept the patrol ship in time. I hope he's all right.

We reach the door that leads off the dock. It slides open, and Skylar holds up a hand for us to wait while she checks it out. She's gone for almost a full minute.

When she sticks her head back in, I flinch. She looks so much like a real official.

"Hallway's clear," she says. "Patrols, keep a hand on your prisoners."

Mal's hand slips around my wrist as we walk out into the corridor. I know he's only playing a part, but I wish he wouldn't grip my wrist so hard.

"You sure this will work?" I ask. Not too loudly, because I'm worried the walls might make my voice echo. The boots the others are wearing clunk with every step.

"Just keep your heads down," Skylar says, "and don't make any trouble."

"And if someone recognizes us?" Logan asks.

"We'll try to convince them they're wrong. If they don't believe us, you need to run back to our ship. No questions asked."

I press my lips together. Only three of us have weapons. Running won't get us very far if we can't even shoot the people chasing us.

"Presuming all goes well," Skylar says as we round a corner, "when you reach the Crust camp, your orders are to stay put until you receive word from one of us. That means no stealing weapons, no sneaking around, no attack plans. Spread the word about what Charlie did with the bomb, and see if you can get some more people on our side."

I remember what Beechy said: He wants me to be a leader. He thinks the others in the work camp will listen to me because I look like them. But if they don't already know what Charlie did, they might think I'm a lunatic.

I'll have to do my best to convince them otherwise.

Around another corner, a number on the wall tells me we've reached loading dock ten. There's a door already open, and I glimpse steam and flashing lights beyond it. A figure in an orange mechanic suit hurries by beyond the doorway. The sound of engines squealing is loud.

Skylar enters first. Mal grips my wrist tighter, roughly pushing me ahead of him through the doorway.

This dock is much bigger than number fourteen. The steam comes from vents in the floor, and from the exhaust pipes of the three transports on the landing platforms. They are massive, the size of the hovercrafts that used to transport me and others from the Surface camp to the fields for work, and to the city for school.

Officials in armor stand here and there, patrolling the area around the platforms. There are more of them than I can count, and they all have guns. My feet stall, and Mal has to nudge my back with the butt of his gun to make me keep walking.

"Act normal," he whispers.

There are lines of people moving up the platform steps and boarding the transports. They're all my age or younger. I can tell by the state of their clothes—tattered, some almost ripped to shreds—that they came from the work camp.

As we walk closer, I recognize some of their faces. Which means they might recognize my face too.

I drop my eyes to the ground. *Don't look at me. Don't call my name.*

I should never have come here. I should never have agreed to this. All I'm going to do is get captured; there's no way around it.

After several more steps, I lift my eyes and notice one of the officials walking toward us from the back of the boarding line.

Dropping my eyes again, I start a slow count to one hundred in my head, because I don't know how else to stay calm. Skylar and the others know what to say to him, I hope.

If they don't—if he figures out I'm a wanted person—I'm ready to run as fast as I possibly can.

His boots come to a stop in front of us.

"Why aren't these two with the group?" he asks. His helmet warps his voice, making it low and mechanized.

"We don't know," Skylar says. "We caught them out in the hall-way. Tell your guys to be more careful about who they let run off." She looks over her shoulder at Mal and Jensen and waves them on with two fingers. "Take them over to the line."

"Yes, sir," Mal says, nudging me forward again. Jensen follows with Logan.

The official takes a short step forward, and I'm sure he's going to stop us. He's going to signal all the other guards, and I'm going to have to run.

But then he steps back and waves us on. "Better hurry and get 'em on board," he says.

The line for the first ship is almost to the end when we reach it. I start up the platform. I can do this; I can fool people into thinking I'm someone other than myself.

On the second step from the top, Mal shoves me forward—so hard, I trip. My knee hits the edge of the next step, and a sharp pain shoots my leg.

"You're a clumsy one, eh?" he says, laughing.

My cheeks burn as he pulls me back to my feet by my shirt-sleeve. Everyone at the top of the platform is staring. Is he *trying* to draw attention to us?

"Is this everyone?" a voice says, not far behind me. It sounds familiar. It makes me pause, even as I straighten and walk up the last step onto the platform.

"Aye, Lieutenant, sir."

"Good. Tell the pilots they're free to depart as soon as the last passengers are aboard."

Every inch of my body goes rigid. I know where I've heard that voice: the Core.

*His hands all over me in the elevator, his tongue in my mouth.*

It can't be him. Not here.

I turn my head a little, enough to see him out of the corner of my eye. He isn't in full-body armor like the others, but a uniform: a gray suit and knee-high black boots. A flash of gold on his chest must be a lapel pin in the shape of a moon. His hair is short and blond, and his smile is fashioned in the shape of a smirk.

Sam.

He's not looking my way, not yet. But he will any second. I'm sure he's going to see me.

I realize Mal's talking. "Make sure these two get on board," he's saying to the guards stationed before the transport entrance.

One of the guards steps forward, and I do my best to stay calm. I pray the sweat beading on my forehead isn't obvious.

"Give me your arm," he says.

I hold it out to him, letting my teeth graze my bottom lip. He grabs my wrist and turns it over. My new ID tag is there for everyone to see. The skin is still a bit red, but hopefully not enough to make him suspicious.

It seems to take a million years for his scan reading to pop up. I glance at Sam again. He's walking past our platform, one hand on the gun in his belt holster, an eye moving in my direction.

Mal shifts his position a little, blocking Sam from view. I turn my head away, hoping, hoping he didn't see me.

Mal was trying to help me when he tripped me, I realize. Sam must've been walking in and looking our way, and Mal knew he wouldn't bat an eye at an official pushing a girl like that; he'd smirk and go on about his business.

"Brea," says the guard, still holding my wrist. That must be the name Beechy used for me in my fake citizen file.

"Yes?" I say.

"You're free to board," he says, and reaches to grab Logan's wrist to scan his ID tag.

"I'll accompany her, if you don't mind," Mal says. "I'd like to keep an eye on her."

"Of course," the guard says. "We're gonna put this boy on the other ship. I think there's more room over there."

"I can take him," Jensen says.

Panic stumbles up my throat.

I open my mouth to tell Jensen he can't, but I stop at the look on Logan's face. *Don't fight*, his eyes are saying.

I want to ignore him; I want to scream. I won't let the guards separate us. I've lost him too many times, and I won't lose him again.

But I force reason into my mind: I remind myself that any fight I give now could blow our cover and ruin everything. It could put Logan in even worse danger.

Mal pushes me up the boarding ramp. My eyes cling to Logan, to his cheeks tanned from the Surface sun and his thin lips and his chest rising and falling. He stares right back at me every second until I have to turn away to walk into the ship.

"Are you sure the other ship's headed for Crust?" I ask Mal.

"Yes. We'll find him again, don't worry."

He'd better be right. Otherwise, I won't forgive myself for not fighting the guards.

I buckle into one of the last empty passenger seats. Mal heads up to the cockpit, no doubt to smooth-talk his way in.

I keep my head down, so I can't make eye contact with anyone in the seats around me. All the passengers aboard this ship are from the camp where I grew up, and I'm sure I know some of them. But I'll be safer if they don't recognize me, not until we're far away from Sam.

Behind me, the entrance ramp slides up. There's a hiss as the door closes. My seat rumbles as the engine picks up.

Relief floods my body. I survived the hardest part of the mission; I made it on board without discovery. Hiding will be easier in the camp among so many people. I won't give Sam another opportunity to catch me. I grip the armrests of my seat as the hovercraft lifts off the ground. With every rise and fall of my chest, my heartbeat steadies, but keeps a fast rhythm. No longer out of panic, but driven with purpose.

I survived in a work camp for sixteen years of my life, and I can do it again. This time I know exactly who I'm up against. So far, I have the advantage because Commander Charlie has no idea where I am, or even that I'm alive.

He wanted me to be a weapon for him, someone who killed on demand. But his serum couldn't break me, and neither could the tortures I endured in Karum. Maybe I've let him control me from far away by giving in to my fear of him. But no longer. I won't give him any more power over me.

Soon he will be the one who is afraid.

# 11

There are no windows in the transport, so I don't know we've landed until the engine dies.

The door at the back of the ship opens, and floodlights stream in. Two officials move up the ramp, carrying pulse rifles. One of them shouts, "Everybody off!"

I unbuckle my belt straps and stand up, along with everyone else. The dark-skinned, pale-eyed girl next to me, maybe eleven years old, looks terrified. So do many of the others around me, at least the younger kids. I don't know what they were told about why they're being transferred. Maybe they weren't given a reason.

Down the ramp, we step off the ship into what must be a flight hangar. It's barely half the size of the one back on the Surface. The floor, walls, and ceiling are made of compacted dirt and rock rather than steel. The floodlights—two of them, mounted on the wall—are the only light source except for the faint glow from the passage-way to the Pipeline, to my left. The only other ships are a few small oval-shaped hov-pods that are sleek and black, and seem big enough for only one or two people. My guess is the officials use them to navigate Crust's tunnels. I remember Oliver said even the city streets aren't big enough for real ships.

I keep my eyes on the Pipeline entrance while everyone disembarks from the transport. The other ship shouldn't be far behind us. Logan shouldn't be far, unless the patrolman's information was wrong, and Mal was wrong, and it isn't headed to Crust.

I ball my hands into fists. Mal wasn't wrong. The ship will be here soon, and Logan will be on it. He has to be.

"We're moving out," an official says. "Follow me."

I don't want to leave yet, not until the other transport arrives. But Mal's standing nearby and he catches my eye. He gives me a look that says, *Don't.*

It's not worth it, anyway. There are too many officials around, and the only ways I can think of stalling the group involve drawing too much attention to myself.

So I follow everyone through a set of sliding doors into a tunnel passageway. Every official I pass looks like he's staring at me, though I can't really tell, because most of them have their helmet visors closed. I'm sure I'm going crazy. But I keep my head down anyway, and push into a denser part of the group as smoothly as I can. Out of the corner of my eye, I notice Mal moving closer to me, gripping his gun a bit tighter. The sight of him eases some of the tension in my arms and hands.

I still don't trust him completely, but I'm glad he's here with me.

The passageway bends and curves. The ice-cold air makes me shiver. Mal and the other officials have their armor to keep them warm, but we have nothing.

Some of the others who came with me on the transport look

deathly pale. A few people are coughing. Maybe because of exposure to moonshine, unless they were ill before the shield went down.

I bet none of them know that a week ago the world almost ended. They probably slept through the whole thing. The scariest part is, if I hadn't been picked for Extraction, I'd be no less ignorant than they are.

We round a corner, and the passageway opens up ahead into an enormous cavern of the sort I learned about in school. I stare up in awe. The ceiling stretches high above us, speckled with stalagmites and stalactites that glow blue in the otherwise dim light. They're covered with arapedas, bioluminescent bugs. I have to hold myself back from walking toward the wall for a closer look. I've never seen anything like this on the Surface.

The path continues across the cavern, but it's blocked on either side of us by a metal railing. Beyond the rail, the ground slopes down to pools of aquamarine and silver water below us. These pools weren't made by man; they were here long before any humans called these caves home.

When the scientists who headed Project Rebuild went to construct Crust, they discovered that caverns already existed miles underground, formed over decades by rivers beneath the Surface. Since people needed to escape the acidic Surface as soon as possible, the scientists largely left the caverns as they were and built living structures inside some of them. Five of the biggest caverns house the adult city, which is said to look like a hive of steel pods. Some of the buildings have man-made tunnels between them, as in the Core, but others are connected by the rocky tunnels that were here before the city existed. People might have to walk from an enclosed, heated cafeteria onto a muddy path to make their way home.

Those who live in the work camp have no steel structures to keep them warm.

On the other side of the cavern, a huge iron gate sits at the end of the path, flanked by two guards. As we approach, one of them taps a code into a console, and the gate swings open to let us inside.

It takes a few seconds for my eyes to adjust as I walk forward. The cave beyond is smaller than the cavern behind us and darker too, with no arapedas giving off a glow. The only light comes from small lamps here and there in the ceiling, and most are flickering as if their power supply is low. Most of the energy in this sector must be allocated to the city.

The cave is full of people on the floor, some curled up asleep on the ground, others leaning against the walls. Their bodies are bony, thinner than the thin I'm used to. Their skin seems dark, whether because of genetics or because they're covered in soot from the coal mines, I can't tell.

Some of them get to their feet at the sight of us. But they don't walk toward the gate, because of the guards with their guns. They stand there staring at us like we're ghosts.

This is the place where Oliver grew up, before he was given a position in the Crust security hub. Before he was picked for Extraction.

A gust of icy air washes over me, forming goose bumps on my arms. It's even colder in here than in the tunnels behind us, and none of the people I see have blankets or pillows. Many are huddled together for warmth, especially the younger ones. They look like refugees, but this is their home.

The air reeks of sweat and sewage. I wrinkle my nose.

There's a loud clang behind me. I turn and see guards locking the gate.

Mal watches me from the other side, lingering after most of the other officials walk away. Then he turns and follows them.

I stare after him until he's gone, disappeared into the tunnels beyond the cavern pools. I'm alone now. I'm the only Alliance member in the camp.

I rub the goose bumps forming on my arms as I turn back to the cave. A few Crust kids are still staring at me and the other new arrivals, but they don't say anything. Those from the Surface slowly drift farther into the camp, to see if the other caves are the same, or to find a place to sleep for the night.

I don't know what else to do, so I walk after them.

Through a short tunnel, I enter another cave room, this one about the same size as the last, and filled with as many people. A cam-bot hovers in the far corner, two red lights blinking on its side. Little ones whimper on the floor. The people around my age are quieter, but some of them give me odd looks as I walk by. More tunnels branch off from this one, leading to more cave rooms with more people. I know there are a lot that make up the work camp's sleeping areas, but I don't know how many. They seem like they might go on forever.

It's hard to find a clear walkway, the place is so crowded. I move along the edge of the room, close to the wall, looking for a place to sit down.

A drop of water hits my nose from above. This part of the ceiling is higher than the rest and darker, so I can't tell where the water came from. But the dirt beneath my feet does seem a bit damp. There could be an underground pool above us. Or a leaky pipe.

I take another few steps, and something crunches loud beneath my feet. Something hard and sharp.

I lift my foot, wincing, and see silver-and-blue bugs skittering across the path in front of me. Hundreds of them, each the size of my pinky.

I jump back, choking down the cry that nearly escapes my throat. These are croachers. They live in dark, damp places like mountain caves. Their bite can damage a person's nerves, even cause temporary paralysis.

My foot doesn't sting, so I don't think I was bitten. Thank the stars. I can't afford paralysis, even temporary, in a place like this. I wish I'd brought my old army boots, even if they don't fit in here. I can handle walking on rocky pathways, but if there are other creatures like these bugs scampering around, I will have to be careful.

I step in a wide arc around the croachers. I train my eyes on the ground ahead as I continue walking, so as not to wander into any more of them.

A boy smirks as I walk past him. He must've seen me nearly get bitten and thought it was funny. I smother the urge to pick up one of the bugs and throw it at his face.

In the next cave room, I look around for a place to sleep. I'm close enough to the camp entrance gate that I should notice if—when—Logan and the other passengers from the transport arrive, unless there's some other entrance they'll use that I don't know about.

I don't know why it's taking so long, but he will come.

I find a spot beside the wall, close to one of the lamps. There aren't any cam-bots around, thankfully. I need to avoid them, in case someone recognizes my face on a screen in the Crust security hub.

The ground is as hard as the floor of my old Karum cell—worse because there are bits of rock everywhere, and there's a pile of rodent droppings a few feet away. No wonder people avoided this spot.

Curling up against the wall, I reach up to pull my hair out of its bun, so it can warm my neck. But I stop, remembering I cut it off, so I would look different and feel different too. Brave enough to survive in this place. I pull my arms inside my shirt. My teeth are chattering, and I can't feel my toes.

The other girls lying on the floor look like me. They fear officials and quarantine like I do. Any one of them could've been picked for Extraction and given a new home. They wouldn't have been crazy enough to throw it all away. They would've been subdued like good citizens, good puppets.

But I couldn't be subdued. And now I'm back where I started.

Only, I'm not the person I was before. I've seen more, and I know more.

I know Charlie can't control me unless I let him. I will find a way to fight him, so he can't control anyone else ever again.

I lie awake for a long time. All around me, people cry and cough and mutter in their sleep. The girl lying closest to me sounds like she's struggling to breathe. I don't think she'll make it through the night.

I squeeze my eyes shut, but the sounds won't go away. Nor will the worry at the back of my mind that Logan's transport took him somewhere different, and I am once again on my own.

I can't shake the feeling too, that creeps up on me like the tip of a knife brushing against my spine—that it was supposed to happen this way. That Charlie knew our plan all along, and I'm exactly where he wants me to be.

✕

"Hold still," someone says.

"What?" I mumble, rolling over in my sleep.

"I said *hold still.*"

The voice sounds gravelly. A young man, I think, but I don't know.

I jerk my eyes open, panicking. It's too dark for me to make out his face, but he must be one of the officials. He must be trying to shackle my hands so he can haul me away to quarantine, or someplace worse.

His hand brushes my skin through a hole in my pant leg, and I kick at where he must be standing. I hit something hard—his shin.

He steps back with a hiss. "Would you cut it out? I was trying to help you."

I push myself off the ground, so I can see him better. He can't be an official, not wearing those tattered pants and a shirt with only one sleeve. He's a boy around my age with a muddy complexion—his skin is almost as dark as Fred's, but not quite—and a mess of black, curly hair. He stands nearly a foot taller than me. He's pinching something between his thumb and forefinger, and he holds it out to me.

A croacher the size of my pinky struggles to free itself from his grip.

I taste bile in my mouth. "Was that thing on me?"

"Yeah, on your leg."

My cheeks warm. "Sorry for kicking you."

"Don't mention it," he says. He drops the croacher onto his other palm and squishes it with his hand, then tosses the remains over his shoulder. He wipes his hands on his pants.

"Is that smart?" I ask.

"It didn't kill me, did it?" His smile crinkles around the edges of his eyes. "You get used to dealing with them, trust me. They're less scary than the wendoes, at least."

"Wendoes?"

"They're sort of like flying muckrats. They live in the caverns on our way to the mines. A kid got a nasty bite the other day, haven't seen him since."

I shudder involuntarily.

The boy laughs. "Doesn't that happen all the time where you came from?"

It takes me a second to remember he thinks I came from another work camp. "Of course people get taken away and they don't come back. Just not because of flying muckrats, usually."

"I see." He holds out a hand. "I'm Hector, by the way."

I give his hand a light shake, my mind racing to recall the name the official used to address me. "I'm Brea." The word feels strange on my tongue, but hopefully I'll get used to it.

"Which sector did you come from, Brea?"

"The Surface."

His eyes widen in rapture. "As in, the moon-and-stars-are-visible-at-night Surface?"

"Yes." I'm distracted now, looking around the cave room at the other people. I don't know how long I slept, but I need to find Logan. He should be here by now, if he's going to get here at all.

"Wow," Hector says. "I've always wanted to see it. I mean, I know the moon's poisonous, but still . . . Why'd you all come here, anyway?"

"We don't really know. But it wasn't just us—the adults came here too. Have you noticed any more kids coming through the gates?"

"No. Why?"

I do my best to breathe evenly, but my throat feels blocked all of a sudden. Like someone shoved a sharp piece of metal inside it. "There was supposed to be another transport on its way, from the Surface camp. It was supposed to arrive right after ours."

We must've been wrong. The transport must've gone to a different sector—Mantle, maybe, or Lower. Logan must be in a camp there.

He is there and I am here, and there is no way for me to reach him.

"Well, it could've gone to Camp B," Hector says.

"Wait." I'm not sure I heard him correctly. "Camp B?"

"Yeah, this is Camp A, and there's a Camp B. It's on the other side of the quarantine facility."

Some of the tension eases in my body. It makes sense that they'd send half of us there, since the caves in A are clearly crowded. Logan shouldn't be far, at least. But I need to find a way to him.

"Okay," I say, moving past Hector. "How do we get there?"

"We can't. There's a separate entrance and everything."

Of course there is. How am I supposed to get in?

Then I remember—Mal. He went off with the other officials, and I have no idea where he is now. But as soon as he comes back, I can tell him about Logan, and he can check that he's okay for me. Maybe he can help me sneak into the other camp, or bring Logan here.

Mal can also fill me in on what's going on with the rest of the Alliance. If all went well and everyone made it onto the last transports leaving the Surface, some of them must be here in Crust. Skylar and Jensen, at least. But until Mal comes, all I can do is wait.

But I'm not going to sit. I'm going to look around and figure out if there's anything in this camp that might be useful. If I can find any of the others from the Surface camp, I should talk to some of them too. I should figure out if they know anything about why Charlie sent us here.

I glance at Hector, who's still standing a few feet away from me, looking uncomfortable and a bit worried. I have no idea how long I've been standing here.

"Thanks for your help," I say. "I'm gonna have a look around the camp, so I'll see you later."

"Are you kidding?" Hector says. "You'll get lost in these caves. Let me give you the tour."

I hesitate, but his smile is too kind, and the last thing I want is to get lost in these caves. "Okay, sure."

"Great! Follow me. Keep your eyes out for croachers."

Still grinning, he leads the way around the people on the floor. Most are waking up now, stretching and sitting upright. They seem fidgety. I don't know what time it is, but it seems like morning. Back in the Surface camp, we'd all be heading to the departure station right about now, for school or to work in the fields.

I grimace as I remember the work people do here—coal mining. That's the reason most of the people I see have black dust forming a crusty layer all over their skin. There's dust all over Hector's neck and arms, though it looks like he managed to get most of it off his face.

"When do we go to the coal mines?" I ask him.

"Actually, we haven't been there in a few days. Not sure why. They haven't let us go to school, either. I really miss it. It's much warmer there."

I frown. "Has this ever happened before?"

"Not that I can remember."

I chew on my bottom lip, thinking. The only reason the mines would stop running is if they suddenly have an infinite supply of coal, or if they've found a replacement energy source. When Charlie made his announcement about the KIMO bomb, he said the Core had become self-sufficient, so it must have its own source, though I don't know what it is. If the Core has its own source, maybe Charlie doesn't care if the other sectors even have energy anymore, because he's going to destroy them all with some new bomb.

But if he doesn't care about the other sectors, why transfer everyone off the Surface? Why not leave everyone for dead?

"How many days has it been?" I ask.

"Three, I think." Hector scratches his head. "It's been a bit hard to tell, since they stopped delivering meal rations every day, twice a day. Now it's only once sometime before we all get too tired to keep our eyes open."

Perfect. I'm already hungry.

But what he said about the three days is important. That lines up with when Darren learned Charlie was transferring people off the Surface too. If everything was running relatively normally before then, something must've happened three or four days ago that made Charlie change his mind. Something big. But the only people who might know what happened would be Charlie, his allies in the Core, and the officials who've been carrying out his orders.

Add that to the list of things I need to talk to Mal about.

"So what have you been doing, then, since you haven't been in the mines?" I ask Hector.

"Sitting around. Waiting. Coming up with a lot of crazy theories about what's going on outside the camp. Then you lot showed up." He gives me a sheepish look. "I was sort of hoping one of you would know what's been going on."

I smile back, but it feels a bit tight. I do know some things. It's obvious Hector has no idea about Charlie's bomb, or acid leaking through the shield when it went down. He has no idea he'd be dead right now if it wasn't for Oliver, Beechy, and me—he and this entire camp would be nothing but bone dust and debris, floating in antigravity. Charlie is probably planning to kill us for real as we speak, after he's used us for whatever he needs.

I should tell Hector all of this, that he and everyone else in the camp are in danger and we need to do something. But I'm worried they won't believe me, or worse, Charlie has undercover officials in this camp. If he does, my warning will be squashed before it has a chance to spread.

Hector's smile might be sweet, and he might've saved me from being bitten by a poisonous croacher bug, but that's all I know about him. I'm not sure I can trust him. And I need to be sure.

# 12

Camp A has almost thirty rooms of caves, most roughly the same size, all of them forming a labyrinth I'll never be able to figure out. But Hector moves through the rooms with ease. He has the whole place memorized, down to the position of every ceiling lamp.

The latrines and baths sit in a cave room at the very center of the camp, inside wooden stalls that look like they might fall apart at any moment. The baths are turned on once a day for half an hour, Hector tells me. With several hundred people needing to use them, it's difficult to get more than a couple of seconds in one, so most people shower less than once a week.

He takes me all the way to the other side of the camp, where another gate separates us from a cavern. But this one doesn't have guards posted outside. The cavern beyond is also different; it's even bigger than the last, with mostly even ground and no pools of water or arapedas. A steel structure fills much of the cavern, beneath the dripping stalactites high above. The building reminds me somewhat of Karum, but instead of one giant facility, it looks more like a series of smaller buildings connected by passageways. Smoke rises from a hole in the ceiling of one of the far rooms.

This is either a factory or the quarantine facility. Hector confirms that it's the latter.

It looks different enough from the one on the Surface that I can almost convince myself it's just a normal building. But not really, because I know what happens inside. I know there are rooms where twenty-year-olds are locked in, where they scratch and scream at the door on their hands and knees as poison gas seeps in through vents in the walls. The gas makes their vision blur and their muscles convulse and their stomachs expel vomit until their bodies can take no more and their lungs stop working.

Their lifeless bodies are thrown in a furnace and burnt. The guards don't blink an eye.

I walk up to the gate and wrap my palms around the bars. They're cold, but I don't let go of them.

Picturing the kill chambers makes me think of my old friend Laila, who died in the Surface camp. I remember how she cried when the officials forced her into the hov-pod outside our shack. How she begged them to give her one more minute to say good-bye. How I couldn't stop the guards from taking her away, and I hated myself for it.

I can feel the familiar panic coming on, the kind I feel when I wake from a nightmare, and what I felt in the jet with Skylar, before I shot Cady. When I lost all control of myself. *Not now, please.*

To distract myself, I solve Yate's Equation in my head, and another equation, and another, until my pulse is almost normal. Until I can think clearly again.

It's not good to get lost in memories, especially the bad kind. I can't save anyone that way. All I've done is hurt more people.

"You okay?" Hector asks, beside me. I can feel his eyes on me, but I don't look at his face. I don't want to see how much he could tell about how I was fighting to keep myself from going crazy.

"Yeah," I say, trying to keep my voice even. "You said Camp B is on the other side of this building, didn't you?"

"Yeah, it is."

Logan might be right on the other side; right now I would do anything to get to him. If only I could sneak through the facility, or walk around it, or climb over it.

My eyes skim the outside wall around the gate, searching for the lock-pad that opens it. There it is, on the wall to my left, about two feet away. I bet I could reach it if I stretched. I strain to see the pad on it. There are only six digits, but I don't know how many are needed to form the passcode. If it's a six-digit code, that's 46,656 possible combinations. I'd need days to guess the right code. There's no way a guard wouldn't notice.

Above all, I can't let any of them catch me doing anything suspicious. I need to keep a low profile. I shouldn't even be standing next to this gate.

I let go of the bars and turn to walk away. But as I look back to make sure Hector's following, the entrance to the quarantine facility opens. Two guards step outside with pulse rifles in hand, stomping up the path toward the gate where Hector and I are standing.

The guards might not be coming for me, but if they're coming to open the gate, it means they're here to take people away. I can't handle seeing anyone dragged to quarantine again. I need to get out of here.

"We should go." I reach for Hector's hand to pull him away.

"Wait, it's okay," he says, laughing a little. "They're just bringing people back from inspection."

I pause. There are people coming out of the building behind the officials—a whole stream of people. Judging by their tattered clothing, they live here in the camp. Girls and boys. All nervous. A little girl rubs a spot on her shoulder where a small piece of gauze is stuck to her skin. It looks like she had a shot.

"Inspection," I repeat.

"That's what they call our health exams. We have them once a month. They give us nutrient pills to supplement our food, and sometimes medicine if we're sick. I think it'll be my turn soon, since today they took the nine- through eleven-year-olds. How old are you?"

I feel like something has drained out of me.

"I'm sixteen." My voice sounds distant, disconnected from me.

"Oh, so you weren't picked for Extraction?" Hector looks embarrassed for asking. "I'm sorry. I know how hard that must be. It'll be my turn next year."

I don't say anything in reply; I'm too distracted.

A health examination might be nothing—it might be for giving people medicine, as Hector said. But the last time someone mentioned medicine to me, it was really the submission serum. These girls and boys don't have strange, lifeless eyes like the people I saw in the Core who'd been turned into mindless, submissive citizens by their monthly injections. They *seem* normal. But that doesn't mean a thing.

After all, it makes sense that administering the serum would be a big step in Charlie's new plan, if he's keeping us alive to do something for him. Subduing all of us makes controlling us easy. A simple shot, and we will follow his orders without a fight.

Hector said everyone up to age eleven has already gone through inspection. That's at least half the people in this camp, and more will go through it in the next few days.

Half the people in this camp might already be mindless. I arrived too late to save them.

---

Sometime in the evening, the guards pass out our daily rations at both camp gates. We have to stand in a long line until it's our turn to receive food. All they give us is a few sips of water and a wafer that tastes more like salty paper than like chunks of whatever meat is mixed in with the baked karo wheat. It makes me thirstier than I was to begin with.

None of the guards who passed out the food were undercover Alliance members, as far as I could tell. I'm still on edge, waiting for Mal to come back so I can find out if Logan and the others are all right. So he can tell me what the plan is.

"Does sunlight really burn people's skin?" Hector asks.

He's sitting beside me on the cave floor, licking wafer crumbs off his dirty fingers. He keeps asking me questions about the Surface, even though I'm guessing he already knows some of the answers from school.

"It can," I say. "That's why I'm covered in freckles. Most people's skin isn't as pale as mine though, at least in the camps. People like you don't have it as bad. But your skin could still peel away if you got a really terrible burn."

Hector's eyes widen in horror. "All my skin?"

I laugh. "No, just some of it. A top layer. It's not as horrible as it sounds. Not as horrible as moonshine burn, that's for sure."

"You're from the Surface?" asks a little girl sitting near us. Her tan cheeks are dimpled and her messy hair is braided.

I nod, nibbling at the last bite of my wafer.

"What does the sky look like?" another girl asks. She's closer to my age, with dark curls and an even darker complexion than Hector.

Another boy is looking at me too. A boy with greasy black hair and a cautious look in his eyes, like he doesn't trust anyone. But his expression softens as I begin to tell the four of them about the sky. I tell them what the sun looks like, and the moon, and the stars. I describe them the way I saw them from the spaceship, beyond the acid shield: the giant moon floating in the sky, drenched in thick, lethal fog; the stars speckling the night with brilliant shades of color.

When I finish, I let my words hang in the air. All four of them are staring at me, mesmerized.

I have their attention, and it's time I used it. I don't know how much I can tell them about what happened a week ago—how Charlie nearly set off the bomb; how he temporarily took the shield down; how he killed Oliver and nearly the rest of us—without giving away that I'm a fugitive from the Core.

But even if they don't believe me, even if they think I'm insane, I have to try. It's why Beechy sent me here in the first place.

When I'm sure the nearest cam-bot has hovered on to the next room, I open my mouth and spit it out: "One of the reasons the officials took us off the Surface and brought us here is because the acid shield went down."

Hector gapes at me in astonishment, as if I've told him half the planet disappeared. "What—why—how—?"

"Couldn't they fix the shield?" the curly-haired girl asks. "It's broken down before, hasn't it?"

I think fast, trying to pull together an explanation that's mostly truthful, that'll serve its purpose. "They did fix the shield, but not quickly enough. And the shield had never broken down like this before. Usually what happens is the particles weaken and the shield starts cracking, so a rehabilitation team has to fly up there to replace the weak parts. This time, the entire shield cut out. One second it was there in the sky, shimmering like it always does, and the next second it was gone. Like someone flipped a switch in a control room and shut it off. None of us knew what was going on. The shield was down for a long time, long enough to let a lot of acid into the atmosphere, and then it came back on like someone had flipped another switch. Like they kept it down just long enough to let the moonshine in."

"That's insane," the curly-haired girl says. "That must've caused a huge amount of environmental damage."

Hector looks uncertain. "Sounds like it wasn't exactly an accident."

"No, I don't think it was," I say, checking to make sure the cam-bot hasn't come back. Still safe. "I think the Developers did it on purpose."

Hector and the two girls share a worried glance. But the greasy-haired boy doesn't look entirely convinced. "Why would they do that?" he asks. "If they'd left you lot to die up there, I'd believe you. But they didn't let you die. They brought you down here, where it's safer. So why go to that much trouble?"

*Because they took the shield down to make me and Beechy turn our ship around, so he could use the bomb and kill us all, and fly away to Marden.*

I want to spill the whole truth so badly. But they have to trust me before they'll believe me.

But they don't need to know everything—all they need to know is that we're not safe here, that Charlie is planning something bad and I'm pretty sure we're at the center of it.

"I don't know why they'd go to that much trouble," I say, "but I know something's going on. Haven't you been thinking it? Three days ago, the mines shut down, and Hector said that's never happened before. Three days ago, I found out we were leaving the Surface, and that's never happened before."

"It could be a coincidence," the greasy-haired boy says, but he doesn't sound like he believes it.

"But Arthur, three days ago is when they started the inspections too," the curly-haired girl says to him. "And we weren't due to have them again for another week or two."

"Exactly," I say.

I didn't realize the inspections were happening early, but that fits with everything, if Charlie suddenly wants all of us subdued. I need to tell these four about the submission serum, but I don't know how.

The cam-bot's hovering back into the room. I'm dead if the microphone picks up what we're saying.

Leaning closer to the others, I lower my voice: "I overheard some of the officials mentioning the inspections, on my way here. They said something like, 'It's about time they're all given the serum, so we won't have to worry about them disobeying orders.'"

The greasy-haired boy, Arthur, narrows his eyes. "What's that supposed to mean?"

"A serum . . . like medicine?" Hector asks.

*A drug made to control us all.*

"I don't know for sure," I say. "That's all they said. Maybe I heard them wrong . . . but I'm sure something's going on, and I have a feeling it won't be good for us."

"I wouldn't believe a word she says," a girl says, behind me. "She's lying through her teeth."

There's something familiar about her voice. I tense as I look over my shoulder. She's leaning against the wall, her arms folded and her lips puckered. Her short dark hair is spiked with something that looks like mud.

Nellie. The girl who tried to kill me the night I was picked for Extraction.

"I came from the Surface too," she says. "The governor told us the shield turning off was a serious glitch in the system. The security tech who let it happen isn't alive anymore."

That night when I scaled the building to escape her, Nellie fled with Grady and the other two boys she was with. When Cadet Waller and the officials arrived to rescue me from a treacherous height, they said they'd find my attackers. They said they'd be punished, maybe even sent to quarantine. But Nellie is here, alive, with no fresh scars that I can see.

Seeing her in front of me again is no relief.

"The governor could've been lying," I say, turning my face away so she won't see it. My heart's thrumming a beat too fast. Even with my curls bleached and my hair short like a boy's, Nellie might recognize me. I doubt she'll be happy to see me. "You honestly believe everything the adults say?"

There's a pause.

"No," Nellie says stiffly. "But why should I believe you? You've got no proof, just theories."

"Maybe so," I say. "But I know what I saw when the shield went down, and you heard what those officials said. I couldn't make that up."

"Not that good of a liar?"

"I have no reason to lie to you."

"Right." Nellie walks slowly around me, until she's in front of me.

Turning my head away again would only make her more suspicious, so I set my jaw and meet her eyes. They are half in shadow because of the way the light from the nearest lamp falls, but I can still see her scrutinizing my features. The freckles I couldn't wash away; the scar that runs along my jaw, a different shape from the one I had when she saw me last, but still on the same side of my face. I can practically see the gears turning in her head. "What did you say your name was?" she asks.

"I didn't," I say. "But it's Brea."

"Brea," Nellie repeats, confusion flickering in her eyes. She must think she knows who I really am, but she also thinks she's crazy because I'm not supposed to be here. I was picked for Extraction. I should be in the Core.

But she seems to come to a conclusion. Crossing her arms, she speaks again in a louder voice. "So let me guess, you think the Developers transferred us down here to give us some mind-control injection, so they can make us do whatever they want? And they're gonna make us do something *bad*, right? Sounds like a load of garbage to me."

Hector gets to his feet, glaring at Nellie. "Just leave her alone, will you?"

I say, "Hector, please—"

"Fine," Nellie says, her mouth curving up at the side in a half smirk. She turns away haughtily and makes a big show of stepping over people's legs to reach the room exit.

As she goes, she calls over her shoulder, "Have fun telling bedtime stories to your new boyfriend, *Brea*."

She knows who I am. The question is whether or not she will tell.

# 13

That night, I lie awake beneath a flickering lamp, listening to the snores coming from Arthur. He lies a few feet away from me, between Hector and the cave wall. The girls, curly-haired Evie and dimpled Lucy, sleep near us too.

The main gate is visible through the short passageway leading to the first room I saw in the camp. The same two guards have been stationed outside the gate since the last meal rations were passed out.

Mal hasn't come yet, and neither has Skylar, or Beechy. I don't know what to think. They didn't say how long it might take them to get a message to me. They didn't say how long I should wait until I start worrying.

But I'm worried already. I still don't know for sure if Logan made it here. And the others could've had trouble getting onto the transports. Even if they made it here, any one of them could've been recognized sometime in the last twenty-four hours. I have no way of knowing.

I might be the only one of us left.

No, I can't think like that. There could be other reasons why no one's come to talk to me yet. The simplest is that they haven't figured out the safest way to send me a message—there are a lot of cam-bots around the camp. They have to be careful and smart about this, because even the slightest slipup could mean the worst for us. And I have to be patient.

I did what Beechy said—I spread the word that we are in danger to other people, but only four listened and believed me. There's little four of us can do in a camp this size, especially with no way out of it. We will likely be taken for the health inspection soon. Evie said the officials and cam-bots work together to track everyone down, so there's no way to hide from them.

We can fight the nurses who administer our medicine, so they won't be able to give us the submission serum, but I don't know how well that'll work. I don't know if it's worth fighting them, if I'll be caught because of it. I already know the serum won't work on me. I'm allergic to the main ingredient, the pollen from the genetically modified aster flower. The serum sets my body on fire with fever, making me so weak, I can barely protect myself. It's brought me close to death before. But it won't make me calm or easy to control.

Unless Charlie's scientists have somehow created a serum with a different core ingredient in the past eight days. It's a slim chance, but one that does make me nervous. I understand the old serum—I know that an energy injection can reverse the effects in some people, even if they aren't allergic. But a new serum, I wouldn't know how to fight.

Beside me, Hector's clothing rustles as he turns over. "Brea?" he whispers.

"Yeah?"

His smile lights up his eyes, even in the dark. "Thought you might be awake."

"It's hard to fall asleep in a new place." Especially without Logan.

"Are you cold?" Hector asks, scooting closer.

I tense instinctively. The comment Nellie said earlier flashes through my head: *your new boyfriend.* Maybe I'm stupid and he's just being nice, but I'm worried Hector might be getting the wrong idea.

I roll over so I'm facing away from him. "It's not too bad," I say, my voice a pitch higher than usual.

The truth is, my whole body is numb, and I've been shivering so much, it's become like second nature. I don't know how everyone doesn't get sick all the time here, with the temperature so low. I suppose their bodies become acclimated to the cold.

Silence passes between us. I almost want to look at Hector's face to make sure he's okay, but I'm afraid that might make it worse. He's only known me for a day. I'm sure he'll get over it, whatever it is.

"Listen," he says. "There's something I want to show you."

His voice sounds firmer, more deliberate. Like he means this is something really important, unrelated to my rejection.

"What is it?" I ask, not turning my head.

"Can't tell you, but I can show you. It's a bit of a walk. We'll have to be quiet."

I tease the inside of my cheek with my teeth. We could get caught, and he makes it sound like this is something we shouldn't be caught doing. And maybe it isn't smart for me to go with him after what just happened.

But I'm too curious to say no.

I roll back over. "I can be quiet."

Hector lifts his head, probably checking the location of the nearest cam-bot. There's one hovering in the passageway to the room with the gate, but its red lights are facing the opposite direction. It's far enough away that its motion sensors shouldn't pick us up if we're careful, at least for now.

"Come on." Hector pushes off the ground.

I stand and follow him, wondering what's so important he has to show it to me in the middle of the night.

—✗—

The stench of human waste stings my nostrils as we approach the flimsy doors of the latrine station. It's even worse than the smell of the latrines in the Surface camp—probably since those weren't enclosed underground—and those were bad enough. I pinch the bridge of my nose. This had better be worth it.

Hector leads the way into the station. There are ten stalls on either side with a high partition between them. He pauses to listen. But the place seems empty. The only sounds I hear are the coughs and snores and whimpers of the people sleeping behind us, in the nearest cave room.

Hector gestures for me to follow him to the right, to the boys' side of the station. Our bare feet squelch in the muddy ground. Water drips from the eaves overhead, through cracks in the limestone where some blackish-green fungus grows.

We stop outside the last latrine stall. Hector carefully pushes open the door to the last stall, checking to make sure no one's inside.

"Are you going to tell me what we're looking for?" I ask.

"It's something I found a while back." He gestures for me to follow him into the cramped stall. "I don't think anyone else knows about it. I've only used it twice, and I'm always careful to make sure no one notices when I do."

The only thing in the stall is a latrine: a hole in the ground with a metal covering. There's nothing special about it, as far as I can tell. I'm about to decide Hector is officially crazy when he says, "There," and I realize he's pointing at the ceiling.

I look up. The light cast by the lone lamp in the room doesn't reach all the way over here, but if I squint, I can see the ridges formed by the limestone. Water or some man-made machine must've eroded it away over time. In some places, the stone hangs in the shape of icicles; in others, it looks like someone cut it into thick slices, but didn't break the slices away.

The stone is brushed with a wash of colors—yellows and whites and pale browns. But directly above the latrine stall, there's a darker spot in the rock, where the ridges slope upward but leave a space between them that almost looks like a hole. I twist my mouth as I stare at it, until my eyes adjust enough that I catch the outline of the handle attached to the hole. It's not a hole; it's a square piece of steel.

A steel door.

I step all the way into the stall, trying not to choke from the smell, though there's barely room for both me and Hector to fit. He closes the door behind us.

"Where does it lead?" I ask.

But I know before he answers. I remember the water dripping from the cave eaves, and the wet spot on the floor last night when I nearly stepped on the croachers.

"The pipes," Hector says. "There's a maintenance corridor up there, but I don't think anyone uses it anymore. The door was all rusted when I tried it the first time. I almost couldn't get it open."

"A maintenance corridor?"

"I think so. It leads all the way to the security hub. I couldn't find a way in, but I heard monitors buzzing and guards talking. The things they were saying . . . " Hector hesitates. "They were waiting for some signal to ditch this sector and head for the Core. Like an evacuation. It was a couple weeks ago, and obviously nothing happened. But that's why I believe what you said earlier, about Charlie planning something bad for us."

My mind races. The guards must've been talking about evacuating to the Core because of the KIMO bomb. A couple weeks ago, preparations were under way. I still wish I could explain all that to Hector, but I can't, because he can't know I came from the Core. Maybe in a few more days I'll trust him enough, but not yet.

But this maintenance corridor could definitely be useful. If I could get to the security hub, I might be able to find Mal or Skylar. I might be able to talk to one of them. Depending on where else the corridor leads, I might even be able to reach Logan.

"Is the corridor connected to the other camp?" I ask, hopeful.

Hector shakes his head. "I couldn't find a way in. The only way into Camp B is through the quarantine facility and the front gate."

There's something odd about the way he paused before he answered, and part of me wonders if he's lying. But it doesn't matter; I can see for myself once I get up there.

I run my hands over the wooden wall on the right side of the stall. It leans almost against the wall of the cave, with a couple inches of space in between. The wall is a few feet higher than my head, but if I could pull myself to the top of it, the ridges in the cave wall could serve as handholds and footholds to reach the door.

The problem is pulling myself up into the passage once I get the door open. The way the ceiling ridges slope, I don't know if I can reach.

"Did you climb all the way up there?" I ask.

"Yeah. There's a short ladder that drops down when you get the door open.

"I'm sure I can make it. If I fall, I might hurt myself, or land in the latrine pit and smell wretched all day. But I don't think I'll fall. I've scaled the side of a skyscraper in the rain, after all.

"Wanna give me a boost?" I ask.

"Are you sure?" Hector asks. "I'm taller than you, so it might be easier for me to go first."

"I can do it. Just give me a boost, and keep an eye out for cam-bots."

Hector crouches a little, clasping his hands flat. I step into them, and he boosts me up so I can reach the first stone handhold I see, above the wall. Digging my fingers into the spot, I heave myself up until my left foot is on top of the wall, and then my right foot is too. The wall creaks under my weight, so I reach for the next ridge in the rock as quickly as I can. My palms are already sweaty, and the stone has some wet residue on it. My fingers slip the first time I grip the ridge. A small noise escapes my throat.

Hector's hands touch my feet, steadying them on the top of the wooden wall.

"Really, I can go first," he says.

"I'm fine," I say in a tight voice.

I can do this on my own.

Reaching for the ridge again, I find a firmer grip. I move one foot to the handhold I used before, and shift my weight off the wall so it won't break. I take a second to steady myself. I can do this; I won't fall. This is what I'm good at. I reach for the next handhold and begin climbing the side of the cave. The ceiling looked higher from the ground. Two more switches from handholds to footholds, and I'm close enough to reach the trapdoor, if I can hold on with one hand and stretch my arm out.

I tighten the grip of my left hand and dig my feet into the stone. Carefully, I move my other hand away from the wall and reach for the door. Sweat drips down the back of my neck and under my shirt.

My fingertips brush the handle. Only brushing—not grasping yet. I have to reach a bit farther.

*Come on, come on.*

My feet are starting to slip; I am going to fall. But I shove that fear to the back of my mind and push my toes against the wall, letting the soles of my feet rise a little to make me taller.

My fingertips brush the handle again. This time, I manage to wrap three fingers around it. I pull as hard as I can.

The trapdoor opens. The ladder drops with a clang.

*Vrux.* Someone must've heard that.

"Go, go, go!" Hector says in a frantic whisper.

Without hesitation, I wrap my palm around a ladder rung and reach my foot onto the lowest one. The ladder reaches only to the top of the latrine station wall, but it'll be easy enough for Hector to climb onto. I see now why it might've been smarter for him to pull it down.

I scurry up the rungs, through the trapdoor. When I check over my shoulder, Hector's already climbing up after me. There's no sign of a cam-bot in the latrine station yet. But I wouldn't be surprised if one is on its way.

At the top of the ladder, I climb onto the floor of a steel tunnel. The maintenance corridor. The place is almost pitch-dark; I can barely see my hand in front of me. The floor feels damp, and I can hear water dripping from somewhere above in a steady stream. I take a step and there's more wetness. No doubt it's seeping through cracks in the floor and muddying the cave dirt.

I stretch a hand toward the ceiling to see what's up there. My fingers brush cold steel; a ceiling. The pipes must be on the other side.

I glance back at Hector as he climbs up through the trapdoor. Once he's standing in the tunnel, he drops to his knee and reaches down to pull the ladder up.

"That was a close one," he says, catching his breath.

"How are we supposed to see?" I ask as the trapdoor closes, drenching us in utter darkness.

"There should be a lamp up here."

"A light switch?" I reach for the wall and run my hand over it, feeling for one.

"No," Hector says, and a light flickers on. He's holding a small metal stick in his hand. A faint beam of light shoots out of one end. It reminds me of the light sticks marshals use in flight ports to help guide ships toward exit tunnels.

"Where'd you get that?" I ask.

Hector grins. "Stole it from a guard."

I raise an eyebrow. "Really?" Impressive, if it's true.

"Nah, just kidding, I found it up here." He points to a small compartment in the wall with a door swung open. "I've seen the guards use stick-lamps before, though."

"Right," I say, laughing at his name for them. He shines the light in my eyes, and I turn my laugh into a cough.

"So," he says, smirking. "Which way?"

Turning, I stare down the dark corridor behind me. The light doesn't let me see very far. But knowing where the latrine station sits in relation to the quarantine facility, I'm pretty sure Camp B—and Logan—are in that direction.

"The quarantine facility is that way, right?" I ask.

"Yes. But the security hub is the other way."

"You're sure there's not a trapdoor leading to the latrines in Camp B?"

"Why do you want to get over there so badly?" Hector asks.

I hesitate, unsure if I want to explain. But why can't I tell him about Logan? Maybe he would help me find him if he knew the truth.

"When the officials brought me here, I got separated from someone," I say. "A friend of mine from the Surface. I think he might be in the other camp. I need to make sure he is."

Otherwise I don't know what I'll do.

Hector looks a bit embarrassed. But he doesn't say anything in reply. He's obviously hiding something.

"You know a way in, don't you?"

This time, he doesn't deny it. "If you follow this corridor, there's a trapdoor leading into the other camp."

"Why didn't you just say so?" I can't help sounding agitated.

"Because it's not a safe way in!" he says. "The trapdoor leads to a room full of explosives. Last time I went over there, I was stupid enough to try to get down even though there wasn't a ladder, and I slipped before I realized what was below me. I had to climb over boxes and boxes of explosives to get back up here. I was lucky I didn't get caught, or blown up."

So he was trying to protect me, it sounds like. But I don't understand one thing. "Why would there be a room full of explosives in the other camp?"

"We use them for mining. I just had no idea the trapdoor led to that storage room. It's right outside the other camp."

My mind's working fast. The stockpile could be useful for Mal and the other rebels—for me, even. If I could steal a few explosives out of that room and hide them up here, in this tunnel, I'd have easy access the second I find something of Charlie's that's better off destroyed.

But there would be security cameras to deal with, and guards. I'll need more of a plan before I try.

"Well," I say, walking past Hector in the opposite direction of the room with explosives. "Then let's check out the security hub."

Hector mutters something that sounds an awful lot like, "Thank goodness." Maybe he read my mind, and was worried I'd ask him to help me steal from the stockpile. I make a mental note to recruit someone else for that, or do it alone.

"Here, let me go first," he says. "I'll shine the light ahead."

"Sure," I say, slowing my feet.

He hurries past me, pointing the light down the passageway. "We shouldn't stay up here long. Sometimes the guards call people for inspection early in the morning, and if they call for us and can't find us, they'll raise the alarm."

"We'll just listen into the hub for a few minutes. See if we hear anything interesting."

———— ✳ ————

The air feels stuffy and cold. My lungs burn like I've been running; there must not be as much oxygen up here. But there's something comforting about the darkness. I almost believe I could hide forever up here, and no one would find me.

But I'd go restless in hiding. I can't sit still, not when I don't know for sure if Logan is safe, not when I still don't know if what Charlie's planning is as bad as before, or even worse.

Not with Hector's explosives stirring ideas at the back of my mind.

When we've been walking for some time—twenty minutes, maybe—we come to a set of steps that lead us down. Twelve steps. At the bottom, the path turns a corner.

"Watch your head," Hector says, flashing his light stick at the ceiling, where one of the steel plates has come loose and is hanging low. "And careful of the wires."

I duck under the hanging piece of ceiling and see what he's talking about. The wall ahead on my right side looks like someone came through here and smashed it open. Big and small pieces of steel are scattered across the floor. Wires poke out of the exposed wall, some thin and forming a tangled web with hundreds, others thicker and lonesome.

As I step carefully over a chunk of metal, a spark runs along one of the thick black wires. I stop moving. These are *live* wires, and water's still dripping from a couple spots in the ceiling. No wonder people abandoned this corridor; it's an electrocution death trap.

"How far is the hub?" I ask.

"We're already outside it," Hector says. "But if you want to listen in on the main control room, we'll have to climb."

He shines his light at the end of the tunnel, just ahead. Thin metal rungs are attached to the wall, leading up through a hole in the ceiling. Not to another trapdoor, I hope.

I continue walking, not taking my eyes off the wires as I step carefully around them. When we reach the ladder, Hector sticks the light between his teeth and starts up the rungs. I glance over my shoulder before I follow, to make sure no one sneaked after us somehow. Not that I can see very far down the corridor. Someone could be hiding anywhere in the dark, though hopefully we would've heard them.

Turning back to the ladder, I climb after Hector. There's no way someone could know we're up here—it's too dark for there to be cameras. I don't have to worry.

The ladder ends a good fifteen feet up, and I crawl into another tunnel. This one is narrower, and the ceiling is low, but thankfully I'm small enough to fit. There's a loud buzzing in the air, coming from whatever's on the other side of these walls.

Hector crawls slowly on his hands and knees in front of me. There's a lot less room for him in here than for me. Apparently he's not claustrophobic.

We crawl in silence for some time. I'd ask how much farther we have to go, but I'm afraid there might be guards close by on the other side of the walls.

Finally Hector stops, and turns around and motions for me to stay where I am, three feet behind him. After setting the light stick down, he reaches and lifts a square piece of the floor with deft, careful fingers. Dust rises with it, and I pinch the bridge of my nose so I won't cough.

Below where the piece of floor used to be is the back side of a vent that doesn't look like it's worked in years. But the slanted gaps in the vent let us peek at what's below: the main control room of the security hub.

A red luminescence fills the place. At the center of the room is a circular table with a lit-up screen on its surface, which shows a map of what I'd guess is the Crust sector. A 3-D hologram of our whole planet floats to the right of the map, spinning slowly.

The opposite wall is covered in small, square monitor screens. They flash between images from the cam-bots and other recording devices placed throughout the sector. There seems to be a whole cluster of screens devoted to the work camps, each labeled A or B. I want to get closer to make out the faces in the images, but I can't.

Two men sit in chairs before the screens, monitoring them. They're dressed in the gray suits I've seen Sam and other officials wear. They're laughing about something, but they stop when a door slides open on the left side of the room and a guard enters.

His blond ponytail helps me recognize him immediately: it's Mal. An involuntary noise almost escapes my throat, but I stop it in time.

One of the security techs rises and gives him a quick salute. Mal salutes him back.

"Cadet, sir, what can I do for you?" the tech asks.

"I came to deliver these plans," Mal says, his boots clunking as he crosses the room. He's not holding his arm like it's broken anymore. "It's important you put them straight into the system."

*Mal!* I yell in my head. *I'm right here. We need to talk.*

"Of course." The tech takes something from him—a data card. "About OS, I'm assuming?"

"That, along with some new information. We've picked up an image transmission."

"Blimey," the second tech says.

"Mind if I slip this in so we can see it?" asks the first tech.

"Not at all."

The tech turns and hurries over to the right-hand side of the room, up a short ramp toward what appear to be more monitors. The vent slits don't let me see that part of the room very well. There are clicks and tapping sounds as the tech slips the data card into a reader.

I keep my eyes on Mal as he moves after the tech. If he's not hiding his face and these men are calling him "cadet," they must know who he really is. He must've made some believable excuse about his short absence from the Surface—or given up information about the Alliance.

"Would you look at that," the tech murmurs. "Looks similar to our T-53 models."

"But bigger," Mal says with a hint of a smirk.

"Wish we had a clearer image. How many days, do you think?"

"Not many." Mal turns and walks to the spinning hologram of Kiel. "That's why it's so important all the inspections are completed as quickly as possible."

His face is stern; commanding. Even when the techs aren't looking at him, his composure doesn't break. I can't help wondering which person is the real him—this official who seems privy to plans and information, or Mal the fugitive, who helped Darren and Cady escape the Surface and escorted me to the work camp?

But if that was only an act and he's been playing the rebels all along, I don't understand why he hasn't turned me in by now.

"And these are the Core fugitives who've been identified?" the tech asks. It sounds like he's clicking through all the data that popped up from the card.

"Correct," Mal says. "We believe some of them may be working in this sector."

"How do you know?"

"There was a situation on the Surface, while the departures were under way. Three patrol ships were sent out to intercept unidentified transports that were believed to be from the insurgent base.

The ships lost communication, and only one came back. There was a second ship on its tail, with a fugitive on board. He was captured. Thanks to him, we know the rebels were trying to sneak into the lower sectors, though we don't know for sure if they were successful."

He's talking about Beechy. Beechy was captured.

"Well, we'll be sure to keep an eye out for any more of them on the cams," the tech says.

"Wonderful. Keep up the good work, gentlemen." Mal moves to the exit door.

"Thank you, sir."

Mal pauses as the door slides open. "Oh, and I was told to inform you that the girl, Clementine, is of particular importance to Commander Charlie. Her official status is unknown; she may not have survived the skirmish a week ago. But if you see any sign of her, it's imperative you let someone know right away."

"Can I ask why she's important?"

"I don't know his reasoning; I don't question my orders. Neither should you. Understood?"

"Yes, sir."

With that, Mal exits the room.

"We should go," Hector whispers.

Vaguely I'm aware of Hector scooting back in the tunnel so he can replace the vent cover. But I can't focus; my mind is moving too fast.

I was right; Charlie is looking for me, even though he doesn't know for sure if I'm alive. He named me before all the others. What does he want with me? I know his plan was to have me return to the Core after my stay in Karum prison, but I never learned why he wanted to keep me alive. And I was sure he'd changed his mind after I helped the Alliance screw up his plans and hijack his bomb.

It doesn't matter what he wants with me. The more important thing Mal shared is that Beechy was captured. He must still be alive—Charlie would keep him alive, since he's married to his daughter, and since he's the only person in Charlie's custody who knows everything about the Alliance and their plans.

Beechy hasn't given us up yet, or I'd be in a holding cell right this second. But I'm afraid he might not hold out much longer. Charlie has ways to break a person. All Beechy has to tell him is that I'm in the work camp and my name is "Brea," and I will have nowhere to hide. Even if I stayed up here in this tunnel, Charlie's men would find me.

I don't have many days left. I need to use them well.

# 14

Hector and I don't say much on our way back down the maintenance corridor. He asks me what I think about what we heard, but I don't give him an honest answer. I'm too worried, and it would take too long to explain why.

Images keep flashing through my mind of Beechy in a dark place like my Karum cell, or on an examination table with electric wires making his body convulse until he tells Charlie what he wants to hear.

*Please stay strong,* I want to tell him. *Please don't die. We'll find a way to rescue you.*

But I don't even know how I'm going to escape this camp alive.

We climb down the ladder through the trapdoor and sneak back to the cave room where Arthur, Evie, and Lucy are fast asleep. I'm so tired from worrying, I knock out seconds after I lie down on the hard floor.

It feels like only a minute later that my eyes are opening again, to the sound of guards stomping into the room.

"Everybody up!" an official shouts. "Inspection time."

The force of his voice urges me to my feet. He and the other officials come around to everyone, checking ID tags. Everyone who falls between the ages of thirteen and seventeen is told to go with the escort guards.

I lower my eyes as a man steps up to me and grabs my wrist. I want to slip away and hide in the maintenance corridor, but there are too many guards and cam-bots around. It'll be hard enough to keep my face from showing up in a recording.

I'll have to think of some other way to keep from getting the serum shot. I have to assume that's what it's for, to prepare for the worst.

The only good thing about this is that there's a chance I might see Logan in the quarantine facility. If all the twelve- to seventeen-year-olds from Camp B have also been called for inspection, he'll be there too. I could learn whether or not he's still okay. That thought keeps my feet steady as I trail after Hector and Arthur, and all the others who will soon do anything Charlie says, if I'm right about the submission serum.

I hope I'm wrong.

✕

The walls inside the quarantine facility are a drab gray color. The front room smells strongly of bleach, the kind of strong that can only mean they're trying to cover up something worse. When they burn corpses in the furnaces, no doubt the stench spreads.

The nurses who greet us are smiling.

"This way, children," one of them says. She has dimples in her cheeks and wears a pale blue lab coat. "Some of you will come with me, and the rest will go with the other nurses."

We follow her down a corridor. I keep my face calm, composed, especially when we're passing the guards who patrol here and there.

Every door we pass could have a kill chamber behind it. But none of them have windows, so I can't know for sure. They remind me of the doors in Karum, thick enough to drown out the screams of the prisoners behind them. There are stains on a couple of the doors, blood someone didn't completely scrub away.

I wonder how many people have died here. How many girls and boys only a few years older than me have seen these bleak walls and known every step they took was one step closer to their last. These are the last hallways they see. The last faces. I get the feeling the smiling nurses aren't around for that; it would only be the stone-faced guards.

"Brea," Evie whispers behind me.

"Yeah?" I whisper back. No one else is talking, so I hope our voices don't carry that much.

"This . . . serum you said you heard the guards say they're giving us," she says, biting her lip. "What did you say it would do?"

Behind her, Lucy seems to be listening in.

I check to make sure there aren't any officials up ahead. The only one I see is still a ways down the hallway.

"They said we wouldn't disobey any orders after they gave it to us," I say quickly. "It sounded like some kind of controlling serum—something that makes us weak-willed. So don't let the nurses give you any shots, if you can."

"They'll call for guards if we don't cooperate," Hector says, in front of me. "How are we supposed to stop them?"

I'm unable to fight the sinking feeling in my stomach. He's right; no one will let us leave this place without the serum in our systems. If we struggle, they might decide throwing us in a kill chamber is easier.

"I don't know," I say.

The nurse at the front of the line stops abruptly and turns around. We've reached a place where the hallway splits four ways. A nurse's station sits at the corner.

"Please stay in the line," our nurse says. "We'll get you all in and out of the examination rooms as quickly as we can."

Another nurse walks over from the station, carrying a tablet. She says something to the first person in line, and directs the girl around the corner, down one of the corridors. The next person is directed around the corner immediately after.

Slowly, the line moves forward. When Arthur is called and I'm almost to the front, I can see around the corners better, enough to tell we're being directed into exam rooms. There's another line of kids at the end of the right-hand branch of hallway. They might be from the other camp. Logan could be down there in line. If I could just slip away; if I could just run to find him without anyone noticing—

"Go into room seven," the nurse says to me with a smile, pointing me down the left-hand corridor. Hector's already been called away, and it's my turn now.

I give the nurse the best smile I can muster, and head to room seven. If there weren't guards stationed outside the doors, I almost really would run. But it would do more harm than good.

Room seven's door slides open when I approach. The guard outside barely glances at me as I walk in.

The room is small with a cushioned examination table against the far wall. To the left is a counter with a sink and jars of supplies—antiseptic patches and strips of gauze—and to the right is the woman who will be examining me, I assume. She's wearing a white coat instead of a blue one, so she must be a doctor. Her dark hair is tied up in a knot at the back of her head. She smiles when she sees me, as she strips off her surgical gloves and tosses them in the trash receptacle.

"Hello, I'm Dr. Piper," she says. "What's your name, sweetie?"

"Brea." I'm amazed I manage to sound normal.

I've hated examination rooms ever since I was a child, thanks to the earliest days of my life, when I lived in the sanitarium until I was old enough to work in the camp. Those days were so long ago, all I can remember are flashes of images: nurses leaning over me; needles glinting in the light; voices saying, *This is for your own good.*

Now, when I look at the exam table, I also see the table I had to lie on for hours in Karum, sometimes awake and sometimes under the influence of a sleeping drug, while the doctors poked and prodded me, and did things I'd like to forget.

"How are you today, Brea?" Dr. Piper asks.

Not okay, not okay at all. I need to get out of here.

"Fine," I manage.

"Can I see the number on your arm?"

I hold it out to her. The skin around the new numbers is still tinged reddish pink, but no one's seemed to notice so far, so I try not to worry. Dr. Piper doesn't scan the number or anything—she just glances.

"You were one of the Surface transfers, correct?"

"Yes." Something about my tag must give it away.

"Okay. If you could take a seat on the bed over there for me, I'll get you out of here real fast." Dr. Piper crosses over to the sink and turns the water on to wash her hands.

Wiping my sweaty palms on my pants, I walk to the table and sit down. I'm going to have to get through this, even if she gives me the shot. It won't make me mindless, anyway. It's the old serum, and all it will do is make me sick for a little while. I can handle that. I can hide it, as I did before, and then Mal and Skylar will help me escape from the camp. I won't have to follow any of Charlie's orders; we will find a way to screw up the next part of his plan.

All these words sound so nice in my head, but I don't believe any of them.

"Now," Dr. Piper says, turning around and sticking the ends of the stethoscope around her neck into her ears, "take a deep breath for me."

She presses the silver disk against my chest. My first breath is a bit shaky, but I control the second one better, and the ones after that, as she moves the disk an inch or two each time. She doesn't need to know how nervous I am.

Soon she pulls the disk away and replaces the stethoscope around her neck. "Good. If you could lie back for me."

I stretch out on the table. There's a small mesh pillow for my head, identical to the one that was on the surgical table in the Core, when the doctor operated on me and made me stronger, and covered up the old scar on my jaw—before Charlie gave me a new one. The memory makes my body tense again.

*Calm down.*

Dr. Piper reaches for the hem of my shirt. "Is it okay if I pull this up a little? I'd like to take a look at your skin, make sure it's looking healthy."

If she's asking me permission, I guess she must not be planning on doing anything too terrible. "Okay."

She rolls my shirt up. With gentle fingers, she touches the skin of my belly, poking it here and there. "Have you noticed a rash, or anything? Or had a fever?"

I shake my head, no.

"Lucky girl," she says, pulling my shirt back down. "I've seen a couple Surface transfers with horrible rashes. Exposure to small amounts of moonshine can cause that. It's horrible that all of you had to deal with that, even if it was only for a few days. They transferred you to the city, right?"

"Right," I say, even though I don't know for sure. But that must've been what happened, or there would've hardly been any work camp survivors.

"I heard there were quite a few tragedies before the transfer, though," Dr. Piper says with a sad sigh. "Thankfully Commander Charlie was able to move the rest of you underground."

Her worry seems so genuine, I wonder if she even knows the whole thing was caused by Charlie in the first place. Maybe he wasn't going to save her, or any of the other personnel in this facility. Maybe they were going to die with us when the world exploded.

"All right, well, you seem pretty healthy," Dr. Piper says, moving over to the sink. "But I would like to give you some medicine before I send you back to the camp. It's a preventive sort of thing. We wouldn't want to bring you down here to keep you alive, only to let you get sick a few days later."

I sit up on the table, digging my fingernails into the cushion. Dr. Piper opens a drawer and pulls out the essentials for the injection—a vial of the serum and a fresh syringe wrapped in plastic. She rips off the plastic.

I can't let her do this. I have to make her stop.

"Is it really necessary?" I ask. "I'm actually allergic to some vaccines."

As soon as I say that, I regret it. Charlie might've mentioned my allergy in whatever description of me he passed around to all the guards.

"You won't be allergic to this one," Dr. Piper says, drawing the serum into the syringe. The serum is a dark, hazy blue instead of the orange color I remember. Must be a new variety. "It's been well tested. It'll be quick, don't worry."

Smiling, she turns around with an antiseptic wipe in hand. I expect her to roll up one of my shirtsleeves, but instead she pushes down the collar of my shirt and dabs antiseptic on the skin around my clavicle, over my trachea. I've never heard of an injection being administered there before, unless someone needed a tube to help them breathe. This can't be good.

"I was afraid of needles when I was younger too," she says, turning to toss the wipe in the trash. She grabs the syringe from the counter. "But it's just a pinch, really. You won't even feel it."

When she steps back toward me, the long, thin needle reflects the light from the overhead lamp into my eyes.

I blink and I see Karum again: I see the doctor sticking a needle into my arm to draw blood; I see him injecting that blood into Fred; I see the lights blurring as I awoke on the table after another operation.

"Please, I really don't think I need this," I say, scooting off the table.

I need to make a run for the door.

"You do, sweetie," Dr. Piper says, smoothly blocking my path. "Everyone needs it. And if you don't cooperate, I'm gonna have to give you something to help you calm down. Can you calm down on your own, Brea?"

She takes a step toward me, and I move back, bumping into

the table. There's only one of her. I'm sure I could overpower her, but there are guards waiting right outside. All she has to do is scream and they'll come running.

"It's just a little prick, okay?" Dr. Piper says, smiling that stupid smile of hers again. She grasps my shoulder with one hand and holds the syringe out with her other, guiding the needle toward my clavicle. "Nothing to fret about."

I knock away her hand holding the syringe and grab her arm in the same motion. I twist it back as far as it can go.

Her face contorts with pain, but she recovers immediately. "Code A!" she yells. "I need help!"

The door zips open and two guards rush inside. The first grabs hold of me, but the second halts three feet away.

I know him. He's Joe, Sam's friend. He stood up for me after we played a simulation game in the Core and I had the luckiest win of my life, but he hasn't been kind to me since. He's been a mindless soldier working for Charlie. Beechy shot him on the hangar deck a little over a week ago, but clearly he survived.

Recognition sparks in his eyes that are clouded over like the eyes of all Charlie's mindless soldiers. Joe remembers me too, though I tried to disguise myself with different hair.

I'm done for.

"Clem—" he starts.

I scream as loud as I can, to drown out his voice. He slaps a palm over my mouth with a growl.

Dr. Piper moves at a fast pace over to the counter to prepare a fresh syringe, since I knocked the last one out of her hand.

I'm an idiot. I should never have fought her.

"Give her the shot, quickly," Joe says. "I need to take her to Lieutenant Sam. Commander Charlie wants her in custody."

"What does he want with her?" Dr. Piper asks.

"She's Clementine," he says. "She's one of the fugitives from the Core."

Dr. Piper stares at me as she takes in this new information. "I see. She lied about her name."

She steps forward, gripping the syringe tightly in hand. The guard I don't know the name of digs his hands into my shoulders, pinning me against him. There's nowhere for me to run, even if I could break away. These three will tell everyone I'm hiding in the camp.

As Dr. Piper pushes the needle into my neck, a booming sound reverberates through my ears. I don't have time to realize what's happening, or brace myself in any way.

The wall behind me rips apart. The force sends me flying forward and slamming into something hard.

Darkness.

# 15

When I come to, my ears are ringing. My body is stiff with shock, and I'm coughing. My temple's pounding like I rammed headfirst into a fighter jet.

I remember what happened: There was an explosion. I can still feel the tremors in my arms and hands and legs.

Dr. Piper was in the middle of giving me the shot. I reach a hand to brush the tender spot on my neck. When I pull my hand away, there are drops of blood on my fingers. I don't know if she had the needle in all the way, if the plunger had released the serum yet.

I lift my head, wincing from the pain, and blink until my eyes adjust to the darkness. The ceiling lamp is dead, but there's a little light coming in from somewhere. Part of the roof in the room behind me collapsed, I think. But the wall in front of me seems mostly intact. We must've been on the edge of the explosion's reach.

The hallway outside is quiet, like everyone evacuated the

building in case of another explosion. It felt like I blacked out for only a few minutes, but maybe it was longer.

The syringe is lying a few feet away from me. The blue serum has leaked out onto the floor—the plastic must've cracked.

Relief floods me. Dr. Piper didn't administer the shot.

Joe is also lying near me, to my left, on his side. His chest slowly rises and falls. His lips are slightly parted, and a thin layer of dust covers his hair and uniform.

He's still alive, and that means he can tell Sam where I am when he wakes up.

Setting my palms on the ground, I push myself to my feet. Pain shoots up every inch of my body, but I ignore it.

Almost everything around me is in pieces. Smoke and dust cloud the air, rising from the debris beyond the blown-out hole in the wall. The sink and cabinets are buried under chunks of gray building.

So is Dr. Piper's body. I can't see her face, but her arm and the sleeve of her lab coat stick out from beneath the rubble. Her arm's hanging at a wrong angle like it fell out of its socket. The limpness of her body is what makes me lose my composure. Cady's body was limp too, when the rescue crew pulled her out of her hovercraft.

This is too much. I want to turn away and run, and let someone else deal with this mess. But I need to know if she's still alive, so I do what I have to do. I pinch the bridge of my nose to fight the nausea, and scoot close enough to reach for Dr. Piper's wrist. I count to twenty as I feel for her pulse.

*Eighteen, nineteen, twenty.*

Nothing. The second guard is buried even deeper under the debris too deep for me to reach. I'm going to have to trust that he's gone too, or at least too injured to tell anyone what happened.

Turning away, I wipe the blood on my pants. This was too close a call. Not just Joe finding out who I am and almost giving me up to Sam, but the fact that I would be dead right now if the other guard hadn't been standing behind me. I would be buried beneath this pile of rubble with no pulse.

I thought I was okay with dying. I accepted the idea when I was on the spaceship with Oliver, and I knew it might be coming when I agreed to go undercover in the work camp. Death would let me leave all the pain in this world behind.

But now that I've barely escaped it again, I'm not sure I want to leave the world yet. Not until I've had the time to fight for the things I care about. Not until I've said good-bye to the people I love.

Death might turn out to be worse than everything I'm running from, and there will be no waking up.

Somewhere far away, there's a booming sound that makes the walls shake. Another bomb.

It makes sense that the Alliance would've targeted this facility, since the kill chambers are one of Charlie's biggest weapons. But I don't understand why no one—not Mal or Skylar or anyone—told me they were planning this. They must've known there'd be people from the work camp in here for inspection. Why would they risk killing us too?

Unless something went wrong with the plan. Someone could've screwed up the bomb timers, set them off early.

Whatever's going on, I need to get the vrux out of here. Another explosion could happen any second.

But first, I have to deal with Joe. He's still lying on his side, his soft breath turning to mist when it touches the air. I'd think he were fast asleep if I didn't know any better.

Maybe he'll wake up and he won't remember he even saw

me, but I don't think he's going to forget. He's going to wake up and tell the other guards I got away, and tell them where to find me.

I can't let him wake up.

I take a slow step forward, lean down, and slip the gun out of his holster. It's a copper like the laser gun I used in the Phantom war simulation game, the day I met him. The day he was almost my friend.

I wrap my palms around the barrel, aiming at his head. My hands are slippery with sweat, barely holding the weapon steady.

I'm not sure I want to do this. It's not Joe's fault Charlie made him a mindless soldier. It's not his fault he ended up here.

But this is about protecting myself. And I can't risk letting him go.

*Don't think.*

I'll imagine someone else's hands are squeezing the trigger. I'll pretend Joe is Charlie, and I'm beating him at last. That will make this easier. But even as I make the decision, Joe's head moves a little. He's waking up.

I have to do this fast.

I slide my index finger through the trigger. Joe's eyes flutter open and he blinks slowly.

A small sound escapes his throat, like he's trying to say something, but he starts coughing instead.

*Now. Do it.*

"Wait," he chokes. "Please don't."

My fingers are glued to the gun, but I can't squeeze the trigger. He was my friend once. How can I shoot him?

"I won't tell anyone I saw you," he says between coughs. "I'll let you go."

I am frozen, my heart hammering in my chest, my arms impossible to move. But I have to shoot him; I have to.

I can't trust him. I don't have a choice.

"No," he says, almost whimpering. His eyes are watering. "Please, please don't shoot me."

He'll say anything right now, but he's still going to follow Charlie's orders. He isn't like me and the others in the Alliance; he can't fight the serum.

But when I start to squeeze the trigger, my hands falter again. *What if I'm wrong?*

Joe's watering eyes seem clearer than they were a couple minutes ago, not hazy like the eyes of the mindless. Almost like he hit his head hard enough to wake up.

"Please let me go," he says again.

"Why should I believe you won't hand me over to Sam?" I ask, snapping the words. "Tell me."

Please give me a good reason. Please don't make me shoot.

"Because I'm on your side," Joe says quickly. "I want to join the Alliance. I've been trying to contact one of you, to let you know. But I didn't have a chance until now."

That makes me pause. I haven't heard anyone on Charlie's side mention the Alliance before. Maybe he's telling the truth. But one thing still doesn't make sense.

"Then why did you tell the doctor my real name?"

"I couldn't control what I said. I didn't want to tell her, but my lips moved and I couldn't stop them."

He was subdued. And now he isn't.

My hands still won't unfreeze. Even if I wanted to shoot him, even if I was sure I had no other choice, I'm not sure they would let me squeeze the trigger.

But he'd better be telling the truth; he'd better not hand me over to Sam.

Slowly, I lower the gun.

Joe struggles to his feet, using the wall to help himself up.

"Thank you," he says.

"You owe me for this." I wipe my sweaty forehead with the back of my hand. "If you get the urge to tell anyone where I am, remember I could've killed you."

"I will," he says.

"Good."

I double-check over my shoulder that Dr. Piper's body hasn't moved. She's still buried underneath the rubble, along with the other guard. I silently thank whoever set off the explosives for taking care of them for me.

Out of the corner of my eye, I notice Joe's hand slipping behind his back. Going straight to the second gun all officials carry with them, the one I forgot to remove from his belt.

There's a split second where panic grips me, where I'm not sure what I'm going to do. But rage hits me with full force, overpowering everything else.

He lied to me. He is not my friend.

I can't let him give me to Charlie.

He draws his gun. I spin around and strike my copper sideways at his head, knocking him off balance.

A shot goes off from his gun, sending a laser beam into the rubble behind me.

As Joe regains his footing, I hit him with the barrel again, yelling through my teeth. Twice more I bash his head, until he slumps, silent, onto the floor. Blood trickles from his hairline.

I stare at him, my hands frozen again, my legs immobile.

The bloody gun slips from my fingertips and hits the floor with a clang.

He lied to me. I had no other choice.

*I'm sorry*, I think.

And then I run.

⚹

I limp down an empty corridor, moving as fast as I can with my legs still aching. The pounding in my temple hasn't subsided yet.

My hands have Joe's blood on them.

I don't even know if I killed him. But I hope I did. Otherwise, he will wake up and tell Sam exactly where to find me.

There are distant cries from corridors behind me, and the sound of boots pounding somewhere up ahead. A rescue crew must be on its way, if it isn't here already. I don't know where the explosions were centered, but they were close enough to the exam rooms that plenty of other people could've been injured. How many kids were trapped under the rubble? Hopefully Hector, Evie, and the others got out of here alive and Logan wasn't anywhere near this place.

Around a corner, the facility entrance comes into view. Three guards stand talking with guns in hand, their backs to me. Behind them, a medical crew carries an empty stretcher through the door, and two more guards follow them. They must be gearing up to begin the rescue mission.

I'm trying to decide what I should do—limp past them and hope they don't notice, or pretend I'm more injured than I really am?—when one of the guards spots me. He says something to the other two and starts jogging toward me, signaling two male medics with a stretcher to follow.

One of the other guards is Sam. There's some distance between us, so maybe I'm wrong, but he's the only one not wearing a helmet, and I'd know his blond hair anywhere. I'm pretty sure he's staring at me.

*Pretend you're hurt.*

"Help!" I double over, clutching my belly. At least when I'm standing like this, I have an excuse to keep my face down.

I wipe my nose with the back of my hand, and rub some of the blood still on my cheeks around a little. Hopefully that will make me look less like Clementine, since I'm sure I'll have to pass Sam on the way out of the building.

"Where are you hurt?" the guard asks when he reaches me. His figure blocks Sam from view.

"I'm fine," I say, but when I let go of the wall I purposely lose my balance. He grabs my shoulders so I won't fall.

"No, you're not," he says, and signals the medics to set the stretcher on the ground. "Where did you come from?"

"One of the exam rooms." I talk fast. "A wall blew apart right after my doctor gave me a shot. I think it knocked me out. I woke up and she was dead. Her blood was all over me. I heard another explosion and I knew I had to get out of there. I was so scared."

"It's gonna be okay." The guard helps me over to the stretcher, and the medics help me climb onto it.

"Who set off the bombs?" I ask, curling up on my side. "How many people died? Some of my friends were in the other exam rooms."

"We got a lot of people out, but we don't know how many were trapped inside, or who made this happen." The guard crouches beside the stretcher. "Listen, uh . . . "

"Brea."

"Brea. These nurses are gonna take you outside and make sure you're okay, and get you back to the camp safely. We're gonna make sure your friends got out. Okay?"

"Okay."

"You'll be just fine," he says.

"Promise?"

"Yes." The thinness of his lips tells me he's lying. He must know Charlie's plans for me and everyone else in the camp. He knows, by the end of it, it's likely we're all going to end up dead.

He straightens as the medics lift my stretcher. We start down the hallway, and I curl up tighter, wrapping my arms around my stomach. Sam is straight ahead. There's no way he won't recognize me, if he gets a good look at my face. Joe did, after all.

Joe's face flashes through my head, with the blood trickling from his hairline.

No, I will not berate myself for what I did to him. This wasn't like what happened with Cady. I was ready to let him go; I was ready to trust him, because I didn't want to kill him. But he gave me no choice.

The sound of Sam and the other guards talking tells me when we've reached the entrance. I open my eyes a little, enough to see Sam giving orders to several more officials who've just entered the building.

"I want teams of two," he says. "You check *every room*. Haul out anyone who's still alive, and try to identify the rest."

He doesn't spare a glance my way as the medics carry my stretcher out of the entrance. But I keep expecting him to. I can't believe he really wouldn't notice me a second time.

Not ten seconds later, we're outside, and his voice is lost in the midst of others. There are a few more officials moving on the wide pathway, but mostly it's filled with the nurses and doctors who must've evacuated. There aren't as many as I would expect—nine or ten at the most. Smoke is heavy in the air; it smells like the whole world is burning. Some of the nurses are crying loudly and hugging each other, like they can't believe this happened.

The medics set my stretcher down on the side of the pathway, where it branches off into another road along the edge of the cavern. It must lead to the city because there are transports parked here—small, silver ones Sam and the extra guards and the medics must've used. It makes sense they'd have a faster way to get here, instead of cutting through the camp.

"They're gonna need us inside," one of the medics says.

"You go," his partner says. "Tell the lieutenant I'll get in there as soon as I can."

As the first medic jogs back to the building entrance, I push myself up with my elbows, ready to stand and limp back into the camp. Sam hasn't come out of the quarantine facility, but he could at any moment. The camp is the safest place for me to hide.

"Hold up there," the medic says, putting a hand on my shoulder to push me back down. "You need to sit tight for a minute. I'm not letting you go until I've had a look at your injuries."

I was afraid he'd say that. "I'm not really hurt. The blood isn't mine."

My head's still throbbing, but I doubt there's a way he can fix it without giving me a shot, and I'm done with those forever.

"I need to at least check your vitals," the medic says, stepping over to the back of his medical transport. "And maybe you'd like clean clothes, or some water? I'd take advantage of this, if I were you. I know your daily rations are scarce."

He has a point, if he's going to make me sit here anyway. "Water, I suppose."

He returns with a bag of medical supplies and a small canister of water. I take the canister and down the cool liquid in only a few swallows. I wish I'd taken my time after it's gone.

The medic chuckles as he takes the empty canister away. He reaches into his bag and pulls out a stethoscope. He listens to my heart, while my eyes stray to the smoke trailing from the ruins of the quarantine facility, up to the mossy stone in the high ceiling of the cavern. I hope the kill chambers are really destroyed, and the furnaces and all the medical equipment too. I hope when Charlie hears what happened here, it makes him furious.

I'm almost smiling to myself when I remember he has Beechy. What will he do to him for this?

"Thomas," someone says behind me.

The medic looks up. "Yes?"

"Lieutenant Sam wants you in there. I'll get this girl back to the camp." The person sets his hand on my shoulder, gripping it a bit too tightly.

It's Skylar, I'm 99 percent sure. But I have to act normal.

Thomas mutters something incoherent, but takes the stethoscope out of his ears and straightens. "All righty, then. It seems you're well enough, Brea."

"Thank you for the water," I say.

"My pleasure." He smiles and tosses the empty canister into the back of the medi-pod, and heads back to the building.

I get to my feet a bit unsteadily and turn to Skylar. She has a helmet on but the visor's open, so I can tell she's glancing over my body.

"You're gonna get me all bloody," she says, and grips my shoulder again and shoves me toward the medi-pod. She lets go of me to climb into the back, to rummage for a towel or something. "Don't you dare move," she adds loud enough she must want people to hear her.

Quieter, she says, "Did they give you a shot? Whisper when you answer, or I swear I'll strangle you."

"No, they didn't," I say in a low voice. "The first explosion cut them off."

"Good thing you made it out of there alive. Paley and Jensen screwed up the timers. The explosives were supposed to go off this morning."

"I wondered if it was a mistake."

"Yeah, well at least it's over."

She steps out of the medi-pod and hands me a towel. I wipe off the blood from my cheeks, though some of it seems already dried.

Skylar checks behind me, then says, "Listen. Charlie's got a lot of people looking for you."

"So I've heard," I say. "Do you know if he wants me dead or alive?"

"Alive."

That's what I don't understand. Charlie was going to leave me to die in the flight hangar the day of the bomb. I'd become too reckless for him to have any hope of turning me into one of his mindless soldiers anymore. The only reason I can imagine he'd let me live now would be to punish me for my crimes before he kills me. To torture me worse than he already has.

"So what am I supposed to do?" I ask.

"I need you to stay undercover in the camp as long as you can. Spread the word to everyone you can that an uprising is under-way. Those in the camps can be a part of it soon."

Now that they're all subdued, I'm not sure how much help they'll be. But hopefully some of them—those with stronger wills—will be able to fight the injection. Those are the people I can still get on our side.

But I don't know how Skylar expects me to be useful if she keeps me in the dark about Alliance movements. "It would help if you'd keep me informed about what you and the others are planning," I say, not hiding the annoyance in my voice.

"It's too dangerous to get messages to you often," Skylar says, grabbing the towel from me and throwing it back into the pod. "But I'll try. Now let's get you back to the camp before someone comes over."

Gripping my arm, she hauls me toward the gate, less than twenty feet away.

We need more time. I have at least a hundred more questions about Beechy, and Mal, and whatever information the Alliance might've found out about Charlie's plan by now. But one thing can't wait.

"Logan. Is he in the other camp?"

"Yes," she says. "He was called for inspection this morning like you, but Jensen checked on him, and he was already out of the building when the bomb went off."

She pushes me through the open camp gate with more force than necessary. But I don't even care. I could laugh, I'm so relieved. Logan is alive; he's all right.

The gate clangs shut behind me. I push myself to my feet and turn in time to see Skylar walking away, before she disappears into the crowd.

She seemed harsher than her usual self. I hope she's not still angry at me for Cady's death. I hope she's just trying to stay in character, even when no one's watching.

As I turn away from the gate, her last words play through my mind again: *He was already outside the building when the bomb went off.*

Every limb of my body freezes.

She was talking about Logan. She said he'd been called in for inspection, but if he was outside before the explosion, that means he finished sooner than I did. He got all the way through his examination with a doctor.

That can only mean one thing: he was given the shot. He couldn't have gotten out of the exam without it.

Logan is one of the mindless.

# 16

The camp seems oddly quiet tonight. People aren't even whispering; they're sleeping, or staring at the walls with uncertain looks on their faces. In the Surface camp, if we'd heard that someone set off explosives in the quarantine facility, we would've cheered.

I can only assume the submission serum is the reason no one here seems to care. Their eyes don't seem muddled or lifeless, like the eyes of most of the subdued I've seen, but there's clearly something different about them. Maybe the effects are taking longer to set in, because there's something different about the injections they were given.

In the shadows, I lean against the wall hugging my knees to my chest. It's been hours since the explosion. I couldn't stay near the building to watch the rescue teams, because of Sam, so I don't know if they're still trying to get people out. I don't know where Hector or Evie or Arthur is. Hopefully not trapped in the facility—hopefully they're somewhere in one of these crowded rooms. I haven't exactly been looking for them. Chances are they were given the injection, so they're probably silent like all the rest of these people. But Skylar's right—there must be a few people in the camp, at least, whose bodies have rejected the serum. There must even be a few who didn't get the shot at all, since the bomb went off in the middle of the inspections. If they aren't subdued like all the others, they must be aware that something is wrong. Maybe they would believe me if I told them what I know. But how can I pick them out from all the rest?

If only Logan were here. Maybe he'd be subdued like everyone else, but at least he'd be with me. Most of the time, things make more sense with him around.

When we first arrived at the KIMO facility, he hardly left my side. We'd been apart for so long since I left for the Core—even when we were reunited, it was in the midst of a fight we almost didn't survive—and both of us were afraid of losing each other again.

The first night in the compound, we'd been assigned separate bunk rooms, and I resigned myself to the fact that we'd have to spend our nights apart. But Logan had a different idea. He told me to wait until everyone else in my room was asleep, slip out of bed, and meet him in one of the training rooms. When I found him, he'd set up a makeshift bed with blankets on the floor mat, in a corner.

"I figured it's still better than where we used to sleep, back in the camp," Logan said with a sheepish smile.

"It's perfect," I said, dropping onto the mat and pulling one of the blankets over me. "Even if people can see us on the security cameras."

"It's dark. Anyway, I doubt the techs pay much attention during the night."

"Hopefully not."

Logan slid an arm around my waist. "I missed you," he said softly.

His words were soft and simple, but they sent an ache straight through me, because a few days before, they'd meant so much more.

I leaned my forehead against his. "I'm here now," I reminded him.

"Good," he whispered, and kissed me. His lips were soft and tasted sweet. I melted into him, pushing off the blanket so it wouldn't be between us. He responded by shifting his body closer to mine. Nervousness trickled down my spine, but I didn't stop him.

All those days I was separated from him, and finally he was right there beside me.

He kissed me again and again, each kiss deeper than the last. My fingers drifted under his shirt and traced lines above the hem of his pants. Logan made a low, guttural sound in his throat. His mouth moved to my neck, while his hands slipped underneath my shirt.

He was kissing me faster now, pressing his lips against my skin once, twice, a hundred times. I fell apart, unraveling at his fingertips. Every breath for him, every touch for him.

He pulled away from me abruptly, wincing.

"What's wrong?" I whispered.

"Nothing," he said. But when he leaned in to kiss me, whatever it was made him stop again. He groaned.

"Is it your leg?" I asked.

His face tightened with pain. "It's been acting up lately."

I helped him lower onto his side on the mat, to take his weight off his bad leg. Laying beside him, I pulled the blanket over both of us.

"Thanks," he said. "Sorry. I didn't mean for it to mess this up."

"You don't have to apologize. This was perfect." I wrapped my arms around him, and he snuggled me back with a sigh.

In the darkness, there was nothing else, only the comfort of his body close to mine. I let exhaustion creep over me and carry me away.

Before I drifted off to sleep, I heard Logan whisper, "I'm glad you didn't forget me."

If I'd been awake enough to answer, I would've assured him I could never forget him, not in a million years, no matter how long we were apart.

The ceiling lamp flickers off overhead, drenching the cave room in darkness. It keeps doing this. Whoever manages the camp's electricity must not care if it's in perfect working condition, as long as the lamps occasionally give off light.

A couple seconds later, the lamp flickers back on. I push off the ground and move toward the door. I can't keep sitting here. I'd might as well check out the quarantine facility again. At this point, I almost don't even care if Sam sees me—but I won't let him.

There's a croacher nest on the ground between the cave rooms. I hop over it, grimacing.

"Clementine," someone says, ahead of me.

I stiffen, my eyes still on the ground. Maybe they're not talking to me—maybe someone else in here has that name. But I'm pretty sure I know that voice. I'm pretty sure she knows exactly who I am.

I slowly lift my head. Nellie stands a few feet away from me, smirking.

"What do you want?" I ask.

"So you answer to your real name too," Nellie says, taking a step closer. "I was starting to wonder if you had a twin, but it seemed unlikely the Developers would let two identical idiots live past age two or three. If there's just one of you, it's easier to believe they didn't notice."

"What do you want, Nellie?" I ask again, louder.

She keeps smirking, like she loves making me mad. But her eyes shift past me and I notice something harder in them. Almost fear. She takes a step to the side of me, keeping her gaze on the room behind me.

"I need to talk to you about what you're doing here," she says quietly. "About why you aren't in the Core. Can you meet me near the latrine station?"

Her voice is entirely different than it was a moment ago, no longer accusing. Maybe she's playing some joke on me, but I think her nervousness is real. I search her face for any signs that she might be subdued. As with all the others in the camp, there aren't any. But she's not acting like them anyway.

"Did you go to inspection today?" I ask. "Did the doctors give you a shot?"

"Yes." She looks confused. "What does that have to do with anything?"

"Just curious."

Either the serum hasn't worked its way into her bloodstream yet, or it didn't work on her for some reason. Maybe she's allergic to it like I am, but in a less extreme way. Maybe she's too strong willed for Charlie's medicine. Maybe that was clear during her test on Extraction day, and that's why she wasn't picked.

"So, will you meet me or not?" Nellie asks.

"Why should I? You tried to *kill* me the last time I saw you. Did you think I'd forgotten?"

"I know," she says stiffly. "I know I did, and of course you don't owe me any favors. But I heard what you said the other day, and I know you're hiding something. Also, I'm pretty sure you don't want anyone to know you're here. Maybe I'll mention your real name to the guards if you won't explain everything."

I flex my hands and tighten them, considering breaking her nose. It's ugly already, but I'm sure I could make it uglier.

"Fine," I say. "I'll meet you by the latrines. But if you tell a single person—"

"I won't unless you don't show up. Meet you in ten."

She slips away into the shadows of the room I was on my way out of. I watch her until she's gone, then head in the opposite direction, letting out a hiss of frustration. Nellie is the last person in the camp I want to trust—and really, how can I trust her? She doesn't care about me, or anyone. She puts her own survival above everything.

But she's the only person here who knows I don't belong, and she hasn't told anyone. If she cares about her survival, my story about Charlie's bomb will make her want to fight him, before he can do something that will result in her death.

I hope I'm right. It would be nice to have an ally.

⚔

We meet beside the latrine station, in a small space between the flimsy building and the wall of the cave. No one's around at this hour, and the nearest cam-bot is in the adjacent room, so there isn't much of a risk of being overheard. Still, we talk in whispers.

I tell Nellie everything: How I showed up in the Core and realized the testing wasn't over. How I had to kill someone and become stronger, faster, smarter to prove I had high Promise. How after the final test, we were all given injections, which turned everyone into smiling puppets and made people believe Charlie when he told lies about moonshine growing stronger, making it necessary for some of us to fly away. How I still had control of my mind, so I didn't believe him. How I tried to destroy his bomb before he could use it, but he caught me.

I tell her about Karum and the things I learned from Fred about Marden. I tell her how Beechy broke me out, and how we hijacked Charlie's bomb and used it to destroy the acid generator—but too late, because Charlie had taken the shield down. I tell her how I've been working with the Alliance ever since, how we came here to launch a coup against him and the other Developers because we know he hasn't given up.

Nellie doesn't interrupt me, but she looks more and more worried the longer I talk. When I'm finished, she slides down the wall until she's sitting, and stares at her hands.

"The doctors gave us that injection you talked about today, didn't they?" she says.

I rub my temple with two fingers. It's still a bit sore from my injury earlier. "I think it's a modified version, yes."

"But I don't feel any different."

"It works best on people who have weak, malleable minds— people who can be persuaded easily to begin with. People with stronger minds can sometimes fight it. At least, that's what Beechy told me."

"That must be part of what they look for in the Extraction tests—weak minds." Nellie laughs softly. "Makes me feel better, actually. But I guess that means they made a mistake with you."

She lifts her head, and one side of her mouth curves upward in a smile. Not a mean smile or a jealous smile, but a kind one. It looks strange, coming from her.

"Yeah, I guess they did," I say with a short laugh.

"Serves them right." Straightening up, Nellie wipes her nose with the back of her hand. "So what do we do now? Your rebels are the ones who took care of the quarantine facility earlier, I assume. What's the next step of their plan?"

The sound of feet squishing through mud catches my ears. Someone must be using the latrine station. I hear a cough, and then a door closes behind me, on the other side of the wall.

"I don't know," I say, lowering my voice. "That's the problem. The others stuck me in here and told me to recruit people for the uprising, but they haven't told me all the plans. They're too afraid I'm going to get caught and ruin things."

"There's gotta be something we can do," Nellie says. "Blowing up the quarantine facility won't stop Charlie from blowing up half the world again, if that's his plan."

"I don't think it is. But I know, you're right. I—" I pause. When Skylar and the others blew up the quarantine facility, all they needed was explosives and people to sneak them in.

We have access to explosives. I look up at the ceiling, at the spot on the other side of the station where the entrance to the maintenance corridor is hidden. It would take us to the room full of bombs in Camp B.

It also leads to the security hub, the main control room for the entire sector. The hub houses the power generators, the security camera monitors, the communication systems—everything. Skylar might be organizing a way to destroy it already, but maybe Nellie and I can do it first.

"I have an idea," I whisper, and Nellie's eyes light up. "It'll be dangerous, though. We're going to have to climb to some high places."

"Whatever it is, I'm game," she says.

I quickly explain what I'm thinking. She offers suggestions, and slowly our plan comes together.

A loud siren cuts us off. It screeches from the walls, from speakers I didn't even know existed, and I slap my hands over my ears to drown out the noise. Nellie says something, but I can't hear her.

I don't know what's happening, but the sound reminds me of the emergency sirens back at the KIMO facility when we thought Charlie's army had found us. The day I slipped up when I was using the fighter jet guns. The day Cady died.

The siren shuts off, leaving my ears ringing. I wait for it to start again.

Instead, a loud voice crackles through the speakers.

"Attention, all workers in the camp. This is Lieutenant Sam of the Core Special Security squad."

My muscles tense.

"As you may know, earlier today we were attacked by fugitives from the Surface," Sam says. "They snuck into the quarantine facility and set off explosives while inspections were under way. Many people were trapped inside. Many didn't survive. We believe the intention of the insurgents was to kill many more of you, but luckily we were able to prevent that from happening."

"Yes, *that* was their intention." Nellie snorts.

I don't laugh. We already know what happened, so Sam must have a reason for saying all this over the loudspeaker. It can't be good.

"Tonight, we've placed extra patrols throughout the camp," Sam says. "They are there to keep you safe. But we need your help in order to prevent such an attack from happening again. If anyone has information regarding the bombers—if you've overhead or seen anything suspicious lately, such as people spreading falsities about the Developers or others who protect you, please tell a patrol right away."

This is how he'll turn everyone against me. "All those who provide substantial information will be offered a once-in-a-lifetime reward—a chance to be picked for a special Extraction in two days' time. You don't need to be sixteen years of age to be eligible, and you may have already participated in an Extraction ceremony."

I've told Nellie all my secrets, and now she could give me up if she wanted, for a ticket to safety in the Core. This could be exactly what she meant to do all along.

"Again, please convey any information you have regarding the fugitive attack to a guard as soon as possible. The Developers, especially Commander Charlie, our righteous leader, thank you for your assistance."

There's a crackle from the speaker, then silence. Long silence, in which I'm terrified to speak.

"Well," Nellie says briskly. "We'd better hurry up and get going."

"You're still in?" I ask.

"Of course." She looks at me like I'm crazy. "Sam's a liar. Did you think I wouldn't get that, after everything you said?"

No, I wasn't sure at all. "I'm glad you did."

"Good." Nellie grins. "Ready to go blow up the security hub?"

"Been ready all my life."

# 17

The air smells dank in the abandoned maintenance corridor. Water leaking from the ceiling drips on my hair as I shut the trapdoor behind us. I've already found the light stick Hector left in the small compartment in the wall, and I switch it on as I get to my feet.

A few feet away, Nellie rubs the goosebumps on her shoulders. "I'm surprised more people don't have frostbite. It's so cold everywhere."

"I'm sure people get it and die from it sometimes, especially when they're working in the mines," I say, shining the light down the right-hand passageway. "But no one cares, since there are plenty more workers to replace them."

"We're just bodies to Charlie, huh?"

"Bodies he almost blew up a little over a week ago."

"I can't believe no one knew. We would've just been . . . gone."

I move past her down the corridor. "The room Hector mentioned should be this way. He said it's on the other side of Camp B."

"You're sure he was telling the truth?" Nellie asks.

"He'd better have been. We can't exactly damage the security hub without explosives."

"Do you know how to detonate them without killing ourselves?"

"I'm sure we can figure it out." I hope we can. We learned a little about how explosives work in school: they're chemically unstable compounds, which release energy when exposed to a lot of heat or a mechanical shock. The ones in the storage room are used by workers in the mines, under supervision, so they shouldn't be too hard to work.

The hardest part will be getting the explosives out of the storage room without getting caught, or setting one off by accident. Hector got lucky last time. I've had some luck too, but I'm sure it's almost run out. After what happened earlier today, there's a 99 percent chance the room will have extra guards, since it's housing the weapon the rebels used, even if they didn't steal from this particular store. The guards should be posted outside, so as long as we're quiet, we should be able to slip in and out. But there will be security cameras. Those will be harder to fool.

At long last, my light hits a wall up ahead. The end of this side of the corridor.

"The door should be just ahead," I say. *If it's really here.*

I shine the light at the floor, bracing for the worst. But there it is—a steel door identical to the other, except there's no ladder pulled up from below. I step over the door and crouch to examine it. Nellie does the same.

"We won't know for sure what's below until we open it," she says.

I set the light stick on the floor, so the light is aimed where I need it. The other door didn't have a handle on this side, since it opened downward from the passageway, but this one does. The handle feels slimy—there's some sort of moss growing on the rusted steel. I tighten my grip, ignoring the wetness. I pull up a little, to test which direction the door opens. That seems to be the way.

As far as we know, no one knows about this corridor or this trapdoor besides Hector, so the guards have no reason to be patrolling inside the storage room. They should be stationed outside. But we can't be certain.

"On the count of three?" I ask.

"One . . . " Nellie clutches the side of the handle.

"Two . . . "

"Three."

We both pull the handle at the same time, straining until the door gives way. We push it all the way open. The room below us is dark and silent. There doesn't seem to be any sign of guards.

Nellie picks up the light and shines it down. The beam trails over the room's contents—metal boxes of various sizes, each with a small moon and the word EXPLOSIVES painted on the side. The highest tower of boxes sits only a few feet below the ceiling, by my guess, but not close enough to reach. One of us will have to climb down without disturbing the explosives, and then get back up.

I glance at Nellie, who's staring at the boxes and biting her lip. She isn't a strong enough climber. It'll have to be me. If an explosive goes off by accident, at least I won't have her death on my conscience.

I sit down and carefully swing my legs through the hole. "Keep the light on for me. And be ready. You're gonna have to pull me back up."

"You sure about this?" Nellie asks. "I bet there are cameras."

"I'm sure there are."

I don't know how I'm going to keep my face away from them, but maybe it doesn't matter. If we manage to blow up the security hub's control panel, we'll destroy all the camera records, and hopefully whichever technicians might've seen me.

If this doesn't work, at least I'll have gone down fighting.

I push off the ledge, bracing myself for the impact of the explosives. I land on a big box in a crouch, relatively stable, but a shudder runs through the pile underneath me. One wrong step and this whole room could blow apart.

Out of the corner of my eye, a tiny red light blinks in the upper corner of the room, near the door. As long as I don't face it, hopefully no one will be able to identify me. But I have to assume someone has already spotted me on the monitor, and will communicate to the guards outside to check if anyone's in here. They could walk in any second.

I need to do this fast.

Straightening—carefully, carefully, so as not to disturb anything—I look around at the nearest crates. The size must designate the model of the explosive inside, but I have no way of knowing which kind are easier to use, or better for what we're trying to do. I can't take more than one or two boxes, if I have to carry them while I climb back up through the trapdoor. I glance at Nellie, who's shining the light down on me.

"Do you think you could catch a box, if I throw it?" I ask in a fast, hushed voice.

"I can try," she says. "Do you think it'll explode if I drop it?"

"None of them should be that unstable, but I can't promise anything," I say, climbing to reach the smaller boxes. I pick up the first one I see, trying my best not to bump the others. The box is about the size of both my hands placed side by side. I notice the number three painted on its underside. The other crates must be numbered too. Not that a three means anything to me.

"You ready?" I ask, holding up the box so I can throw it to Nellie.

"Yeah," she says. Her voice is muffled by the light stick, which she's holding between her teeth. She lowers her hands through the hole, about five feet above me. As long as she isn't a clumsy catcher, this should be easy.

I toss up the box. Her hands fumble, and she lets out a squeal. But she doesn't drop it. She lifts it all the way up through the hole and sets it aside.

"How many more?" she asks with the light stick still in her mouth.

"Just a couple. We need to get out of here."

Maybe it's only my imagination, but I'm pretty sure I can hear voices through the door. Guards talking. If I make any loud noise, they'll be able to hear me too.

I reach for another small box and toss it up to Nellie. Then two more. The security camera's light blinks at the edge of my vision. My palms grow sweaty. My whole body is tense, waiting for one of the guards to bust the door open. Surely they will any minute now. I've been in this room too long.

"Last one," I say, tossing Nellie another box. She catches it easily.

"Okay, get back up here," she says. "I'm getting the feeling we should really hurry."

I don't mention I've had that feeling for some time. Glancing at the room's exit door, I climb back over so I'm on the highest pile below the hole in the ceiling. I'm still at least three feet below where Nellie's hands can reach. For the millionth time, I curse how short I am. Hector or Beechy could probably jump and grab the ledge.

Hissing through my teeth, I look at the other crates all around the room. I'm going to have to make this pile higher, so I can reach.

I scramble off the pile and gather similar-sized boxes, and stack them on top of the others. I've managed to make the stack grow a good foot and a half when a small *whir* reaches my ears, and I pause. It's coming from the security camera in the corner. I turn my head just as the camera stops turning. It points directly at me, making my face clear and bright for whoever's watching the monitor screen.

*Vrux.*

After turning away, I pack two more crates on top of the pile and climb to the top of it again. It's not as steady as I'd like it to be, but it'll have to do. I straighten slowly at the top of it, and lift my eyes to the hole above me. Nellie stretches a hand down.

"Hurry," she says.

There's a loud shout from the other side of the wall.

I lift onto my tiptoes and grasp her hand. The explosive crate I'm balancing on slips out from under my foot as she heaves me up. She uses her other hand to pull me up the rest of the way, until only my legs are dangling.

The storage room door opens as I pull my legs into the corridor. Nellie and I slam the trapdoor shut.

"The guards know where we went—they can follow us," she says.

"We won't let them." I grab one of the boxes with explosives and find the place to open it—a keypad on the bottom side with only numbers one, two, and three. I'm guessing it's a three-digit code, so there are twenty-seven possible combinations. Easy if we had time, but we don't have time. The guards are taller; they just have to climb onto the pile I made and bust the trapdoor open.

My fingers fly through the codes:

1-2-3, 1-1-1, 1-1-2, 1-1-3, 1-2-1, 1-2-2, 2-1-1

2-1-1 works. The crate unlocks and I lift it open. Inside are three cylinder-shaped explosives in silver packaging, with black and blue wires connecting them, beside a small black object that looks like a comm box, which must be the detonator.

"Take the other crates and run," I tell Nellie.

"What are you gonna do?"

"I'll be right behind you. Go."

She doesn't argue. She leaves the light stick behind. I arrange the three explosives on top of the trapdoor, grab the light and detonator, and get to my feet. The shouts from the guards in the storage room are loud; they sound like they're right below the door.

"Are you coming?" Nellie asks from down the corridor.

"Yes." I turn and run after her with my hand hovering over the detonation button. I don't know how far the range of the explosives will be. I don't know when I should set them off.

There's a banging sound behind me, and faint light streams into the corridor. Over my shoulder, I see a guard stick his head up through the trapdoor.

Faster, faster. I have to go faster.

"Hey!" he shouts.

There's no way to know if I'm far enough away yet, but there's no more time to wait.

I press the detonation button and wait for the fire to swallow me whole.

# 18

*B*<sup>OOM!</sup>       I duck my head as fire bursts through the tunnel behind
me, ripping the floor and ceiling apart. It sends a ripple of heat
through my body. I must've made it out of range, since I'm still on
my feet. But my ears are ringing. Nellie's up ahead, running with
the boxes over her head like they'll protect her.

*BOOM!*

The second explosion is even louder. The entire tunnel quakes,
sending me crashing into the wall to catch my balance. There's a
popping sound in my left ear. Pain sears through my head, and I
scream. I can't help it.

*BOOM! BOOM! BOOM!*

The explosives in the storage room must be setting each other
off. I can't hear anything out of my left ear—the eardrum must've
ruptured—and I'm blinking fast to keep from crying.

I have to keep moving. I need to get far, far away before this
whole tunnel blows to smithereens.

As I run, one hand pressed against the wetness of blood on my ear, I realize, faintly, what a horrible plan this was. We were never going to get explosives out of that room without raising an alarm—not without disabling the security cameras. But we didn't disable them, and now my face is on the feed. Sam will know soon that I'm responsible for this mess, if he doesn't already.

Ahead of me, Nellie slows down. We've reached the door to our side of the camp. I didn't realize we were running so fast.

"What now?" she asks. "Someone knows we're up here, even if those guards are dead."

"I know." I touch the wall to steady myself, trying to focus on anything except the pain in my ear. I can still feel warm liquid leaking out of it, flowing onto my fingers. My other ear echoes with endless ringing.

We have minutes, maybe, before someone pieces the clues together and discovers this tunnel. Not enough time to reach the security hub, set off the explosives, and make it back here in time to slip into the camp without anyone noticing. If we have any intention of hiding, we need to give up what we set out to do and hurry down the ladder right this second.

Angry tears leak from my eyes when I open them again. I can't hide anymore. Sam is going to catch me, whether it's in a few minutes or a couple of hours. He must know I'm in the camp now; all he has to do is come looking.

There's no point in running anymore. But maybe I can still pull off one more stunt, even if it's crazy. Only, I have to do it alone. Nellie doesn't need to take the fall.

I wipe the tears from my eyes, push off the wall, and move to the trapdoor. "You have to get out of here," I say, kneeling beside the door and shoving it open. "No one saw your face. If you climb down and slip back in with everyone else, no one ever has to know you were up here."

A quick glance at the latrine station tells me the stalls are empty. No one has found this entrance to the tunnel yet. I stand up and push the ladder down for Nellie.

"What about you?" she asks. One of her hands is clenched at her side. The other still clutches the explosives I asked her to carry.

I step forward and take them from her, keeping my left ear pointed away from her, so she won't notice the blood. "I'll be fine," I say. "It'll be easier for me to sneak back into the camp after I blow up the security hub if I'm on my own." I'm sure Nellie can see the lie in my face, but I keep my jaw firm anyway. She chews her lip. The selfish part of me hopes she's going to insist on coming with me even if it means she'll be caught.

Instead, she doesn't say anything at all. She wipes her nose with the back of her hand and climbs down the ladder.

I was right; she cares more for her own life than for anyone else's. Logan would say she's smarter than me. I'm not sure I disagree.

She hops down into the latrine stall, landing with a squish in the mud. She wipes her hands on her pants before pushing through the stall door and glancing around.

As I pull the ladder back into the corridor, Nellie looks up at me. I can't see her eyes clearly from here, but I can tell she's saying her good-bye with them. She knows the chances of me sneaking back into the camp after I finish my mission are almost none. She knows I'll likely be in Charlie's custody by morning, if I don't die in the hub explosion.

Lowering her eyes, she moves out of the latrine stall and out of sight.

I shut the trapdoor as securely as I can, grab the light stick, and make sure the explosive packages are secure under my arm. A third hand would be useful to keep pressure on my bleeding ear, but I don't have one.

The corridor seems darker now that I'm alone. I shine the light ahead of me as I half limp, half run. My ear aches so badly I'm afraid it's going to burst, but I won't let anything slow me down.

As long as I'm free, I will keep fighting.

⤝

Down the stairway with twelve steps, I duck under the gap in the ceiling and pause in front of the corridor. Wires poke out of the damaged walls on either side of me, electricity still running along them.

When I was here last night, Hector said we'd reached the security hub already. I can't see what's on the other side of these walls, but these wires remind me of the kind that run from the back of circuit boards. And circuit boards of this size mean they're running important machinery—maybe even the main power plant for the entire sector. Even if I'm wrong, setting off the explosives this close to the hub control room is bound to cause some damage. Hopefully it will be enough.

The cases holding the explosives each require a different code to unlock them. It takes a couple minutes for me to guess them all. But instead of growing more and more anxious, as the seconds pass, I feel calmer. I'm finally doing something with my hands, something that feels like it will make a difference. I want to make sure I do it right.

I pull the explosives out of the cases in their silver wrapping and place them in groups of three along the wire-filled wall of the corridor, spaced evenly. The fourth set, I place beneath the ladder at the end of the corridor. I don't bother to pick up the empty cases.

With four detonators in hand and the light stick under my elbow, I walk back up the stairs to the main corridor. I've placed the detonators in order, so I know which one will set off each set of explosives.

At the top of the steps, I press the button for the set below the ladder.

*BOOM!*

I drop the detonator I used and continue walking, slowly counting to ten in my head. I press the next button.

*BOOM!*

Drop the detonator. Count to ten. I press the last two detonators at the same time, and drop them as I start to run.

*BOOM! BOOM!*

I jam my fist into my left ear, because it's still bleeding. The pain is almost too much to bear.

Behind me, smoke and bits of scorched metal rain through the air where the corridor blew open. People are screaming somewhere in the distance. Or maybe that's just the ringing in my not-deaf ear.

It feels like a long time has passed already, but I haven't reached the trapdoor yet. I must be limping more than I'm running.

When the exit comes into view, I see someone has already opened the door. A tall, lean figure climbs up the ladder into the corridor.

"Brea showed me this place, and the room with the explosives. I'm sure she's up here," he says.

It's Hector.

"There she is," he says, pointing at me as he gets to his feet.

White-hot anger courses through me. "You're helping them?"

He doesn't answer.

He's the one who told me about this passage and the room with the explosives. Now he's turning me in? He must be doing it because of Sam's announcement. He must've decided a shot at Extraction was too important.

Another figure climbs into view and steps off the ladder. This man is a patrolman, all armor and authority—the kind of official who terrified me as a child. A carbon copy of the official who gave me the old scar on my jaw, before Charlie replaced it with a fresh one, down to the hazel eyes flashing at me through his helmet visor. But officials almost always look the same to me.

He lifts a rifle that's nearly half my size. When he speaks, there's an expert coldness to his voice, a stony hardness to his jaw. "Don't move," he says.

I almost want to laugh. I have nowhere to go. Doesn't he know I blew up both ends of the corridor?

"Drop your weapons," he says.

"I don't have any." I show him both my hands—the one covered with blood, the other holding nothing but a light stick.

"Drop the light," he says.

I hesitate, weighing my options. The light is the only weapon I have, though it isn't a good one.

But two more guards climb into view. I can't take on three of them. I can't let them shoot me; I need them to take me to Sam alive.

There's one more play I can make for the rebels—an important play. If I can earn an audience with Commander Charlie, I can kill him before he orders my execution, or uses me for whatever he's planning. I might be the only one who can.

"I give up," I say, dropping the light stick.

The first guard and his second-in-command move forward. The second secures my hands behind my back. The first shines the light from a fixture on his armor into my face, nearly blinding me.

The third guard takes a few steps down the other side of the passageway. "This is the right corridor," he says. "You can smell the smoke."

"Good work, Hector," says the head patrolman, the one pointing the light at my eyes.

"Thank you, sir," Hector says.

There's a hint of regret in his voice. It only makes me angrier. I don't even care if he's only doing this because of the shot the doctors gave him earlier. He means nothing to me now.

"So," the head patrolman says. "Brea. Are you aware a storage room full of explosives was broken into tonight?"

"Of course," I say, forcing calm into my voice. I don't want these officials or Hector to know I'm afraid. "I broke into it myself. And my name isn't Brea." I look directly into the guard's eyes. "It's Clementine."

"We guessed that," the patrolman says smoothly. "We'll need to run some tests to confirm your identity, of course. First, you're going to tell us where your friends are. We know you couldn't have pulled off a stunt like this alone."

I'm not going to let them find the others. Not Nellie, not Logan, not anyone.

"You're wrong," I say. "I broke into the room on my own tonight. I blew it up afterwards, as you may have noticed, and then I blew up part of the security hub."

A hiss of air escapes through the guard's teeth.

I let out a light laugh. "Didn't hear about that yet? You should really work on speeding up communication, or important things will be overlooked."

"None of this explains the destruction of the quarantine facility," the patrolman says, ignoring my comment. "I know you played a part in that, and I know you had help. Give me the names your friends are using."

He must think he'll get a bigger reward when he turns me over to Sam, if he's already made me talk. But I don't even know what names Skylar and the others are using so they won't get caught. Mal's using his real one, but he must've convinced everyone he's not a Core fugitive.

But it's better if this patrolman thinks I have information and I'm just not telling him, so he'll keep me alive longer.

I look him in the eye. "My name is Clementine. My citizenship number is S68477. I was born on the Surface, and I was picked for Extraction—"

"Give me names," the patrolman repeats, "or I'll give your leg a bullet."

He lifts his rifle and aims it at my left leg.

My head won't stop throbbing, and dots speckle my vision no matter how many times I blink. But I keep my voice calm as I keep talking: "You won't hurt me. Commander Charlie wants me alive and unharmed."

The patrolman laughs. "That's a bit of an exaggeration. 'Alive' is all I've heard anyone say."

I need to keep talking. I don't know if that will help me, but it's all I've got.

"My name is Clementine," I say. "My citizenship number is S68477. I was born on the Surface, and I was picked for Extraction—"

The patrolman lifts his rifle again. I see the butt of his gun flying at my face and feel pain exploding across my temple.

Then nothing.

# 19

My hands are bound behind my back with shackles—I can tell before I open my eyes. The skin of my wrists already feels sore from rubbing against the metal.

My head is hard to lift. I wince as pain shoots across my forehead.

I remember what happened: the explosions; Hector turning me in; the official knocking me out.

I don't know where I am now, or how long I've been here.

It takes several seconds for my eyes to adjust. There's hardly any light in here, only a flickering bulb high above. The room is small—a holding cell, most likely. But a strange cell; one of the walls is made of mirrorlike glass, and there's an identical room on the other side of it.

I stare at my reflection, slumped against the wall. There's nothing left of my curls but a few stringy strands of pasty blond. My eyes seem empty and desperate. I've had nothing to eat or drink in stars know how long. There's a bandage over my left ear that someone must've put there while I was sleeping. There's less pain in my ear, only a dull throbbing, but it feels like it's plugged up with gauze. I can't hear a thing out of it.

Even in the dim light, I can tell my skin and hair and clothes are covered with soot. Worse than the dirt is the blood I've collected over the past day. Blood on my pants, blood on my cheeks, blood on my hands. My own, and Joe's. I have no way to wash it away, nor fresh clothes to change into. I have to wear his blood like a scar, a constant reminder of the way I am changing.

*He lied to me*, I remind myself. *I didn't have a choice.*

But was it even worth it? I won a few extra hours of hiding and time to use those explosives, but I don't know how much damage they did. I still ended up in this cell.

I force my eyes away from the mirror. I need to stay calm. I need to figure out as much as I can about where I am. Information will help me feel like I have some control over what's going to happen to me, though I know I have none.

I use the wall to get to my feet. It's difficult with my hands behind my back, but I manage.

There's a security camera with a blinking red dot in the upper right corner of my cell. The exit door is to my left, a few feet away from me, but there is no handle or lock-pad, as far as I can tell. My guess is the only way out of this cell is if a guard opens the door from the other side.

I'm stuck in here until someone comes for me, and that will most likely be Sam, or someone coming to take me to him. I hate that I've escaped from him so many times, only to end up right back in his grip.

If my wrists were thinner, I could slip out of my handcuffs. If the glass wall weren't so thick, I could break it and use a piece for a weapon. But someone would see me on the security camera anyway, and they'd stop me.

A door slams shut somewhere nearby, and my whole body stiffens. He's coming.

*Calm down.*

I need to think about something else, anything besides what Sam's going to do to me. The first good memory I think of, I play out in my mind like it's happening again.

✗

I'm ten years old. The sky is turning violet as faint stars speckle across it. Logan and I are sitting on a set of boulders on the edge of the Surface work camp. We're sitting in silence, waiting for the moon to rise, when the guards will make us go inside.

Logan's left hand rests on his knee, and his right hand rests on a boulder. I keep finding myself looking at his hand, instead of the sky. I'm used to holding his hand by now—he grabs my hand all the time, whenever we're walking down the street to the departure station, or on our way to the fields, or heading home. It always feels like he's trying to keep me from getting lost in the crowd. Like he thinks I'll get hurt if I let go of his hand.

Tonight, we aren't in any crowd, and I'm in no danger of getting lost. But I feel like holding his hand anyway. I'm not quite sure why. Because it feels nice, I suppose.

Part of me wonders if Logan will think I'm strange for holding his hand without a reason, but I decide I don't care. I reach out and gently turn his hand over, and slide my fingers through the spaces between his. His palm is sweaty, but so is mine.

Logan doesn't look at me, but he tightens his grip, gluing our fingers together. When I glance at his face, he's smiling at the stars. And I know I made the right choice.

There's a muffled sound of a door opening, and I ball my hands into fists. It's not my door, though—it's the door to the other holding cell, on the other side of the glass wall. A figure in guard armor, minus the helmet, steps in and flips a light on. His blond hair is tied in a ponytail.

Mal.

His eyes shift to mine for an instant, then away.

"Bring him in," he says to someone behind him. The glass wall muffles Mal's voice.

I wish I could get inside his head, so I would know for certain where his loyalties lie. He swore he's on our side, but he has the other side believing he's on theirs.

Another guard enters the room, pushing someone else in front of him. The person has a sack cloth over his head, and his hands are bound like mine. He wears trousers and a shirt covered in mud, and has no shoes.

The guard shoves the prisoner forward—so hard, his head hits the glass. He doesn't even grunt; he must be unconscious. The guard unties the sack and rips it off the prisoner's head.

It takes everything in me not to cry out.

Logan's limp body slumps against the glass. Fresh blood trickles from his nose, and the skin around his left eye is black and blue.

I knew this would happen, sooner or later. Sam must've guessed he was also hiding in the camp and scoured the place for him, or someone gave Logan up.

Mal and the guard leave the room without sparing me another glance.

As soon as the door shuts behind them, I drop to my knees beside the glass. There's so much blood on Logan's face. His nose looks like it was broken and someone set it badly. I wonder if he fought the guards, or if he went quietly and they hurt him anyway so I would see.

Angry tears fill my eyes. I press my palm into the cold glass. I want to smash the wall and make the glass rain down on everything.

"Logan, I'm so sorry," I say. "Whatever they do to me, whatever they do to you, please know I . . . "

*I love you.* I haven't said that to him yet, not in the right way, at least. Not since I realized how much he meant to me.

Now I want to say it, but he can't hear me. He's so close, and I can't even touch him.

There's a soft click behind me. I whip my head around as the door to my holding cell opens. I struggle to my feet, blinking fast so hopefully it won't look like I've been crying. Two guards I don't recognize enter.

Sam walks in behind them. He's wearing his slick gray uniform, and there are gloves on his hands. White, like Charlie's.

"Wait outside," he says to the guards. "Tell them to turn off the cameras."

"Yes, sir." The guards leave. The door clicks shut behind them. My feet feel like they're stuck to the floor. I'm practically trembling from anger and the memory of what happened the last time Sam and I were alone together.

He takes a step toward me, a cold smile forming at the side of his mouth. He has no weapons that I can see—no guns, no knives.

Almost as if he was worried I'd find some way to steal them. That makes me relax a little. It reminds me that he's scared of me. He hates me because I'm a threat.

"Did you think hair like this would suit your face?" He snorts. "If so, you were sadly mistaken."

He takes another step and reaches for my head. I know he expects me to react, so I stand still, though I desperately want to run. He grabs a tuft of what's left of my curls and pulls them up, inspecting them.

I keep staring straight ahead, at the small flecks of stubble on his face. The pain comes a few seconds later, when he wrenches my hair up from my scalp before he lets it go.

"You're so dirty, it's disgusting." He wipes his gloved hand on his pants. "Worse than an animal."

I give him what I hope is a blank face. Inside, I'm praying this means that will be the only time he touches me today.

Sam's eyes narrow a little, like he finds something unsavory about my silence. He smooths out the creases in his gloves and makes himself tall. The smirk returns to his mouth. "So, how did you like my present?"

I must let a flicker of confusion cross my face, because Sam says, "The one behind you."

Of course. I ball my hands into fists behind my back, wishing I could use them. Sam deserves a bloody nose to match Logan's.

"Commander Charlie had a feeling you both would be hiding in the vicinity of each other," Sam says. "But I have to admit I didn't expect you to be stupid enough to go into the camp. We couldn't have planned it more perfectly with the inspections."

I keep my expression calm, steady. He doesn't need to know mine didn't go smoothly.

"Oh, we did a test, and we know you avoided the injection," he says with a smile, and my stomach dips. "Your friend didn't, though. And we have something more fun in mind for you. Worked out pretty well, I think."

I touch my teeth together, then pull them apart. I can't keep listening to him anymore. "What do you want, Sam?" I ask.

"Oh, is this not fun for you?"

"Just tell me."

He takes two steps forward, until his face is inches from mine. His breath is hot against my cheeks. Instinct makes me want to press back against the glass, to get as far away from him as possible, but I fight it. The cruel amusement in his eyes tells me he knows what I'm thinking. I hold his gaze and lift my head higher.

"I want you to tell me the location of your other friends," Sam says. "We have a list of their names, but I doubt they're using their real names. And some of them are better than you at hiding."

"What makes you think I know where they are?"

"I could be wrong." Sam removes his right glove and inspects his hand. "But let's just say I'm hoping you know their location, for your sake and the sake of your boyfriend."

He lifts his bare hand to my neck and caresses my skin, even though it's covered with soot. He shifts his body so it lines up with mine.

I'm all too aware of how gentle his touch is—and how much worse it could get. The security camera isn't blinking anymore; no one can see us. Someone might hear me if I scream, but I doubt they'll come.

I need to answer him—I need to tell him something so he'll stop touching me, and so he won't hurt Logan. But I don't even know where most of the rebels are. The only people I've seen since I arrived in Crust are Mal and Skylar. I could give him Mal, but he's playing his part so well, Sam might not even believe he's Charlie's enemy.

I'm not even sure I believe it.

Breathing through my nose as normally as I can, I look Sam straight in the eye. "I don't know where they are. I came here with the rebels, but I haven't heard from them since I entered the camp. I don't know how they blew up the quarantine facility, or what they're planning next. I swear I would tell you if I knew. Please don't hurt Logan."

Sam studies my face, his expression unreadable. Then he drops his hand and slips his glove back on. "That's not something I can guarantee, since you didn't give me any names."

"I don't know them," I say again, louder. I want to yell; I want to scream. "I swear I don't know anything. Beechy was making all the calls."

"Too bad he gave himself up."

"He didn't give himself up—you caught him."

Sam laughs softly. "Oh, you've got it wrong. He flew straight into our arms."

I stare at him, searching for the lie in his eyes. "That's not possible."

"Believe whatever you'd like."

"If he gave himself up, why did it take you two days to figure out where I was? How come you don't know the entire rebel plan by now?"

"I didn't say he gave himself up to *chat*. You're making false assumptions." Sam checks the time-band on his wrist. "Anyway, this has been fun. Looks like I'm running late for a meeting."

He turns and walks over to the door. He raps twice on the door, and steps back as it opens.

He's lying about Beechy, or stretching the truth—he must be. If Beechy gave himself up, it was because he had no other choice. But I have to know for sure.

"Please tell me what you meant," I say.

"It's much more fun to leave you hanging," Sam says with a smile as he walks out.

The door shuts, and he's gone. Turning, I see Logan still slumped against the glass with his eyes closed.

I ram my shoulder against the glass and let out a yell of frustration.

# 20

No one brings me food or water.

I don't know if it's day or night anymore. I don't know how much time has passed since Sam came in here, but it feels like it's been several hours at least. I hope he won't come back.

All I know for sure is I'm freezing cold and my clothes barely offer any warmth. My mouth isn't producing nearly enough saliva to satiate my thirst.

I'm not sure I should sleep when I'm this weak. I might not wake up.

To keep my mind working, I run through the symptoms of dehydration, from what I saw in the work camp on the Surface. Once my thirst reaches an extreme point, I'll likely develop severe confusion and delirium, along with rapid breathing and a rapid heartbeat, and a fever. I'll stop producing sweat and tears. If it gets bad enough, my brain cells could swell and rupture from my body trying to pull too much water back into my cells, or I could have kidney failure or go into shock from low blood volume. Any one of these could lead to death.

Surely someone will bring me water soon. Charlie doesn't want me dead—not yet, at least. Sam said he has something fun in mind for me.

My gaze moves to Logan, who's still knocked out on the other side of the wall. His cool breath forms misty circles on the glass. Maybe Charlie's going to make me kill him, like he made me shoot an Unstable my first day in the Core.

I won't do it, no matter what he threatens me with. I won't let anyone hurt Logan again, and I won't hurt him myself.

"Clem," a muffled voice says.

I sit up more, snapping my focus back to Logan's lips. They move again, forming a soundless word. Slowly, his eyelids flutter open.

"Logan, it's me," I say through chattering teeth. "I'm here."

"You're hurt," he murmurs.

I almost laugh. Of course that's the first thing he would say, when he's the one who's been knocked out with a black eye and a bloody nose.

"I'm okay," I say, pressing my fingertips to the glass. "Are you?"

"Been better." Logan lifts his head with effort, looking around. He blinks a few times, until his gaze seems steadier. "How long have I been out?"

"I don't know. As long as I've been in here."

He lets out a short cough and winces, touching a hand to his side. "Did Sam come in yet?"

"He did. We had a nice chat."

The color fades from Logan's cheeks. "He didn't . . . " His voice trails off. Memories of Sam's hands and elevators linger in the silence.

I pull my legs closer to my body. "No."

"Good," Logan says, his shoulders slumping in relief. "As soon as I got to the camp and couldn't find you anywhere, I thought you might've already been caught. I was afraid Charlie had you."

"I thought you were far away in one of the other sectors," I say in a small voice. "I didn't know when I would see you again."

A soft smile tugs at Logan's lips. "You can see me now."

He presses a hand to the glass, showing me the calluses in his palm, the hard edges where he cut his skin working in the camp on the Surface. The dim light overhead casts shadows on his face, making the bruise around his injured eye even darker. I want to run my fingers across his skin and heal his bruises with my lips.

He coughs again. The movement rocks his whole body, and suddenly I remember what Skylar told me the last time I saw her: Logan received the injection in the quarantine facility.

"They gave you a shot, didn't they?" I ask.

Logan's mouth thins. "How did you know?"

"I saw Skylar the day the explosives went off. She said something that made me think you must have."

"She was right," he says. "But it's not what you think. It wasn't like the shot you were given in the Core."

"I know, I could tell it was different," I say. "But it still did something. It made everyone weirdly quiet."

"I think that was an effect of the pill everyone took after their injection. I had to pretend to swallow mine, and spit it out and bury it when I got back to the camp."

"Wait. What pill?"

"This chewable vitamin. My doctor said it's something all the child workers in Crust are given every week so they won't die of malnutrition. I asked around and I'm pretty sure she was telling the truth. But I think it also subdues people a little—probably not a strong dosage, but that would be why the atmosphere changed afterwards."

I didn't notice any pills during my examination, but it sounds like my doctor would've given it to me on my way out the door. If Logan's right, that explains why Nellie wasn't quiet like everyone else—she too must've spit out her pill. But it doesn't explain what the injection was for.

"What about the shot?" I ask. "How do you know it didn't contain any submission serum?"

Logan stares at nothing, like he's trying to decide whether to reveal something. Then he looks back at me. "I was told what was in the shot on my way here. I was also told not to tell you, or Sam would administer the injection to you. And I can't let that happen."

I press my lips together, hard. "That's not fair to me, and you know it."

"I'm sorry. I just . . . I can't lose you yet, Clementine."

"But you think I'm okay with losing you? Logan, we're in holding cells. Sam's going to kill us himself or deliver us to Charlie, for him to kill us. You're going to lose me soon anyway, so why not just tell me?"

An emotion I can't read flickers across Logan's face, but he says nothing.

"Fine." I turn away from him and press my back against the glass, crossing my arms.

"I'm sorry," Logan whispers.

I stare at the gray wall opposite me, wanting to tell him everything that's been in my head for so many days—how I lost control and killed Cady, and how I might've killed Joe. How part of me is afraid I'm becoming exactly what Charlie wants me to be.

Logan and I are both keeping secrets. But I'm not brave enough to spill mine yet, and he cares too much about me to spill his.

"Me too," I say.

⁂

A boot kicks me hard in the ribs. "Get up," a voice says.

"I'm up," I mumble, forcing myself to lift my head even though I'm only half awake. I don't remember falling asleep, but I must have. My body hurts from lying curled up on my side, with my arms behind my back.

"I meant up *all the way*," the official says, wrenching me to my feet by my elbow.

I see his face and flinch. The hazel eyes; the stony hardness to his jaw. This is the patrolman who found me in the maintenance corridor.

"Sorry," I say quickly.

I lick my dirty, chapped lips to moisten them a little. My eyes dart to the cell on the other side of the glass, as I attempt to steady my legs. *No!*

The cell is empty. Logan is gone. There's a bloodstain on the glass, where his face was leaning against it when he was still unconscious.

He's gone; he's gone; he's gone. Where did they take him? They can't have gone and killed him already.

No, when they kill him, they will make me watch.

The patrolman pulls me toward my cell door by my elbow, but I pull back.

"Where's the prisoner who was in the other cell?" I ask.

He doesn't answer. He pushes me ahead of him out the door, and this time I don't have the strength to fight back.

There's another guard waiting out in the corridor. He's holding a sackcloth like the one Logan had over his head when Mal brought him in.

"Please don't make me wear that," I say. "I won't struggle, I swear."

"Put it on her," the patrolman says, securing my arms behind my back. He's much too strong.

The other guard jams the cloth over my head, blocking out all the light. I'm stuck in all-consuming darkness that reminds me of my first cell in Karum, and how I woke up there disoriented, all alone. The guard ties the cloth too tight around my neck. I can still breathe, but it takes some effort. As long as I can breathe, I won't die.

"Let's go," the patrolman says, and kicks the back of my ankle to make me move. A sharp pain shoots up my leg, but I walk.

I wish I could see where we're going. I don't even know what building we're in—we could be anywhere.

All I know inside the hood's darkness is the cold feel of the ground beneath my feet. I still can't hear much of anything out of my left ear, which makes me even more disoriented.

After a long time, or maybe not long at all, I hear the *whoosh* of a door sliding open in front of me. Familiar sounds arise in my ears: hammers pounding and drills buzzing, and ship engines roaring to life.

A strong smell of sweat and engine oil wafts through my nostrils as the patrolman moves me along, through the doorway. We're in a flight hangar, and that means Sam is putting me on a ship. Either he's sending me to the Surface to die from acid exposure, or I'm on my way to the Core. To Charlie.

The roar of the transport's engine grows louder as we near it. I trip on my way up the boarding ramp, but the patrolman pulls me right back up, rougher than I'd like. I picture myself ramming a boot into his face, like he keeps ramming his into my leg. It would give me great satisfaction.

At least the air inside the ship is warmer, and the seat I'm forced to sit in has a cushion. The patrolman buckles me in. The sound of his boots clunking tells me when he walks away. He didn't remove my hood. I was counting on that happening soon; I don't know if I can deal with claustrophobia the whole flight.

It's going to be okay. I. Will. Not. Faint.

There's a sound like suction behind me. The ship door closing. The engine roar grows even louder, and I press back against my seat as we lift off the ground.

I need to know where Logan is. Did they put him on a ship already, and take him away?

I hope they took him wherever I'm going. It must be the Core. At least I'll be familiar with the place. Hopefully I won't be executed right away. As long as I'm alive, there's still a possibility, however small, that I can escape.

As long as I'm near Charlie, there's still a chance I can kill him.

# 21

When we reach the Core, I'm led into an elevator. My legs are half asleep from the hour-long ship ride, but my guard forces me to walk. He loosens his grip on my arm as we speed down the vertical shaft and then switch to a horizontal one. I don't know where he's taking me.

*Ding.*

"Restricted Division," a cool female voice says as the elevator doors slide open. He could be taking me to a cell. Or he could be taking me straight to Charlie. I have a bad feeling it's the latter.

As my guard leads me forward, I remember: Beechy is here. I don't know where Charlie's keeping him, or if I'll even get to see him, but knowing he's already gone through something similar to what I'm about to go through makes me less nervous. It reminds me there are still people who believe I am strong, and need me to be strong for them.

If any opportunity arises for me to put an end to Charlie, I have to be ready to do it. I can't hesitate as I did with Joe.

Charlie has never been my friend; I owe him nothing. The only thing he deserves is a bullet through his chest.

My guard makes me stop walking again. There's a soft tapping, like he's tapping buttons, followed by a snap.

"Who is it?" a muffled voice says. It sounds like it's coming through a speaker.

"Lieutenant Dean," my guard says. "I'm accompanying the prisoner, Clementine."

There's a click and the whoosh of a door sliding open. We walk forward again, into a corridor with a dull hum in the air. There are ridges in the floor, and the air feels cooler.

The last time I was here, Charlie spilled the truth about his plan to destroy half the world, and gave me a shot to make me sick, and threw me in Karum. I don't know what he'll do this time to make things worse, but I'm sure he'll find a way. I only hope he won't involve Logan.

But why else would he have had Sam keep him alive?

I count thirty steps and two corners we have to turn until we stop again. Another door slides open.

Lieutenant Dean lets go of my arm and gives my lower back a light push forward. I take careful steps down a short ramp to a flatter floor, but I'm afraid to go farther. He's not guiding me anymore, and I can't see a thing. I'm not sure I want to see.

"Welcome," a hoarse voice says. I know it too well.

Two hands brush my back from behind—Dean's, I hope—and loosen the sack around my head, and pull it off. I squint at the harsh light.

"Take off her shackles," the hoarse voice says again. "She won't need them."

That makes me open my eyes. Commander Charlie's standing

on the other side of the room, but I don't look at him yet. First I take in my surroundings as Dean unlocks my shackles and slips them off my wrists. The source of light comes from blue lamps in the floor, which give the whole place an eerie glow. There are several desks with blank monitor screens built into the walls on either side of me, along with a wall panel covered with buttons of various shapes and sizes. Ahead of me, a short set of steps lead to a wide, rectangular table with holograms of ships and our planet spinning above its surface, like the table I saw in the Crust security hub's control room.

Charlie stands on the other side of the table, and beyond him is another screen covering the wall and part of the ceiling. The screen is speckled with a night sky full of endless stars, like this is a spaceship and I'm looking out a window. But there are no real windows in the Core; this screen is either transmitting an image of the sky captured from somewhere else, or it's a fake moving image.

A memory comes to mind of what a scientist said once in the Core, during Charlie's big announcement, and I realize what this place must be: the control room that turns the Core into a battleship once the outer sectors have been blasted away.

"Do you like my ship?" Charlie asks, gesturing to the room. He moves around the table, stepping into full view. He's wearing his standard navy uniform and white gloves, and his face has as many wrinkles as I remember. His hair seems a darker shade of gray in the light.

With my wrists free, I flex them and rub the tender skin. "It's not a ship yet."

"Ah, *yet* is the key word."

"It won't ever be."

Charlie walks down the steps with a subtle limp in his left leg, where Beechy shot him with a laser before we hijacked his ship. He's trying to hide it, but it's still noticeable. The damage must've been deep enough that his surgeons couldn't fix it completely.

Good. He deserves to have a scar, too.

"I missed your delightful retorts, Clementine," Charlie says when he reaches the bottom of the steps. "It's good to see you again."

I don't reply. I can't tell if this cool exterior of his is a ploy or not. I expected him to be furious with me after how badly I ruined his plans.

He keeps walking forward, closer and closer. I step back, but Lieutenant Dean takes hold of my shoulders to keep me where I am.

Charlie steps to the left of me, heading toward one of the desks. "Would you like something to drink?" he asks. He reaches the desk and taps a button on the wall beside it. A large piece of the wall slides away, revealing a hole with three pitchers and a stack of empty cups inside. "We have yazo juice, arebara, and water. Have you tried arebara? It's my personal favorite, though some people find it a bit strong."

Maybe this is a trick and all the pitchers are poisoned, but I'm so thirsty, I don't even care.

"Water. Please."

Charlie pulls out the middle pitcher and lifts the cup from the top of the stack. He pours the water, taking his time, and sets the pitcher down back in the hole. He taps the button again, and the wall closes back up. Turning back to me, he smiles as he walks over and hands it to me.

The last time I had water, I downed it all at once, but this time I know I might not get more, so I take one sip at a time and savor the coolness on my tongue.

No one speaks until I'm finished. I wipe my mouth with the back of my hand. As I move to return the cup to Charlie, I pause. It's a plastic cup, and the rim is a bit sharp—almost sharp enough to be useful as a weapon.

Charlie's lip twitches in amusement. He wraps his fingers around the cup. "I give you water after your guards have kept you thirsty for two days, and now you want to kill me?" He makes a *tsk*ing noise.

I loosen my grip with only a tinge of annoyance, and let him take the cup away. It would've made a shoddy weapon anyway.

Moving to the opposite wall, Charlie dumps the cup into a trash chute. "Now, come over here. I'd like to show you something."

He heads back up the steps to the table with the holograms. I don't want Dean to force me to move again, so I follow Charlie without argument. Though I'm not stupid. I know Charlie didn't bring me here for small talk and a glass of water.

At the top of the steps, he moves around to the other side of the table, but I stay on this side, staring at the slow-spinning blue hologram of a planet that must be Kiel. Up close, it's bigger than I realized, nearly half my size. It shows the Surface in detail: miniature mountains and forests; a vast expanse of ocean; the buildings that form the city and work camp. And those are only the places I've seen in real life—there's a whole back side of our world that I've never seen before, with plains and rivers and jungles. There's a whole other half to the ocean.

"Beautiful, isn't it?" Charlie says. "Our world is rich and full of life. It's easy to understand why our ancestors chose to leave their old home and settle here to build a civilization."

My mind plays back the conversation I had with Fred in Karum, when he first told me about our ancestors' original home, Marden.

"We came here because of a war," I say. "We didn't get along with the people in our old home."

"Don't call them 'people.' The Mardenites are savages, not humans. We should never have let them run us out of our old home. We should've slaughtered them all and ended this whole mess before it began."

"The acid shield is destroyed, so the mess with them is over. You're the one who wants to prolong it."

"You're wrong," Charlie says calmly. "I want to end it, so we can put it all behind us and start over."

"Then end it! Marden's savages don't care about us anymore. Stop caring about them."

Charlie's cheeks pinch, letting me glimpse the annoyance behind his calm exterior. He turns his back and moves to the desk below the massive screen of stars. He fiddles with something, and the stars speed by as if this room is really a ship and he's speeding us across the sky, or scrolling back in time.

My eyes drop to the table in front of me, to something I noticed without really seeing it. There are three thin, pointy pieces of metal, similar to nails but without a flat end, lying below the spinning hologram of Kiel. They blend into the screen, but I'm sure they're real. I shift my body an inch to the right so I'm blocking them from the view of Dean, who's still waiting back by the ramp. Charlie freezes the star screen on an image, and pulls a laser pointer out of his pocket. He directs the laser at a small cluster of objects in the sky, which look like several stars clumped together.

"Keep your eyes on those," he says and rolls the image again, this time much slower.

I set my palm on the table as I step around it to see the screen better. My fingers close over one of the pieces of metal. It fits perfectly inside my palm.

My eyes remain on the clump of stars on the screen. These stars look like they're moving faster than the rest. Almost like a clump of satellites, but if we have any in the sky right now, there aren't that many. And they wouldn't be moving together.

"What are those?" I ask, moving my hand off the table. I clutch the nail with my fist.

Charlie switches the laser pointer off. "Those are ships from Marden. A whole fleet of them, headed toward our planet."

"Excuse me?"

"Marden is sending an army to wipe us out."

I wait for him to laugh, to give away that this is a joke. An army can't be coming.

But those dots moving fast on the screen do look an awful lot like a fleet of ships. And there's a flicker of real fear behind Charlie's stony eyes; he believes the fleet is a true threat.

"You can't be serious," I say.

"I assure you I am." He steps back to the table and sets his hand on the lit surface. It's a touch screen. He flips quickly through some images and pulls up a new hologram, this time of a small fleet— the one among the stars. "My astronomers spotted the fleet five days ago."

Five days ago. That was the day before he began transferring people off the Surface, and the day before the Crust coal mines shut down.

"We've been tracking its position," he says, "and we've created a model of what we believe their ships look like, based on sketches we recovered from old records."

"Why would they be sending an army, after all this time?"

Charlie's nostrils flare slightly. "Well, you did destroy the weapon the Mardenites placed on our moon. It could've been sending a signal to them, one they lost as soon as the generator was destroyed. That would've made them realize we're still very much alive, and possibly still a threat."

No, that makes no sense. "We destroyed their weapon eleven days ago. Fred told me it would take a few *months* to reach Marden by ship. Unless their technology is far, far superior to ours, they couldn't get here in eleven days. Which means they were already on their way."

Charlie draws his gaze away from mine. But something tells me he already knew.

The pointy ends of the nail in my fist dig into my skin. *Not yet.* "If you want me to trust you, don't lie to me. Tell me everything you know."

Charlie rubs the spot above his nose with two fingers and gives me a wry smile. "Sorry, there is something I failed to mention. The last time we sent an army to Marden, we captured a few of the savages and brought them back with us. One in particular is a rather important figure to the Mardenites. A savior, they call him. He is the god and leader of their people. He's the reason they put that generator on the moon, and the reason they're bringing a whole fleet."

I pause to process this new information. An alien god? "What, so they know we killed him?"

"It's possible they think we did, yes, and that's why they're coming to wipe us out," Charlie says stiffly. "It's also possible they know he's still alive, and they're coming to rescue him. Your guess is as good as mine. All I have to rely on for information about the Mardenites comes from the military records we have from the time of the last war, and what information we've extracted from the savage in our custody."

Either way, it doesn't make sense to me. All of this—us flying to Marden, capturing their god and bringing him here—happened hundreds of years ago. Why would they retaliate now? They already put a generator on the moon and tried to wipe us out. Did it take them three hundred years to realize they failed?

In fact—"They put the generator on the moon to wipe us out," I say. "The acid could've killed their god too. I doubt they wanted that."

"The savages are immune to the acid, so he wouldn't have died," Charlie says.

"How do you know?"

"I am privy to more information about Marden's inhabitants than you would care to know, since the war records have been passed down to all the Developers. But we performed a test recently to confirm it."

"On the Mardenite prisoner, you mean?"

"Indeed."

Memories of the tests Charlie had the Karum doctors perform on me flash through my head, and I feel sick to my stomach. "How is he still alive, if we captured him three centuries ago?"

"The Mardenites have life spans far superior to our own."

If they're really coming for us in warships, I need to know more about them. I'd like to meet the one we captured and talk to him myself. "Where are you keeping him?"

Charlie swipes his hand across the table screen, and the hologram of the fleet disappears. "That's classified information. If you agree to aid me in the war against the fleet, I may choose to disclose his location. But you haven't yet."

He looks at me expectantly.

It almost doesn't even matter if he's wrong about this and the Mardenite army isn't coming to wage war against us. He believes it is, and he is in control of everything.

"You want my help," I repeat, in case I misunderstood.

"You must've guessed that's why I brought you here and explained the situation, instead of having my men dispose of you."

I study his face and the wrinkles around his mouth. This is a trick, I know it. This is the man who had every intention of his bomb detonating and ripping me to shreds.

"You don't need my help. Why didn't you have them kill me?"

Charlie frowns. "It has never been my intention to kill you, Clementine. I thought I made that clear before. I'm the person who picked you for Extraction, who plucked you out of your decrepit existence and gave you a new one. I chose you for one simple but important reason: because you possess one of the highest intellectual capacities of any individual I've ever known. Ever since you were a small child, your brain scans and Promise tests have shown us what all the doctors agree are simply remarkable genes. Not only are you quick-witted and capable of understanding even the highest concepts in terms of mathematics and science, but you are also quick on your feet. And your reaction to the submission serum? Truly extraordinary. I've never come across another individual so capable of fighting it in its many forms."

I don't believe him. There are plenty of others as smart as me, or smarter.

"I have an allergy, that's all."

Charlie lets out a light chuckle. "Dear, you should take my compliments when I give them to you. I don't hand them out often."

"It's hard for me to see the merit in them when I recall how you nearly left me to die the day the bomb went off. You weren't so quick to save me for my 'remarkable genes' then."

"Do you not recall that I had sent Beechy to rescue you from Karum in order to return you to the Core? I meant for you to survive. It was your misdoings that made you end up on that flight deck. And I admit although I was not in the most forgiving state of mind that day, I assure you I would've regretted your death."

"How comforting. But what, so you've decided to forgive me now?"

"I believe now, as I did then, that you are more useful to me alive, at least for the time being. No, I don't need your help to vanquish Marden's army. But I want it. I want you to put your intelligence to good use and help my army leaders determine the best course of action. I want you and Beechy, who agreed to help earlier today, to influence your friends to turn their fight against the bigger enemy." The light from a lamp beneath Charlie's feet casts eerie shadows under his eyes. "Marden's fleet is coming. The savages created the acid that's threatened to batter our planet for decades—can you even imagine the weapons they must have at their disposal by now? They will make our race extinct if we're unable to hold them off. I assure you, killing me won't stop them."

Beechy agreed to help him? He must be subdued. There's no other explanation.

Charlie might be saying all these pretty things about how he wants to keep me alive, but they don't apply to anyone else, and they won't apply to me forever. He is responsible for Oliver's death, as well as the deaths of thousands and thousands of people in the work camps, all the years he's been the ruling Developer of Kiel.

When Marden's army comes, surely Charlie will have no

difficulty sacrificing more people for his cause. He meant to do it before, and he will try again until he succeeds.

"Tell me your plan of attack first." I cross my arms. "I know about the injections you gave all the people in the Crust camp. I was there. You're going to use them for something, aren't you?"

"You don't miss a thing, do you? Yes, the child workers have a role to play, as do we all."

He doesn't have to explain the specifics. I know whatever their role is, he doesn't expect them to survive to the end of the war.

Squeezing the nail tighter in my palm, I set my jaw. "I understand Marden's army is coming, and I will do my best to fight it. But I'm not going to stop fighting you, and neither will any of the other rebels. You're no war commander—all you are is someone who murders people for his own means, and feels no regret." I take a small step forward. "You're a selfish man who's afraid of dying. But you will die, and when you're turning to dust, believe me, the people will cheer. You'll only be remembered as a tyrant."

Charlie brings his hand up to rub his temple. "I can't say I didn't see this decision coming."

Out of the corner of my eye, I notice Dean walking over from the door. He's almost to the steps, and he's carrying the shackles.

I don't wait another second—I move toward Charlie and bring my hand up, holding the nail like it's a knife. I aim at his neck, but he moves both hands to stop me, so I direct my weapon at his arm instead. The sharp point meets his forearm skin through his uniform and draws blood. Charlie barely reacts, which makes me pause.

Before I can make another move, Dean grabs me from behind. I struggle, trying to hurt him with the nail too, but he's too strong. He rips the nail out of my hand and tosses it on the table beside us, then forces my arms behind my back. I feel a shackle close around one of my wrists, then the other. There's saliva on my chin, but I can't wipe it off. All I can do is glare at Charlie.

He remains calm and composed as he removes a small patch from his pocket and tears it open. There's an antiseptic patch inside, which he uses to wipe the blood off his arm.

"I admire your boldness," he says. "But next time I'd suggest using a bigger weapon. Now, since you denied my initial request for help, let's move on to Plan B. You said you'd like to know what was the purpose of the injection administered in the Crust camp? I'd like to show you. Lieutenant Dean, bring her along."

"Gladly, sir," Dean says.

Charlie moves around the table and down the steps, heading for the exit from the Core ship bridge. Dean kicks the back of my ankle to make me follow.

# 22

We take an elevator up to the health ward. I struggle against Dean the whole way, even when he grips my arms so hard, my skin burns. Charlie said he's going to show me what the injections were for. He's going to give me one, I'm sure. He's going to have people hold me still so I can't run, and this time there won't be any explosion to make them stop.

*Ding.*

The elevator door opens. Charlie leads the way out into a corridor. There's no receptionist's desk ahead, and no one in sight except two officials talking outside one of the doors. This must be a back entrance to the ward.

The guards straighten and salute Charlie as we approach. I recognize one of them: Colonel Parker, with his mustache thin and black. He's the official who oversaw my physical training during Promise Elevation. He barely glances in my direction.

"Commander, sir, everything's ready for you inside," he says.

"I also have an update on the status of OS, whenever you're ready for it."

"I can hear it now," Charlie says.

I fidget with my hands, trying to slip free of my shackles, but it's no use.

"I've just received word that the final inspections in Crust and Lower have been completed, and the ones in Mantle are near completion," Parker says. "Also, the fugitive, Skylar, has arrived and is being transferred to cell block A."

I let out a noise before I can stop myself. They're putting her in a prison cell. They caught her. *How?*

"Very good," Charlie says, ignoring me. "We'll speak more later. You two are dismissed."

"Yes, sir."

With another salute, Colonel Parker and other guard head down the corridor.

Charlie steps up to the door and presses his thumb into the lock-pad on the wall beside it. There's a click, and the door slides open. He enters the room ahead of me.

I want to ask him about Skylar, but I shouldn't. I can't tell him anything he doesn't already know, or I could jeopardize everyone else in the Alliance. He has four of us now. I have a feeling it won't be long until he's discovered the rest.

Through the doorway, the room is small and plain. There are cabinets and a sink against one wall, and a door ahead leading to the room beside us, which is separated from us by a wall made of glass. A monitor screen sits at the top of the glass, in the center of the wall.

The room beside us is much bigger. It has blinding white walls, an operating table, and blue lights and a monitor screen hanging from mechanical arms on the ceiling. Two nurses and one surgeon move around the operating table, the surgeon and one of the nurses completely blocking their patient from view.

"What is this?" I ask.

"You wanted to know what's inside the injection. I'm going to show you."

I glue my eyes to the operating table, waiting for the surgeon to move aside so I can see whom she's operating on.

*Thump thump* goes my heart.

"Watch the monitor," Charlie says.

The screen above us switches on, showing the hazy image of a person's face. The image slowly sharpens. My spleen feels like it rips in half.

Logan is wide awake, and there's a sheen of sweat on his forehead. A black strap keeps his head against the table, and his arms and legs are also strapped down, but he's still struggling. His lips are stretched apart, held open by metal clamps. The gloved hand of the surgeon holds a thin white tube above his mouth. As I watch, the hand guides the tube down his throat.

"They're hurting him!" I cry, wrenching against Dean's grip. I want to fly through the glass; I need to make the surgeons stop. But Dean pulls me right back against him, an arm around my chest to hold me still.

"The procedure causes only mild discomfort," Charlie says. "As long as he keeps still."

The screen switches to an image of what can only be the inside of Logan's throat—pink, fleshy, wet. There must be a camera at the end of the tube.

I look through the window at his full figure. The surgeon isn't blocking his face anymore. The skin of Logan's face has turned deathly pale, and his chest rises from the table like he's convulsing. He must be choking.

This can't go on. It has to stop. "Make them stop—please. I don't need to see this—you can just tell me what was inside the injection. You can let him go."

"No, I think it's good for you to see."

I want to find the sharpest piece of wire and tie it around Charlie's neck, and pull and pull and pull until he suffocates.

Logan has stopped convulsing, but the rapid rise and fall of his chest tells me he's breathing much too fast. His heart rate must be far above normal. If the surgeon doesn't stop this soon, if his body keeps panicking, he could have a heart attack.

Charlie steps closer to me. I flinch away from him, but he grabs my chin firmly and lifts it so I'm forced to look back at the screen.

"Tell me what you see," he says.

The screen shows the same fleshy pink material as before, forming a tube that must be Logan's esophagus. The image zooms in further and further until I make out a minuscule gray object embedded in the tissue. It looks like a microchip small enough to fit inside an injection needle. It looks like something that doesn't belong.

"Is it a tracker?" I ask.

Charlie releases my chin. His fingers were squeezing so tightly, I'm sure they left a mark. He smiles at me, a wide, vicious smile that makes me want to strangle him again.

"It's an advanced weapon developed by a team of my best scientists and weapons technicians, including a friend of yours, Colonel Fred. It's similar to a microchip. We call it a Stryker. Once injected through the trachea, the Stryker embeds itself into the gastrointestinal tract. It has no effect on the normal functions of the body. But each Stryker is programmed to respond to a remote signal, which triggers a chemical reaction inside the material, followed by an explosion that will impact the surrounding area within a two-mile radius."

There's a bomb inside Logan. There are bombs inside everyone who received this injection in the work camps—thousands and thousands of people.

"You're going to kill all of them." It's not even a question.

"It's unfortunate, but yes. It's a calculated move. The Strykers are the primary weapon for the first stage of our attack against Marden's fleet. According to our calculations, the fleet should arrive within three days' time. Tomorrow, we're transporting all the child workers back to the Surface. We're telling them a neutralizing agent has been released up there, to decontaminate the air. We've decided to shut down the work camps indefinitely, but in reality they'll be living in the city only until the fleet arrives."

"And then what?" I ask. "You wait for the fleet to land, and once they're all within a two-mile radius of the city, you can blast them all to bits before they kill everyone?"

"Essentially, yes."

"What if the ships blow up the buildings from the sky first?"

"It's not necessary for the child workers to be alive for us to activate the bombs." Charlie's eyes shine, not in a kind way.

The anger coursing through my veins makes me feel like my whole body is a bomb and I'm on the verge of exploding. "You could be placing normal explosives in the city to accomplish the same thing. You don't have to kill all those people."

"They are hardly useful to me anymore, now that the Core is self-sufficient. And you forget that Marden's savages don't know about our underground cities," Charlie says just as calmly as he's revealed everything else. "We're hoping they will assume the slaughter of the child workers has been a slaughter of our entire civilization, and they will go back home without delving deeper. The deaths of the children could save us from a brutal, endless war. Don't you see the good in that?"

I turn my head away, back to the window into the operating room. Logan is still on the table with the tube in his mouth; his chest is still rising and falling rapidly. He's helpless and probably terrified.

"I've seen what you wanted," I say. "Tell the surgeon to take the tube out."

"Not yet," Charlie says. "He's going to stay like that a little longer."

"He's scared. His heart's beating too fast. He's going to *die*."

"Maybe, maybe not. My guess is he'll survive. But if he does, I'm putting him on the transport to the Surface in two days' time, and I'm betting he won't survive that expedition."

"Please don't. Send me instead if you want, but please, please let him go."

"It's sweet of you to offer for his sake, but no." Charlie walks over to the exit door. There's a comm box on the wall, and he presses the Speak button. "Send Nurse Irene in with the B-strain."

"She's on her way," a voice says through the speaker.

"Wonderful." Charlie lets go of the button. When he turns around, I notice there's a bloodstain on his uniform sleeve where I cut him with the nail earlier. I want to relish in the fact the stain might not even wash out, but I can't.

All I can think about is the bomb inside Logan ripping him apart. In my head, he dies like Oliver, in a burst of fire. But Logan wouldn't even get to float among the stars. His remains would mingle with the remains of all the other child workers.

I don't want any of them to die. But I don't have a way to save all of them—right now the only person I can save is Logan. And I will do anything.

"What do I have to do?" I ask Charlie in as calm a voice as I can manage.

"You will pledge your allegiance to me. You will agree to assist me in developing our attack plans against the fleet, and you will carry out my orders without any questions."

The thought of working for him, of helping him make plans and pretending I respect his decisions, is more than I can bear. But I am out of options. My only hope is that he's right about my "remarkable genes," and I will come up with better attack maneuvers Charlie will approve that won't involve killing thousands of innocents.

"I swear," I say without hesitation.

"A nurse is bringing an injection over. You will take it without a struggle."

My skin prickles all over. There's the catch. "You're going to put a Stryker in me."

"Actually," Charlie says, "I'm referring to a submission serum my scientists have been developing—a special formula created just for you, with a new base ingredient. You won't be allergic to this one. You can thank Beechy for helping us get the formula right. He was an excellent test subject."

It feels like there's a block of ice stuck in my throat. He wants to subdue me; he wants to invade my mind. It's never worked before—before, his serum gave me a headache and fever so strong, I was afraid I was going to die.

Turning me into one of the mindless will be even worse. I've seen it; I remember Oliver with his muddled, foggy eyes, how he attacked me and Beechy when we found him guarding Charlie's bomb. When my other friend I made in the Core, Ariadne, was under its influence, she let Sam kiss her and do things she never would've agreed to do if she were in her right mind.

If Charlie's right and he's perfected this new formula, I might change my mind and decide his plan to kill all the child workers for the sake of the rest of us is pure perfection. Even if some part of me still knows it's wrong, I will go along with it anyway. I will follow his orders without question. I will lose my free will.

"My terms are nonnegotiable," Charlie says. "Either you agree to both of them, or I'll make sure Logan is in the first batch of child workers delivered to the Surface. And I will make sure he doesn't come back."

On the operating table, Logan is struggling again. The water trickling from his eyes is visible from here, and he looks like he's trying to spit out the tube, but it's too far down his throat.

"You'll take out Logan's Stryker if I agree?" I ask.

"Yes, once you've taken the serum. You have my word."

I don't want to let him give me any injection. But if I don't, it's not like he'll let me go free—he'll lock me in a cell, and I won't be able to do anything while he puts Logan and all the others on the Surface to die. At least if I agree to help him and let him subdue me, there's still a chance I can fight the injection afterwards. There's still a chance I can regain my will and find a way to stop him.

Really, what choice do I have?

The door opens, and the nurse enters. She's carrying a plastic tray with a small stack of gauze, an antiseptic patch, and two syringes, each in an individual plastic wrapper.

"Here's the B-strain serum, Commander Charlie, sir," the nurse says.

One prick and all this will be over. I might not even remember it happened.

"Perfect," Charlie says. "Prep to administer the injection. Let's do this quickly, please."

The nurse sets the tray on the counter beside the sink. She's already wearing gloves, so she picks up the antiseptic patch and steps over to me. Dean pulls my left sleeve up over my shoulder. The nurse dabs my skin with the wet patch, humming as she works.

I can't watch her do this. I stare at Logan and picture how his body will finally relax once the surgeon takes the tube out of his throat. I don't think he'll be happy when he finds out what I did, though. He won't forgive me for taking this serum willingly, even though I'm doing it to save his life.

There's a ripping sound as the nurse tears the plastic off a syringe. When she turns around, the needle glints in the light.

I blink and the glint of light turns blue, like the lights in Karum.

"Wait," I say.

The nurse pauses with the needle an inch from my shoulder.

I can't let another doctor or nurse give me a shot. Not ever again.

Charlie's eyes are narrowed.

"Can I do it myself?" I ask. "It'll be easier."

"You won't use it as a weapon?"

"No, I'll take the shot—I have to save Logan. Please, just let me do it myself."

Charlie's lips thin slightly, full of distrust, but then he nods. "Uncuff her," he says to Dean.

Dean releases my arms, unlocks my shackles, and slips them

off. I rub my sore wrists before turning to face the nurse. She holds out the syringe to me.

I slip my fingers around it and take it from her. The glass casing feels cool in my grip, lighter than I expected. The liquid inside the barrel is silver.

I position the syringe above my left shoulder. All I have to do is push the needle in, press the plunger, and the surgeon will take Logan's tube out. Charlie will let him live.

Gritting my teeth, I focus on the syringe again, making sure my thumb is ready on the plunger. I have to do this fast, before I change my mind. I'll find some way to fight the submission—I know it.

Before I can change my mind, I push the needle through my skin. It spreads an ache through my shoulder and neck, but it hardly bothers me; I've felt much worse. I press the plunger all the way down. The silver liquid slowly empties from the syringe. Charlie watches with a small smile.

When the syringe is empty, I pull it out and drop it. It makes a small clink when it hits the floor.

# 23

V ery good," Charlie says.

"Tell the surgeon to stop," I say.

Turning away, he walks over to the door leading to the operating room and opens it. When the door shuts behind him, I can't hear the command he gives the surgeon. But a nurse says something that looks like, "Yes, sir," and the surgeon begins removing the tube.

My throat sticks when I swallow. I don't know how long it will take for the serum to start working.

I look down at my hands, and my legs and feet below them. There's no slow spread of fire through my body, like I would feel if my allergy were kicking in and making me dizzy with fever. But there is something else: a dull pounding in my temple; a hammering inside my eardrums. Charlie beckons to me from the other side of the glass. He wants me to join him.

As I push through the door, the world tilts a little, and the edges of my vision blur. *Is this what it feels like?*

But I blink a few times, and the world rights itself. So I keep walking. Lieutenant Dean follows me, even though he doesn't need to. I'm not going to run anymore.

In the operating room, Logan's coughing loudly as the last of the tube lifts out of his mouth. Phlegm and bile drip from the end of the tube, which the surgeon hands to a nurse to take away.

Logan notices me as I walk forward, and tries to turn his head against his restraint.

"Clem," he chokes, "what are you doing here?"

The glass wall is shaded on this side, too dark to see through, so he couldn't have seen me standing there. He didn't have any idea I was here.

I want to tell Logan I took Charlie's injection, and I'm sorry, and I don't know what's going to happen to me, but I did it to save him. But I don't think Charlie would want me to tell him that, and I have to do what Charlie wants. I have to keep Logan safe.

"I'm sorry they hurt you, Logan," I say. "But everything's going to be okay now." My tongue feels thick and heavy in my mouth, like cotton. Almost like it doesn't belong there.

The hammering picks up inside my head.

"She and I just made an arrangement," Charlie says. "She'll follow my orders in exchange for saving your life. Won't you, Clementine?"

"Of course." My mouth curves upward in a smile. But I didn't tell my mouth to smile.

It's starting: I am losing control of my body.

"You are loyal to me, aren't you, Clementine?"

"I will always be loyal to the Developers," I say automatically. The smile remains on my face like it's been stuck there. I can't make it budge no matter how hard I try.

Alarm sweeps through Logan's eyes. "What did you do to her?"

"She did this to herself," Charlie says, not hiding his delight. "A nurse handed her the syringe, but she stuck the needle in and pressed the plunger."

I shouldn't have done this. I shouldn't have given Charlie my mind.

"Change her back. Give her an antidote."

"I'm afraid I can't. The serum isn't poison."

"I'll kill you," Logan spits, struggling against his restraints. "The second I get my hands free."

"I have a feeling Clementine might stop you." Commander Charlie glances at me, that same expectancy in his eyes.

"You can't kill him," my mouth says without my permission. "He's going to save you. You should thank him."

"The surgeon's going to remove the bomb from your esophagus lining," Commander Charlie says. "I'm afraid I can't let you roam the Core free, but you'll be given a nice cell. Clementine can visit you as long as you cooperate."

"She's not Clementine," Logan says through gritted teeth.

"She's more obedient, is all," Commander Charlie says. "Clementine, why don't you help the nurses put him under for his operation?"

My feet move automatically, walking around to the other side of the table. I can't make them stop.

I can't move my legs. I can't move my hands. I can't move my arms.

The panic inside me makes me feel like I'm suffocating. But I have to stay calm. I knew this would happen; I knew what I was getting into.

I did this to save Logan.

One of the nurses directs me to the sink at the back of the room to wash my hands. I turn the water on, wet my hands, and scrub them with soap. Layers of grime and dust from the Crust camp swirl in a dark funnel down the drain.

When I'm finished, I dry my hands with a paper towel and pull on a pair of gloves. I walk back to the operating table. "What next?" my lips ask, though I didn't tell them to say anything at all.

The nurse points me to a clear mask on the tray of medical tools. The mask is connected by a thick white tube to a machine in the wall. A similar mask was used to put me under, when I had my operation here in the Core, so I remember what the nurses did. I pick up the mask and step over to Logan, while one of the nurses goes over to the wall to turn on the sleeping gas once the mask is on properly.

My hands feel unsteady, but I don't think it's visible. The part of my brain that has control over me isn't frightened of what's happening; it is obedient.

The other nurse moves to Logan's other side and sets a hand on his forehead to keep him still. His eyes water as I lift the mask over his mouth and nose.

*Please, don't cry,* I want to tell him. But my lips are dead and useless, no longer my own.

"Why are you helping him?" he whispers before I press the edges of the mask against his skin. He doesn't sound mad anymore; he sounds lost and defeated.

*He was going to kill you otherwise. I didn't have a choice.*

"Don't worry," is all my lips say. "Everything's going to be okay now."

A tear slides down his cheek. "You're wrong," he says through the mask.

All of this is wrong. I should've been smarter and found a way to overpower Charlie before he could put me in this situation, before he could threaten to kill Logan.

When I'm sure the mask is secure, I tell the nurse by the wall, and she presses the button to start the gas.

Slowly, Logan's eyelids droop until they close. The tear on his cheek slides down the side of his face and settles on his ear.

The nurse switches off the gas. "You can remove the mask," she says sweetly.

I do as she says, taking the mask away and setting it back on the tray. Logan's lips remain slightly parted, stretched from the tool that was holding them open earlier. His arms hang limp at his sides, and his chest rises and falls at a more normal pace.

At least he's not panicking anymore, and he's not in pain. Soon the bomb will be removed from his chest.

"Let's leave them to their work, Clementine," Charlie says as I move away to let the nurses and surgeon take over.

"You're welcome, sir," I say automatically.

I don't want to leave. I want to make sure the nurses do as Charlie promised.

But my body turns without hesitation, and I turn and follow him back through the door. Dean trails behind us. The nurse is still waiting in the smaller room. Commander Charlie walks to the tray with the stack of gauze and the extra syringe still on it.

"This particular form of the serum currently wears off in a much shorter amount of time than the previous formula," he says, and glances at his time-band. "It's eleven o'clock now. You'll need to readminister the serum in twenty-four hours, and again twenty-four hours after that, and so on. I'll have a nurse bring you more tomorrow."

He holds the tray out to me. I pick up the syringe and tuck it inside my hand, and my lips form another smile for him. "I'll make sure to give myself a shot in twenty-four hours."

"Of course you will," Commander Charlie says, his eyes twinkling. "I have full faith in you. You're going to be a great help in our strategy planning. I have some ideas I'd like to run by you later this evening."

"I look forward to hearing them."

Charlie sets his hand on my shoulder and pats it twice.

I flinch away from his touch; I shove him inside my head. But my body doesn't react in the slightest. My smile remains wide as ever.

"Why don't you run along and let Lieutenant Dean show you to the room I've prepared for you, so you can wash up," he says. "The cafeteria is open for lunch. I'm sure you're hungry."

I am starving, and my mouth is dry even after that cup of water. But I don't want to go to the cafeteria because Charlie told me to. I don't want to do *anything* he says, but my lips are already moving.

"I am hungry," I say.

"We'll have plans to discuss soon, but I'll have someone send for you."

"Okay," I say. "Thank you for everything."

"It's my absolute pleasure."

Lieutenant Dean sets a hand on my lower back. I walk with him out of the room, into the corridor.

I try to unclench my fingers, to drop the syringe. I want it to clatter to the floor and break, and spill Charlie's serum so it can't control anyone. I want to jam the needle into Charlie's neck. Would he listen to me then? If I told him to take his own life, would he do it?

But my hands remain tight around the barrel, like it's glued to my palm. Some other part of my brain, which is subdued and allegiant to Charlie, has control of my motor nerves, and I don't know how to free it.

We reach an elevator, and Lieutenant Dean lets me step inside first. I push my hand toward the buttons on the wall to close the door before he can come inside, but of course my hand doesn't even move; it remains limp at my side.

I'm a prisoner in my own body.

As the door closes, and Dean presses a button and pays me some compliment that makes the other me laugh and blush while disgust curls in my stomach, it hits me how utterly and completely helpless I am.

A boy could tell me to kiss him and this subdued, other me might do it. Charlie could tell me to kill someone and Other Me would squeeze the trigger. I can solve puzzles and make calculations in seconds; I can climb better than almost anyone; I scored high on the Core Official Development Aptitude test.

I will be the perfect soldier, as Charlie always intended.

How am I going to fight this?

# 24

In my assigned bedroom, after Lieutenant Dean leaves, I set the extra syringe on the hovering tray beside my bed.

Twenty-four hours, I remind myself. I have twenty-four hours to regain control of my body and keep myself from administering another shot.

I wonder how many crimes Charlie will make me commit in the next twenty-four hours.

Shoving that thought away, I focus on my surroundings, since Other Me is already taking everything in. There's a small Corpo-Bot screen in the corner. There's only one bed—huge and round, heaped with blankets even softer than the carpet—but the room is almost twice the size of the one I shared with Ariadne. Charlie must've decided I deserve a higher status of living, since I've pledged my allegiance to him now.

The four walls around my bed have a strange silver sheen, and no lamps, as far as I can tell. But there's a light-panel by the door. I press one of the buttons, and the walls transform into what looks like a real sunset. Clouds drift around me, through a haze of pinks, oranges, purples. I feel like I'm standing in the sky.

My hand moves to press the other button before I decide I want to, but the next second I forget I'm angry. Endless stars surround me with their brilliant light, hues of red and gold and bluish green. A million suns floating in distant galaxies.

Other Me revels in the calm the stars give her. But my calm splinters fast. Even under the influence of the submission serum, the stars bring back flashes of that night on the spaceship—the night I lost Oliver. The stars might've been the last thing he saw before he died.

Commander Charlie is the reason he's gone. He's the reason I lost him.

I hate Charlie for giving these stars to me after he's taken almost everything else away, as if he thinks he can make up for some of it. He can't.

Other Me switches off the stars to take a shower and finally scrub the dirt off her body. I switch them off out of defiance and revel in the feeling, for an instant, that I'm in control again. Even if it's a lie.

※

Lunch is almost over when I arrive in the cafeteria. My cheeks are no longer bloodstained, and I'm wearing knee-high black boots. My skintight gray suit clings to my body, showing off the places where I still have a bit of curve and some muscle. The fabric isn't uncomfortable, but if I had the use of my hands, I would rip it apart and go naked before I'd wear this uniform. Core officials wear gray suits; Sam wears this suit. Charlie is making me associate myself with everyone I've ever hated, and I can't do anything to stop it.

I walk straight to the touch screens on the wall, to order my meal. My fingers tap through the menu without my permission, detached from the nonsubdued part of my brain. Thankfully, they pick food that looks appetizing: woreken ribs smothered in spicy sauce, a side of yellow beets in tangy dressing, and a large canteen of water.

Tray in hand, I head to the nearest table. All but one table in the cafeteria is empty, and I don't recognize the people at the table—teens who are talking and laughing while they eat. I'm not ready to run into anyone I know yet. Not when Other Me is smiling about her new uniform, and I can't trust my mouth to say the right things.

I slip onto the bench, set my tray down, and slice off a piece of the ribs with my fork and knife. The first bite is juicy. Spicy sauce trickles down my chin, and I wipe it away with a napkin. I can't deny the food here is better than anywhere else. Even the canned food we ate in the KIMO facility, which was tastier than my daily rations in the Surface camp, tasted like plastic compared to this.

The cafeteria door opens, and I try to turn my head to make sure I don't need to avoid whoever walked in, but Other Me won't budge her eyes. She's scarfing through her ribs, apparently as starving as I feel. I grind my teeth together as she chews.

If I'm going to be trapped like this awhile, at least for the next twenty-four hours, I need to figure out as much as I can about Charlie's defensive strategy against Marden's fleet. Information is all I have, and it's the only good thing about my predicament; now that I'm subdued, he will hopefully trust me enough to tell me everything. The more I learn, the easier it'll be to sabotage his strategy once I figure out how to overcome the serum.

He already told me the first stage of the defensive plan involves the Strykers and relocating the entire population of the lower sector work camps to the Surface. No doubt he'll make me help relocate them, because he is cruel and knows how much I hate that he's sacrificing all those people. Some of them are my friends—Nellie, Evie, Lucy, and Grady, if he's still alive. Even Hector, who turned me in. I don't want to see any of them die.

Nellie, at least, knows everything Charlie's already done, and knows she's in danger. But she doesn't know how much. Even if she tries to hide someplace when officials come to put her on a transport ship, as long as the Stryker is in her body, the bomb will go off with all the others. She will die no matter where she is.

My hand lifts another bite of food to my lips. I half wish I could make myself stop eating—why should I get food like this when Nellie and the others get almost nothing?—but I can't afford not to eat. Maybe half the reason I can't fight the serum and regain control is because I've grown so weak in the past few days, in the work camp and then in my holding cell. Charlie might've told the guards to starve me on purpose for that very reason.

I need to get stronger, so I can make my mind strong too. I don't know what exactly Charlie is going to make me do—he could make me do anything. Before I knew about the submission serum, he told me he wants me to work with Beechy to convince the rest of the Alliance to fight for him, once he captures them, I assume. Surely he already knows where they are, if Beechy's subdued like I am. He must've given everything up, including the location of our headquarters.

Charlie could've lied to me, though. Killing the fugitives would be easier than convincing them to change their allegiance, unless he has enough of this new serum to administer to all of them. All the rebels used to fight his old injection, but this new kind would make them do anything Charlie wants, same as me.

As I stand to dump my empty tray in the trash chute and exit the cafeteria, I hope the others in the Alliance were smarter than I; that they were prepared for something like this. Mal knew Beechy was captured, so he could've informed the others in Crust and figured out new covers for them, ones Beechy wouldn't know about. Maybe Mal even somehow got word to the KIMO facility and told Sandy and the others to relocate, so when Beechy gave up their location they wouldn't be found.

This is assuming Mal is still on our side, completely undercover. Maybe he's been fighting against us all along, and he's the one who gave Logan and Skylar up.

But I hope I'm wrong. I hope we won't be able to find the other rebels, so Charlie can't subdue them and he can't make me kill them.

✕

I don't know where I'm headed after I leave the cafeteria until I end up in Training Division, in the room with the track and the obstacle course, where I passed CODA. Other Me wants to work on her physical conditioning. At least this will feel somewhat natural, since I ran and lifted weights almost every day in the KIMO facility. But I don't want to think about what exactly Other Me is planning on doing with her strength.

A young man in official garb—a gray suit identical to mine—holds the door open for me as I enter. His eyes drink in my figure, and a smile twitches at the edge of his mouth. I curse my stupid lips for smiling back.

Is this what it feels like for everyone after they receive their monthly injections? Oliver and Ariadne used to smile incessantly too, and agree to things they wouldn't normally agree to. After

Oliver snapped out of his submission, he seemed to remember the things he'd done while under the influence—agreeing to help Charlie; trying to shoot me; becoming overpowered—but he didn't make it sound like he'd been trapped inside his body. He knew what was going on and he thought it was strange, but he didn't know why.

Maybe self-awareness is the side effect of the new strain of serum. Or maybe it isn't even normal—maybe it's a sign my brain is fighting back.

I run on the track for almost an hour, until my calves and lungs are burning and I'm sure I'm going to be sore tomorrow. But Other Me isn't finished. Her feet carry me to another training room a few doors down, where punching bags hang from the walls. There are other people already inside—young boys, all of them. An older official is coaching two boys who are sparring on the floor mat, while the rest practice the same techniques against the punching bags. I must've interrupted a training session.

"Always size up your opponent before you engage," the coach says.

His voice makes me start. I know him. He's not just any official—he's Colonel Parker. His eyes never look hazy or muddled, like he's subdued. But he's Commander Charlie's right-hand man. His loyalty must be because he believes in Charlie's plans.

I tell my body to turn around, to leave quickly, but of course, it doesn't listen. My feet linger in the doorway.

A couple of the boys notice me first, and then Parker does. It takes him a minute to recognize me.

He stops frowning and smiles a little, like he knows my secret. Charlie must've told him I took the injection.

"Clementine, join us, if you'd like," he says.

"Thank you," I say, walking into the room.

Colonel Parker refocuses his attention on the sparring pair on the mat. The boys can't be more than twelve or thirteen, but they're throwing punches and block attacks like they've been doing it for years. They have gloves on and mouthpieces, but no helmets.

I listen to Parker's coaching tips as I wrap sparring tape around my hands. I'm still getting used to hearing out of only my right ear; I have to face that side of my head toward him to hear him best.

"Remember to set up your opponent before you strike," he says. "Set high, strike low, and vice versa. You'll get more hits in."

Facing one of the punching bags, I flex my hands before curling them into fists. I wet my lips, bouncing on the balls of my feet to make my movements light. All things I would normally do, but they feel strange when the wrong half of my brain is in control. At least I can still imagine the bag is Commander Charlie. When I aim my first punch, I hit him square in the nose. He slaps a gloved hand over it with a groan. When he pulls his hand away, there's blood all over the glove, so much it will never wash away.

If I could move my mouth, I'd curl my lips into a smile.

I practice each of the punching styles—uppercut, hook, cross, straight, and jab—until my hands hurt and the boys around me have finished their training. They trail out of the room, laughing and still practicing their jabs, and leave me alone with Colonel Parker. My eyes are so focused on the punching bag that I don't notice him watching me until I'm pretty sure he's been standing there for some time. His arms are crossed, and there's amusement in his eyes.

Other Me stops to catch her breath. The tape is covered in sweat and a few bloodstains from my knuckles, and falling off my hands. I'm relieved when I pull the tape off, because it means I'm finished.

"Your form is pretty good," Colonel Parker says. "It could use work, but it's getting there. Seems like you've been practicing."

"A bit," I say, and I hope my lips won't tell him anything more. Maybe he already knows the location of Alliance headquarters, but if he doesn't, he doesn't need to know.

"Do you have somewhere to be?" he asks. "We could spar a little. Officials are usually expected to spar with a partner each day. I don't want to force you, since you're new to this. But I think it would be good for you to get into the rhythm of things."

I'm not an official, I want to tell him. But I'm wearing the uniform, aren't I?

"I agree," Other Me says with a wide smile. "Let's spar."

Parker smiles in turn. "I'll get you a pair of gloves."

He walks into the small supply room on the other side of the floor mat. He must be encouraging this because he believes I'm a permanent addition to Charlie's team. He knows Other Me came in here with the intention of practicing to fight Charlie's enemies—my friends.

I will try my vruxing hardest not to let her do it. But Colonel Parker thinks I won't be able to stop her.

He brings me gloves that must be meant for someone younger, but they fit my small hands perfectly. He gives me a mouthpiece too. I face him on the mat.

"Ready?" Parker says.

"Ready," I say through the mouthpiece.

And we begin.

# 25

Commander Charlie sends for me in the evening. A guard finds me after dinner and escorts me to Restricted Division.

It's the first time I've been able to walk through the corridors when I'm not fearing for my life. At first the hallways look no different from those in the rest of the Core. But as we move farther in and take a set of stairs to a floor below, the corridors become narrower, reminding me of the passageways in a spaceship. Some of the doors we pass have markers over them: HALL OF COMMANDERS; CREW QUARTERS; ENGINE ACCESS.

Even though I'm subdued, I'm amazed Charlie's letting me see these rooms. Most of the doors require access codes, but now I know exactly where the engines are, and the hyperdrive systems. All the equipment that might someday allow the Core to run as a battleship and survive on her own.

If the systems were destroyed, that would never be an option.

We come to an unmarked door, a short way beyond the Hall

of Commanders. The guard types a code into a lock-pad on the wall, and the door slides open. I follow him inside.

The room is large, with a huge round table taking up most of the space. A meeting room. Only eight of the twenty or so seats are taken. I pull out the nearest chair, glancing around at the other faces.

Most of the people here are familiar. Two of the officials I've never seen before, but Colonel Parker is here. He gives me a nod and a smile when he sees me. My knuckles are bruised from our sparring match earlier, but I'm glad I agreed to it. It made me feel more confident, capable of defending myself with my hands.

Cadet Waller sits a few seats to my right, her long, black hair tied in a high ponytail. A couple seats beyond her is the scientist who helped Charlie make his big false announcement about the increase of moonshine in the atmosphere, in the Core pavilion several weeks ago. Sitting in the chair beside him is Fred.

Fred's wearing a simple gray tunic and pants, even though he was once a colonel and I bet he has an old uniform. His eyes seem less dead than I remember, but his skin is just as sunken and scarred. When he looks at me, a flash of guilt crosses his face. He is the scientist who developed the KIMO bomb; my friend died because of him. He is the one who gave Logan's name to the doctors; Logan was tortured in Karum because of him.

I forgave him for those things. I knew that he was weak and desperate, looking for a way out. But now he's on Charlie's side again, helping him design Strykers and other weapons capable of destroying Marden's fleet. He's helping commit genocide, and this time it's not a trick; he knows it's going to happen.

It's hard to keep forgiving him.

I look away from him, to the person I've been wanting and also dreading to see. Beechy sits across the table from me, to the left of Commander Charlie. He's wearing his old skintight suit made of dark leather. He smiles at me—an unnatural smile; it stretches too wide and doesn't completely fill his eyes, because they're layered with film—and I smile back.

My insides churn. I want to know what happened at the Surface security hub—how, exactly, someone caught him. Did he turn himself in, as Sam said? Did he not have any choice?

Beechy folds his hands together and looks at Charlie, who's speaking.

"Now that we're all here, let's get started," he says. "Colonel Parker, please update everyone on the status of Operation Stryker."

I want to ask what Charlie did to Beechy after he was caught. I want to know if being the test subject for the submission serum was painful at all, because if it was, I want to tell him I'm sorry. It's half my fault, since Charlie developed the serum because of me.

I want to ask Beechy if he feels as trapped inside his skin as I do. I want to ask him if he has any idea how to break free.

Colonel Parker's talking, and I realize I should be listening to what he's saying. Hopefully Other Me looks like she's being attentive.

"All officials in Crust, Mantle, and Lower have received the order to begin loading workers from the camp into transports at nine tomorrow morning," Parker says. "It will take a few trips to transport everyone, and they'll be staggering the trips between sectors, so as not to clog the Pipeline. The commanding officer in each sector will keep in contact with me throughout the morning. I'll be following them to the Surface with a small squadron of officials, departing at approximately ten thirty, or sooner if it becomes clear reinforcements are needed. Cadet Waller, I believe you said you'll remain here in the Core to be my primary contact once I've reached the Surface."

"Yes, sir," Cadet Waller says, clasping her hands on the table. She has her tablet with her, as always.

"Let's go over the plan once the transports reach the Surface," Charlie says.

Colonel Parker runs his palm over the table, which is made of the same touch-screen material as the table in the Core bridge. Small, holographic buildings pop up from the center of the table. A miniature city builds itself. The Surface city. I can pick out the education tower, the sanitarium, and the building I scaled the evening I was picked for Extraction.

"We'll be unloading the transports in the city," Parker says. "The child workers will be told this evening that they're being transferred to the Surface because the city will be their new home and the work camps are dissolving. We're allowing them to sleep in the resident buildings. Our goal is to make this seem like a new kind of Extraction for them—a reward. This will lessen the risk of them giving us trouble. We've also ensured that the nutrient vitamins the workers in the lower sectors usually receive every week were replaced by a different kind of pill, which contained a small dosage of submission serum. That should make them docile."

Lies, lies, lies, that's all people in the camps are ever told. The horrible thing is, most of them will fall for this. Most of them would give anything for a chance to spend even one night in a city building instead of in a shack or on the floor of a cave. Even if they don't believe the Developers would really shut down the work camps, once they're in the city, they'll want to believe it so much, they'll forget how strange it seems.

"The pill form of the serum wears off within a few days, though," says the scientist I don't know the name of. He's tapping his hand on the table like he has a nervous itch. "If we're wrong about the arrival of the fleet, I hope you realize we could run into a serious problem. Some of the workers are bound to question this and try to make trouble, especially if we give them free rein of the city. I don't like that we're putting all of them together—their numbers are *huge*, and they have the highest percentage of potential Unstables. There are more of them than the entire Core population."

Ariadne recited the numbers when we first arrived in the Core—she said the population is roughly ten thousand. The Surface camp had about four thousand people, and the other camps must have a similar number, maybe a bit smaller. That means there are about sixteen thousand people in all the camps, combined.

Hope stirs in my chest. With that many of them, surely there's a chance they can band together and form an uprising. Surely there are lots of people like Nellie among them, who don't trust the Developers or the officials, even if they don't know about the KIMO bomb.

But even if they fought back, they don't know about the Strykers, and they have no way to remove them from their bodies.

"We're not letting them run free," Commander Charlie says calmly. "We're locking them inside the resident buildings. The air is still contaminated by moonshine—though we're telling them it's been decontaminated. The recreation options they'll have available to them should distract them from the reality of their situation."

"And officials will remain on the Surface to keep things under control," Colonel Parker says, flipping off the hologram of the city. "As soon as Marden's fleet appears within close range, which should be within three or four days, they'll evacuate immediately. Once the fleet arrives, it won't matter if the workers break free of the buildings. All that matters is that they remain within the bounds of the settlement and don't have access to any ships."

The only hope of survival for the workers would be to hijack ships and fly down here to the Core, so Charlie wouldn't detonate the Strykers for fear of destroying his precious home, and dying himself in the explosions. But as long as I'm trapped in my body, I can't warn them about this. I can't help them. Three days isn't enough time.

"Clementine," Commander Charlie says, snapping me out of my thoughts. "Do you see any serious issues with this plan? Do you have any suggestions?"

I try to close up my throat so I can't answer. I try to convince Other Me to say what I really want to say: *Don't go through with this plan.*

But the words escape my mouth anyway: "While you're transporting the workers into the buildings, you should have a demonstration. Make it clear to all of them that moonshine is still a threat, and they'll be too scared to venture outside."

"I like the way you think." Commander Charlie adjusts one of his gloves. "Colonel Parker, I'll let you take the initiative on that."

"Yes, sir." Vrux, vrux, vrux. How could I suggest that? He's going to listen to me; he's going to kill some of the workers in the worst way possible, and it will be all my fault.

*You couldn't help it,* I remind myself. But that doesn't make me any happier.

"Now, let's move onto the other important topic: the fugitives," Commander Charlie says. "They're part of an insurrection group they call 'the Alliance.' We have two members in our company, and two other rebels in custody. I will be interrogating one of them when we're finished here, but for now, the information we have about Alliance operations comes from Mr. Beechy here, as well as what Lieutenant Sam has determined while dealing with the recent destruction of the Crust quarantine facility. Beechy provided the list of names of those who were working with his company."

Charlie taps the table screen, and the list appears in a floating hologram big enough for all of us to read. There's a picture and an identification number beside many of the names, but not all of them.

Sandy*
Skylar
Clementine
Logan
Jensen
Darren*
Buck*
Rita
Fiona*
Wright
Ansel
Wanda
Ellen*
Richard*
Clarence

The small star beside some of the names seems to designate the people who remained at headquarters. But there are missing names. Our company didn't have only fifteen people, last I checked.

I scan the list again. Mal's name is definitely missing, along with

Paley's. Did Beechy forget about them, or leave them out on purpose?

To leave them out, he would've had to fight his injection. *How?*

"Clementine," Charlie says.

"Yes?" I say automatically. *No, no, no.* If he asks me for more names, I'll give them. I won't be able to stop myself.

"Can you tell me the location of any of these people?" he asks.

"I know Jensen is somewhere in Crust," I say. "He was disguised as a guard the last time I saw him. As for the other names, I'm sorry. I don't know. I was separated from most of them before I boarded the transport for the work camp."

I've never been more grateful for the way Charlie phrased a question.

Out of the corner of my eye, I notice Cadet Waller's cheeks pinching.

"That's unfortunate," Commander Charlie says. "But I'm hoping our most recent prisoner, Ms. Skylar, will be able to fill in some of the blanks. She denied having anything to do with the recent Crust incident, but during our interrogation this evening I'm sure I'll get the truth out of her. I'm confident she knows the location of at least a few other Alliance members. The rest will appear with time when they attempt another form of sabotage, and we'll have our friends here to help us identify them."

"Shouldn't we attempt to prevent more attacks from happening, sir?" Cadet Waller asks.

"Lieutenant Sam is putting suitable precautions into place," Charlie says. "And we've made sure the word has spread about the capture of certain fugitives already, so as to discourage the others. At the moment, I'm less concerned about the fugitives in the lower sectors and more concerned with the ones who remain at their headquarters. They are, as yet, unaware of the situation with Marden's army. If they remain where they are without knowledge of this, their reaction to the fleet's arrival could be devastating for our cause. They also may be coordinating an attack to penetrate Core defenses as we speak. My daughter is among them. I believe it's in our best interest to bring them all here for questioning, to see if their skills can be useful to us, if we subdue them with the new B-strain serum. The facility where Sandy and her team are based is well fortified, but Beechy assures me it has its weaknesses."

"Where is this facility?" Fred asks, speaking for the first time. His voice is as deep and hollow as I remember.

"I'll show you," Beechy says. His voice sounds different; short and clipped.

His fingers move expertly over the table touch screen. He brings up Kiel's surface and zooms in until the mountain range takes up the whole table. He zooms in farther, making one mountain bigger than the rest.

"The Alliance is based in an old facility once occupied by members of KIMO, the Kiel Intelligence Military Operative," he says.

Fred lets a hiss of air escape through his teeth.

"Early tomorrow," Beechy continues, "Clementine and I will fly here with a squadron of patrolmen. We're going to break in, capture everyone inside, and destroy the facility."

When I swallow, there's a sick taste in my mouth. I don't want to do any of that.

Cadet Waller cuts in: "Commander, sir, forgive me, but do you really trust these two enough to send them on this mission?"

"Yes," Charlie says. "And they will be accompanied by Lieutenant Sam and several capable soldiers, should the mission face any challenges. I trust they'll get it done. Do you disagree with my judgment?"

She presses her lips together. "No, sir."

If I had control of my hands, I'd be digging my nails into the fabric of my seat. Sam is coming with us.

I can't help wondering if this is a trick, if really Charlie is sending me and Beechy away so we can help Sam and the other soldiers break into the facility, and then they'll kill the two of us and everyone inside.

Even if that's the truth, I can't do a thing to stop him. My actions are not my own anymore.

Commander Charlie turns off the mountain hologram. "More detailed instructions for those of you involved with either mission will be given tomorrow, through the supervising officers. Are there any more immediate questions?

The silence lingers.

"Good. You're all dismissed." Charlie pushes his chair back and rises. "Clementine, come with me."

I rise before I even process his order. I don't know where we're going.

But he walks out of the room, and I follow.

# 26

He takes me to Cell Block A, a corridor of doors with no handles or windows. The guard who escorts us down the block presses his palm against a small blue panel on one of the cell doors, and the door slides open.

I know now why we're here: Charlie said he was going to interrogate Skylar after the meeting. I don't know why he brought me along, but he must have a reason. I doubt it will make me happy.

Charlie pauses outside the door and removes the gun from his holster. It's a copper, but sleeker than the model I've used before. He holds it out to me with his gloved hand.

"Hold this for me," he says.

I take it without a word. But I don't trust myself with a gun, not when he's controlling my hands. Not when he's about to interrogate Skylar, and he might make me use this gun to force her to give us information.

I won't use the gun. I won't shoot her. I will resist with all my strength.

The guard pushes the cell door open, and Charlie walks inside. I follow him.

If only I could lift the gun and point it at him. If only I could squeeze the trigger.

He steps to my left, and I see Skylar sitting in the corner of the cell, her head leaning against the wall. Her eyes are closed, and the skin around her right one is horribly bruised, black and blue. There's a cut on her lower lip and a deeper one on her bare left arm, which is chained with her other arm above her head. She's not wearing an official's uniform anymore; she's wearing a tunic with ripped sleeves and pants that are too long for her, and there are no shoes on her feet.

She always seemed so strong and ruthless in my head, the kind of person who could overpower anyone who tried to break her. If she's broken, I don't know what that makes me.

Commander Charlie fixes his gloves as he walks slowly up to her. He pauses, observing her with a distasteful expression.

His boot comes down hard on her ankle.

Skylar wakes with a start. Her face twists in pain, but she recovers quickly, taking in both of us.

"How was your nap?" Charlie asks.

She barely looks at him. "Clementine," she chokes.

"Yes, I believe you've met."

I try to force my lips apart to say something—*I'm sorry. He made me come. I won't let him hurt you.*—but what my lips do instead is smile. The fake, happy smile I'd like to rip off my face forever.

"What did you do to her?" Skylar asks.

Charlie waves her concern away with a hand. "I gave her a little shot, that's all."

"Of course. That's how you deal with everyone."

"It's how I deal with people who don't understand the importance of loyalty." Charlie clasps his hands behind his back and turns to me. "Clementine, do you know the definition of the word 'loyalty'?"

"It means supporting someone, no matter what," I say immediately. "Remaining faithful to them. Fighting for them."

Skylar drops her eyes and narrows them.

"Very good," Charlie says. "And what are some words that mean the opposite of that?"

"Treachery. A disloyal person is a traitor."

"Yes, 'traitor.' That's the word I was aiming for."

"I'm *not* a traitor," Skylar says through her teeth. She lifts her head again, focusing her stern gaze on Charlie. "I've been nothing but loyal to you. I went through all of this for you!"

I frown. I expected her to lie, but not like this.

"Tell me what you went through, exactly," Charlie says. "Because Lieutenant Sam gave me a different impression. Be specific."

Skylar looks like she's fighting speaking, but not because she doesn't want to tell Charlie. It's because she doesn't want me to hear what she's going to say.

"You told me your suspicions about a Core insurrectionist group a month before you launched the bomb," she says, her voice a bit strained. "You told me to learn what I could, and make the members trust me. I've always been friends with Beechy and your daughter, so it wasn't hard to make them think I'd changed my mind about you. But they didn't tell me their plan to invade Karum or attack you the day of the bomb, not until it was happening. And when it seemed like they might actually win, you told me to go with them. So I went to their headquarters. A couple Alliance members had been stationed there for a while. The place was well secured, and I tried hacking into the main system to find some way to contact you, to tell you where we were. But I couldn't make it work."

Skylar pauses. I stare at her, not understanding a word of this. I can't tell if she's lying or telling the truth.

She keeps going. She tells Charlie about the week we spent there sending out recon pilots and waiting for them to return, and how she used her time wisely, befriending as many rebels as she could and gaining their trust. How she gained my trust.

"When the scouts returned with the news about you transferring everyone off the Surface," she says, "naturally Beechy jumped on that and put a whole plan together. We'd sneak onto the transports, get to the lower sectors, and wreak as much havoc as we could. In a systematic way, of course. I helped him and Sandy plot out the parameters. I thought if I could get all the rebels to the lower sectors, I'd be able to contact you and hand them over. But I had to make sure nothing went wrong on our way to the Surface city; I had to make sure the rebels couldn't change their minds once they left. So I leaked half our fuel supply the morning we were supposed to leave and started a small fire. Blamed it on someone else. It was easy enough."

She laughs a short, mirthless laugh that makes my jaw harden in anger. She leaked the fuel; she caused the fire. She must've done it right before I ran into her early that morning. But when she blamed it on Buck, we all believed her.

Commander Charlie is watching me, I realize. He's watching my face to see if I will react to this, but my face feels as calm as ever. Inside, I want to scream.

"Let's skip to what happened in Crust," he says, turning back to Skylar with a rueful smile. "Why didn't you contact me as soon as you arrived?"

"I tried, I swear I did. But I couldn't get into the comm rooms—not without proper ID. I was afraid someone would recognize me. You had my name on all the rebel lists; you had people looking for me. Look what happened when they caught me."

"So you decided to blow up the quarantine building in the meantime?" Charlie asks calmly.

"I had *nothing* to do with that," Skylar says, pulling against her chains in her anger.

"Beechy said you were supposed to take over as the rebel leader once you realized he'd been captured."

"I did take over, at the beginning. I told everyone it was best if we stayed low for a few days, since I was hoping to make contact with you before they did something. But I was subordinated by Cadet Mal."

*No, no, no.*

Commander Charlie looks surprised. "The cadet currently assisting Sam with the rebel investigation?"

"The very same."

Now Charlie is the one searching for the lie in Skylar's face. "Cadet Malcolm transferred from the Surface security hub, where he's been stationed for the past two years. To my knowledge, there's no record of him leaving his post."

"With all due respect, sir, he's an expert hacker. He could've easily wiped his records clean."

"It's possible . . . ," Charlie says. He turns to me. "Do you know a Cadet Mal?"

I swear my heart is pounding, but when I focus on my real one, I count seventy-two beats in a minute. A perfectly normal rate.

"Yes, sir," I say. "He helped transport me into the Crust camp."

Charlie's lips form a thin line. "I see. I'll send word for an investigation about him to begin right away. Thank you both for the tip."

Just like that, I've given someone up.

"I can help you find more of them," Skylar says. "If you let me free and you send me back there, I swear I'll help Sam bring them all in."

There's subtle desperation in her voice, but I can tell she's being truthful. She didn't get a chance to turn me in—I turned myself in first—but she would have. I wondered if Mal was the one on Charlie's side, but I was wrong. It was her all along.

With a sigh, Charlie turns away from both of us, walking slowly to the wall before turning around. "I would like to trust you, Skylar," he says. "But I know how you like to spin stories. I'm afraid you may have left some things out."

"I didn't," she says immediately. "I swear. Commander, please—"

"You aren't useful to me anymore, if I can't trust you," Charlie says. "Clementine, do you trust her?"

"No," I say, and I'm surprised there's real venom in Other Me's voice. "No, I don't."

Before I realize what I'm doing, I've taken three steps forward. I've lifted the gun Charlie gave me, and I'm aiming it at Skylar. He didn't tell me to do this, but I know in my deepest core this is what he hoped I would do.

Panic races through me like wildfire. *What am I doing?* I'm angry with her, but I don't want her dead. I don't want to shoot her.

She's staring at me with wide, cautious eyes. She's frightened, but she doesn't think I'll do it. She doesn't realize how my hands have turned against me, making me a weapon for Charlie.

Charlie has a look on his face that tells me he's reveling in his control over me.

But is this really him in control? I'm afraid it might be me too, even if it's only a small part of me. I spoke the truth—I don't trust Skylar. She isn't my friend, like I thought she was. She's my enemy, like Joe was my enemy.

And I hurt Joe. I had to, so he couldn't hurt me.

"Clementine," Skylar whispers, her eyes almost watering. She's realized I'm not faking this. "I shouldn't have lied to you. I'm sorry. But please, don't do this."

A hand falls on my shoulder. Charlie's hand. "Do what feels right," he says.

*Do what feels right.*

I take another step and push the barrel against Skylar's forehead. Her iron shackles clink as she moves her hands a little. She blinks fast, and a single tear rolls down her cheek.

My index finger brushes over the trigger.

"Please," she says.

I don't want to do this. I don't want to kill her.

Charlie didn't give me a direct order, so he's testing my instincts. He wants to see whether I'll make the right decision.

Why would he want me to kill her?

To prove I will do what he says. To prove I will be a mindless soldier, fighting for him.

But Skylar would be more useful to him alive. And I've already proved I'm a mindless soldier, haven't I? I've proved it by pressing this barrel against her forehead, by brushing my hand over the trigger. The real me would not have done this. I don't need to go all the way through with it, not this time.

Skylar isn't Charlie's enemy—she's mine. But I don't want to kill her.

My jaw is still set; my finger is still on the trigger. Slowly, I slide my finger away. I remove the barrel from her forehead and turn to Charlie and hold out the gun.

"She gave us Cadet Mal," I say. "She'll give you the other rebels too. She might be the only one who can. I don't think it's wise to kill her yet."

Charlie doesn't answer for a long time, his blank face giving me no sign of what he's thinking. Finally, he says, "A smart decision," and takes the gun from my hand.

I wonder if he means it.

He tucks the copper into his holster and tells Skylar he'll have the guards bring her some food. Her shoulders slump in relief.

"Come," he says to me, and I follow him out of the cell.

"Tomorrow morning," he says, once we're in the hallway. "I need you to report to the health ward, room fourteen, ten minutes before eleven o' clock. I'll be there to oversee the readministration of your injection. I'm sure you'll have no trouble with it, but I care about your safety, so I want to make sure you don't make any mistakes."

What he means is, he cares about making me easy to control.

"I won't be late," I say.

"Come ready to depart, as I'll be escorting you to your mission transport immediately afterwards."

We round a corner and reach an elevator I can take to leave Restricted Division. Charlie presses the button for me, then turns and sets a hand on my shoulder. His eyes bore into mine, like a black hole trying to suck me in. But when he speaks, his voice is kind.

"Thank you for your loyalty, Clementine."

The way he says that word—*loyalty*—almost sounds like a subtle threat.

"I will always be loyal to you," I say automatically.

"I'm glad to hear that," he says.

The elevator arrives, and I step inside. As I press the button for my floor in Slumber Division, a sour taste fills my mouth. The taste of fear.

It seemed like he was speaking to the real me, the one trapped inside. It seemed like he can tell I'm trying to break free because I didn't shoot Skylar.

He's reminding me he can tell one of his loyal followers to shoot me, and they won't falter as I did. They will pull the trigger.

# 27

In my dream, I lie in the dark of the Crust camp, surrounded by croacher nests. My body is paralyzed; I can't move.

The silver-and-blue bugs skitter close to me, brushing my bare arms and legs with their feelers. If they bite me, their venom will keep me paralyzed forever. I will never be able to get out of here.

Nellie and Hector are standing nearby. They could help me, but all they do is laugh.

A giant croacher crawls up onto my palm, its long legs scurrying over my skin. I scream. I shake my hand to get it off me, but my hand remains limp on the ground.

The bug pauses at the center of my palm. Its body twitches, and its silver eyes gleam in the dark.

It sinks its teeth into my skin and a garbled scream erupts from my throat.

⁎

I wake with sweaty palms, shoving and kicking my sheets away like they're the croachers. But it was just a dream. I'm not in the camp anymore.

*You're okay*, I tell myself. Everything is okay.

I close my eyes until my breathing slows down. When I'm lying here, it feels like I'm in control again. I almost forget I'm trapped inside my skin.

Then my arms push me up into a sitting position, and my legs kick the sheets back the rest of the way without my permission. And I remember.

I remember Charlie is making me take another dose of serum today. I remember he's putting me on a ship and making me capture my friends. I almost wish I were still trapped in the croacher dream. At least I would wake up.

Today is real; it is happening.

After standing, I walk into the bathroom to wash up. I pause in front of the mirror to stare at my reflection. Some of the bleach washed out of my hair with the dirt yesterday—the steam-clean chemicals are powerful—so the few strands of hair curling from my scalp aren't as white-blond as before, more golden. The blue in my eyes has turned almost gray, a murky color that stretches over the pupil of each eye, as well as the iris. When I smile at myself, the smile looks like the smile I've seen on other mindless citizens: so big, it looks fake. I look like a shell of my real self, and that's what I am.

But there's something real inside me still, something that wasn't created by the serum in my bloodstream. A part of my brain that influences my actions, even when it feels like someone else is controlling my hands. That's the reason I almost shot Skylar last night—I can't deny it. Charlie didn't tell me to shoot her; he told me to follow my instincts. My instincts didn't come from an injection; they came from my anger about Skylar's betrayal.

I use the steam-clean to wash my hair and face and neck. The cleaning chemicals wash out most of the remaining bleach in my curls, bringing more red out. The red makes me look more like myself in the mirror, but I'm not sure that's a good thing.

Back in the main bedroom, I pull my outfit out of the clothing slot in the wall. It's the same gray uniform as yesterday, freshly washed, but today there are accessories with it: a black padded vest, a thick belt with a gun holster, and a pair of protective gloves. This is an outfit for a soldier being sent on a war mission.

That's where I'm headed today: a war mission, against the wrong enemy.

My hands don't falter as I pull on the uniform, snapping on the vest and slipping on my knee-high boots. Other Me has calmed down, but beneath her exterior I am not calm at all.

The time on the band around my wrist says it's nine thirty. I have one hour and forty minutes until I'm supposed to meet Charlie in the health ward. One hour and forty minutes to fight the serum enough that it wears off, so I can refuse the other injection. I can still regain control.

But *how?*

My legs make me walk to the hovering tray beside my bed, where I set the second syringe yesterday. I pick it up and turn it over in my hand, staring at the silver liquid inside. Almost hesitating, but that can't be it. Other Me wouldn't hesitate.

What would make her hesitate?

Logan's face drifts into my head, the way it looked when I held the gas mask over his mouth and nose. His watery eyes were devoid of hope. I have to see him before I leave for the KIMO facility. If things don't go well up there, I might not come back. And I have a feeling things will be different, if I do. I might've hurt people; I might've done things I swore I would never do. Even trapped inside this body, I will feel guilty if I hurt anyone.

My hand tucks the syringe inside a small zipped pouch on the left side of my holster belt. I turn away and walk to the door. I beg my feet to take me to someone who knows where Charlie is keeping Logan.

Other Me loves him too. Surely she doesn't want to leave without saying good-bye.

⊁

First, she takes me to the cafeteria. I am hungry, but I'm worried I'll get stuck at one of the tables for a long time. That lieutenant who escorted me here from Crust, Dean, is sitting nearby, and he already noticed me come in. The look on his face makes me think he might ask me to join him and his uniformed friends.

Thankfully, Other Me seems like she's on my side for once. I leave the cafeteria without sitting down, a breakfast bar sprinkled with sweet seeds in my hands. My feet carry me to an elevator, and when it arrives, my finger presses the button for Restricted Division, near Cell Block A. I don't know exactly where Logan is, but Charlie said he'd put him in a cell, so he must be in Block A or B, which I passed on my way to A with Charlie last night.

There aren't many holding cells in the Core; most Core prisoners are branded Unstable and sent to Karum. Now that Karum is silent and the Surface may soon be under attack, execution seems a likelier sentence for everyone Charlie can't figure out how to control.

The elevator door slides open when I reach Restricted Division.

I walk out into the corridor, swallowing the last bite of the sweet bar, and turn two corners before I reach Block A.

There's a guard outside the main door—the same guard who let us into Skylar's cell last night. He stiffens and sets a hand on the weapon in his holster as I approach.

"This is a restricted area," he says.

"I'm allowed here," I say.

Suspicion touches his eyes, but finally recognition sinks in. Still, he doesn't move his hand from the barrel of his weapon.

"Are you looking for someone?" he asks in a gruff voice.

"I need help finding a prisoner. His name is Logan."

"Why do you need to find him?"

"Commander Charlie said I'm allowed to visit him, and I'm shipping out on a mission today. I want to say good-bye. Please," I add.

He sighs and removes his hand from his weapon.

"Fine," he says. "Just this once. Follow me."

He unlocks the door behind him. I give him a grateful smile.

He leads me down the cell block, past Skylar's cell to the end of the corridor. I can't believe Logan was so close when I visited her last night, and I didn't realize. I didn't even think of him.

Part of me is glad I didn't see him, though. He would've seen me too, maybe when I was about to shoot Skylar. He would've thought I was a monster.

The guard unlocks the last door and opens it. He glances toward the opposite end of the corridor.

"Make it quick," he says. "I'll be back to get you soon."

"I will. Thank you," I say, stepping through the doorway.

Logan's cell isn't what I expected. It's small and mostly bare, but it has a cot with a real mattress and a toilet in the corner. He's sitting on the bed reading on a tablet.

I'm amazed Charlie let him have all of this. He kept his promise; Logan isn't in a transport on his way to the Surface. There's no longer a Stryker inside him. I shouldn't want to thank Charlie for anything, but I want to thank him for this.

When Logan notices me, he sets the tablet aside quickly and stands, surprised. "Clementine."

"That's me," I say.

He's wearing the same clothes as the last time I saw him, but his face and hair look like they've been washed. He looks awake, aware, anxious.

"Are you—?" He takes a step toward me, but hesitates, his eyes searching my expression. There's too much eagerness in his, though he's trying not to show it. "Are you okay?"

*Are you subdued?* That must be what he means. He thinks I'm not anymore, or I'm just pretending to be. He thinks that's the only reason I would come to visit him.

"I'm perfect," says Other Me with a smile. It feels so fake. "You're safe, so I'm happy."

It's not completely a lie, but it's not at all what I want to say.

Logan falters. Distrust replaces the eagerness in his eyes. He turns his head away, maybe so I won't see it.

"I'm glad you're perfect," he says, and his voice is stiff, almost breaking. He was too hopeful I would've broken free by now; he thought I was stronger than I really am.

There are words on the tip of my tongue—*I'm still here, Logan, but I need your help. I'm trapped and I can't get out.* But when I try to force them out, they become like raindrops I can never grasp, though they fall on me and will drown me if they don't stop.

I can't say what I want to say. All I can do is stand here staring at him until Other Me decides to move her lips or feet or hands.

Other Me takes a small step forward. "They're sending me on a mission today," she lets me say. "That's why I came. I wanted to say good-bye."

Logan's head snaps back to me. "What? Where are you going?"

"I'm sorry, I can't tell you," I say. "The mission is classified."

He groans in frustration. "You can't give me anything more than that?"

"I won't be gone long. I'll visit you again when I come back."

"*If* you come back," he says.

"I will."

"Can you promise me?"

My lips don't say anything at first. Then a single word escapes: "No."

"Yeah, I thought so."

"But you don't have to worry," I say, taking two steps closer to him. "Commander Charlie saved you, and he'll save me too. We have to trust him."

I reach out my hand and brush his cheek. I'm grateful he doesn't flinch away; it feels good to touch him.

"You really believe that?" Logan says in a soft, bitter voice.

I slip my arms around his neck. "Yes."

"It's the injection talking."

"I don't care."

His eyes are locked on mine, though there's hesitance in his. Other Me doesn't seem to care; I rise onto my tiptoes and pull him down a little, until his lips are mere centimeters from mine.

I can feel him struggling with himself, deciding whether or not this is right.

Thank the stars, he gives in. He kisses me, and everything else falls away. There's nothing but his lips and mine, and the energy coursing between them.

*It's me,* I tell him over and over with my lips. *I'm still here.*

He pulls away too fast. Not yet, please. I want him back, and so does Other Me. But when I lean into him again, he lets go of me and moves back, all the way to the wall.

"I'm sorry," he says. "I can't. You're not her."

I stare at him, my lips unmoving. Anger trickles into my veins, soft at first, then crushing me. *Why can't I make him see?* The serum should be wearing off by now, not overpowering me so much. Seeing him again, being with him was supposed to snap me out of this. But it didn't work; I'm still not free.

*I'm sorry too,* I want to tell him. I'm sorry I did this to myself. But it was my only option, the only way to keep Charlie from sending him to the Surface to die.

I would give myself the serum again, a hundred times, to save Logan.

Other Me still hasn't spoken, I realize. She's at a loss for words for once, like me.

Logan is still watching me, his expression somewhere between anger and guilt. He rubs his temple with his thumb and forefinger, then slowly closes the space between us.

"I'm sorry," he says again, softer this time. Setting his hands on my shoulders, he leans forward and presses his lips against my forehead. Tenderly. This time he doesn't pull away.

Can't we stay like this forever?

Right on cue, I hear the sound of the cell door unlocking behind me.

Logan steps back, keeping his hands on my shoulders. His eyes plead with me.

"I know you can fight this," he whispers. "Come back to me, Clem."

"Let's go," the guard says.

I pull away from Logan, but I look back at him on my way out. Though I can't bring my mouth to say anything, I hope he sees the answer in my eyes: *I'll try.*

# 28

At exactly ten minutes to eleven, I enter room fourteen in the health ward.

My stomach is full of nerves. I hope the fear isn't in my expression. I don't want Charlie to know I'm aware of everything that's happening until I'm in control again and I can strangle him for all of this, though I'm worried he's already guessed I'm aware after what happened with Skylar.

The room is similar to other Core exam rooms, with a cot on the right-hand side and a sink, counter, and cabinets on the left. The lights are dim and blue, casting eerie shadows on the faces of the two men standing in here, speaking in low voices. Commander Charlie and Lieutenant Dean.

I stiffen. The lieutenant must be here in case something goes wrong, in case Charlie needs someone to hold me down while the nurse gives me my injection. These are the two who forced me into my cage. They both want to be sure I remain inside it.

Charlie stops talking when he sees me, holding up a hand to hush Dean, as well.

"Here you are," he says, glancing at his time-band. "Right on time. Do you have the syringe?"

I unzip my belt pouch and pull the syringe out to show him.

"Good," Charlie says. "And here's the nurse."

I hear the soft click of shoes behind me.

"Here's the next batch of injections, as you requested, Commander Charlie, sir," the nurse says, setting three syringes on the counter by the sink. Her hair is long and blond and familiar.

Ariadne's smile is wide, and her cheeks are rosy. The last time I saw her, she was in a bed with Sam. They were kissing, and I ran because I didn't know what else to do. She couldn't have wanted to be with him; she knew he was cruel. But she'd been injected with the mind-control serum, and he took advantage of that.

She is still mindless. There's a glaze over her eyes like the glaze over mine.

"Clementine, it's so good to see you!" she says. "I heard you were sick. I'm so glad you got better."

Sick. She thinks I was sick, and that's why I haven't been around. Charlie would tell her that; he used to tell everyone Unstables had a sickness that couldn't be cured, even though all they were were people who tried to fight him and sometimes won.

"It's horrible that Oliver didn't get well." Ariadne's smile fades. "I wish I'd been further along in my medical training when that happened. I wish I could've saved him."

I stare at her, thankful my lips aren't moving for once. Charlie looks amused out of the corner of my eye.

He makes me furious. Lying about why I was gone is one thing; lying about Oliver's death is another. Charlie could've saved him.

He could've stationed someone else on the spaceship to guard the KIMO bomb, or no one. He could've let Oliver stay here in the Core, where he'd be safer, but he put him on the ship because he didn't care about his safety. He knew it would kill me when I found out.

He brought Ariadne here on purpose too, so I would hear her say this. He knew I would get angry. I can't clear up the truth for her, not when my mouth won't do as I tell it.

"It's nice to see a happy reunion," Charlie says, not bothering to hide his sarcasm. "But let's hurry this along, shall we?"

"Of course, sir," Ariadne says, wiping the sadness from her face like someone pressed a switch on her back to flip it off. She turns away to rummage through a drawer.

I'm not ready for this. I need to figure out how to control my hands first, how to make them turn against Charlie instead of doing what he says. I'm running out of time.

When Ariadne turns around again, she's ripping open an antiseptic patch. She set a few more on the counter with the extra syringes. "If you'd please roll up your sleeve," she says with a smile, "I'll clean the injection site for you, and then you can administer the shot."

My hand moves automatically to do as she says.

I will make it stop. I struggle until beads of sweat trickle down my forehead, until I feel like I'm going to explode from trying so hard.

The struggle lasts only a second in reality. My hand rolls up my left sleeve, exposing my bare shoulder. Ariadne presses the cool patch to my skin and wipes the area gently.

Lieutenant Dean has his hand on the weapon in his holster, just in case. Charlie's body is tense as he watches me out of the corner of my eye, his gaze so hard and focused, I'm sure he's looking right through my skin. He's looking at the girl who wants to scream at him and tear his skin open with her fingernails and use the syringe in her hand to make him listen to her for once, and take his own life if she says.

*You can't make me do this. I won't let you.*

The slight twitch of his lip tells me he heard me, or saw the words in my face. But all he does is smile, that smile that says it doesn't matter how hard I struggle; he will always win.

Ariadne takes a step back. "All finished."

"Go ahead, Clementine," Charlie says.

*I won't.*

My fingers rip the syringe's plastic open and hand the wrapper to Ariadne. They pull the needle covering off next, and hand it to her as well. She tosses both articles in the trash.

My hand guides the syringe to my shoulder.

I don't know how to stop it. I don't know how to make the other half of me listen.

There's still time. In twenty-four hours, I'll have to give myself another injection again. Maybe I'll have figured out how to regain control by then.

But I don't know where I'll be in twenty-four hours. I don't know what the war mission will make me do, or turn me into.

My hand guides the needle closer to my skin. My hand is visibly shaking. That must mean I'm doing something right; I'm starting to break free of this. I will every fiber of my body to make my hand stop moving, to break free all the way.

It doesn't work. The needle pricks my skin, and my thumb presses down on the plunger. The silver liquid flows into my body. I lost again; the clock has restarted.

Out of the corner of my eye, Lieutenant Dean takes his hand off the weapon in his holster.

"Very good," Charlie says, almost relieved.

If he's relieved, that means he saw me fighting the injection; he saw me close to escaping from my cage. For at least a moment, he thought I would win.

"Let's head to the flight port," he says. "You have a ship to board."

Ariadne hands me the supply of extra syringes and antiseptic patches. She waves at me on our way out, and my lips move on their own to offer her a smile in return.

I have twenty-four hours until my next injection. Twenty-four hours to figure out a way to stop this from happening again.

✳

Two officials haul a metal crate up the ramp of the hovercraft. The crate has the word EXPLOSIVES on its side.

I walk past the ramp with Commander Charlie and Lieutenant Dean to meet Lieutenant Sam and Beechy, who stand beside an X-wing fighter jet. We're taking six X-wings on the mission, along with the hovercraft. Mechanics are still loading fuel into two of the jets through hoses. Most of the pilots are already in the cockpits going through the preflight checklist, and the last few are climbing up the ladders.

Skylar freezes at the top of one of the ladders, her cheeks paling at the sight of me with Charlie.

I nearly falter in my step. *What's she doing here?*

I thought Charlie still had her locked in a cell. I didn't think he trusted her enough to send her with us on this mission.

I don't want her coming. I will never trust her again.

Skylar sets her jaw, climbs up into her seat, and jams her helmet over her head.

Lieutenant Dean dismisses himself before we reach Sam, saying he'd better help with the cargo. He must be coming on the mission too, then.

When we reach Sam, he's telling Beechy to make sure all the explosives are on board the hovercraft.

"The men just put the last crate inside," Beechy says.

"Double check. If any are missing when we need them later, the blame will fall on you."

"Of course, sir." Beechy salutes him and Charlie before hurrying away, up the ship's ramp.

Sam smiles coolly, clearly enjoying his authority over Beechy. The smile falters a little when he sees me, though. I don't think he likes me standing so close to Charlie.

"Commander, sir, how can I help you?" Sam says.

"Did you secure Cadet Malcolm successfully?" Charlie asks. "I've received no updates."

"Yes, we have him in custody. He's in the Crust cell block. My men will get him to talk, and I'll have him transferred here once he does, as soon as I return from the mission. Your orders were to shoot the other Crust fugitives if they don't surrender, correct?"

The deepest pit of my stomach lurches.

"That's correct," Charlie says. "Good, I'm glad to hear it."

Sam can't shoot them. I won't let him.

"What's the mission status?"

"We're double-checking that all the equipment has been loaded," Sam says. "We're set to leave in T-minus fifteen minutes."

"Good," Charlie says. "I put this mission in your hands, and I expect you to accomplish it without a hitch."

"I assure you I will, sir."

Charlie purses his lips slightly. "Get to work, then."

"Yes, sir," Sam says, but I swear he mutters something under his breath as he struts away.

Charlie turns to me. His eyes sweep over my figure. "We need to get you a gun. You won't be much help on the mission with an empty holster. Follow me."

My feet lead me after him to the bottom of the hovercraft ramp. Lieutenant Dean comes down the ramp, ducking his head under the low doorway.

"Lieutenant," Charlie says.

"Yes, sir?" says Dean.

"Are there any coppers on board?"

"I believe so."

"Retrieve one for me, please."

Dean turns around and disappears inside the ship. I wonder why Charlie didn't let me walk up the ramp and get the gun myself.

When Dean returns, he hands the copper to Charlie. "Anything else?"

"That'll be all."

A slight crease touches Dean's forehead. But he nods and heads back up the ramp.

Charlie weighs the copper in his palm, checking the mechanics. This model has a small scope that he opens and closes.

"This should do nicely," he says, and hands the gun to me. "I'd like you to test it out first, though."

I grip the copper, unsure what he means. He keeps glancing at the door we walked through to enter the port. He's been doing that for some time, but it didn't strike me as odd until now.

"Is there a target nearby?" Other Me asks.

"Yes, there is," he says, relaxing, his eyes still on the doorway.

I look over there again. Two guards are leading in a prisoner. A young man who limps with every step.

Logan.

"What's he doing here?"

Logan's eyes land on me as he draws closer. There's something urgent in them, something fearful.

"I told Logan he was going to be able to see you off," Charlie says. "But I brought him here for a different reason."

"Why?" my lips ask of their own accord. I'm not sure I want to know the answer.

Leaning in, Charlie brings his mouth close to my ear. "To remind you that no matter what you may think, I'm still in control," he says softly. "And I always will be."

Fear is a serpent twisting inside me, wrapping around my lungs. Charlie steps away from me, and his eyes land on mine, dark and cruel. "Logan is your target. Shoot him in the leg."

It takes too long for his order to sink in.

The world turns into slow motion. Panic splinters through me, but my feet take two steps forward; my hands lift the copper and find their target; my fingers settle on the trigger. I can't put the gun down.

I cry out, but the sound is lost inside me.

A look of understanding—and terror—crosses Logan's face. He opens his mouth, but my finger squeezes the trigger and a laser flies before he can speak. It doesn't miss my target.

*No no no no no no no no*

Logan falls forward with a cry, his face contorting with pain. Blood gushes from his left leg, from the gash on his thigh where the laser seared his skin.

I didn't. I can't have.

I shot him.

I want to scream. I want to say, *It wasn't me, not really,* and *Please forgive me.*

Charlie steps around me until he's facing me, and my gun is almost pointed at him. I can't lower my hands; they're immobile. Even Other Me can't believe this.

"It's all right," Charlie says, and sets his hands on my wrists and gently lowers them.

I want to knock his hands away. I want to put the gun back up and shoot him. But my hands won't listen.

Charlie turns around, so he's no longer blocking Logan from view. Logan is on his side on the ground, unable to move. The tears are visible in his eyes, but he's blinking fast to stop them.

I hit his bad leg, at least. I could've crippled his good leg, but I didn't and that's something. But it's not enough.

"Take him to the health ward," Charlie says to the guards.

The guards heave Logan to his feet. He yells in agony. His eyes meet mine, and there is no pity in them, no understanding. There is only hurt.

"How could you?" he asks.

His words rip my chest open. My heart feels like it's going to bleed out.

I don't know how I'll ever forgive myself for this.

Something wet trickles down my cheek. I must be crying. I've never cried under the serum before.

I hesitate, unsure what this means. I decide to try something. Focusing hard, I send the signal to my hands to ball into fists.

They *listen*.

Whatever broke inside me must've been big enough to break the part of me controlled by the serum too. Am I free?

Charlie turns back to me. He sees my teary-eyed face and sighs, disappointed. "Clementine, listen to me."

He reaches out and takes my hand in his, like he's my friend. He is not my friend; he will never be.

I tell my hand to pull away from his. I wrench as hard as I can. My hand pulls away a little, but not enough. I'm still partially under the serum's control.

"This demonstration was to help you understand: The more you fight the serum, the more you will lose," Charlie says. "I hope you will be smart enough to spare yourself this hurt. I trust you will make sure to readminister your injection when a new dosage is required, every single time. I trust you won't fight it, or do anything to jeopardize this mission."

How can he expect me to do any of this? I will never stop fighting.

"If you slip up," Charlie says, softer, "I will have no choice. I will kill Logan. And you will live with the guilt for the rest of your life."

I feel a knife in my chest again. Deep, twisting my insides.

I shake my head, but it hardly shakes at all.

"You can't," I only manage to make the words come out in a whisper. I want to scream them.

Charlie can. And he will.

# 29

Sam makes the final boarding call. Charlie lets go of my hand. The imprint of his fingers leaves a raw ache like a burn in my skin. I don't want to leave yet—I won't leave until Charlie takes back what he said. But my body moves without my permission. I slip my gun into its holster, turn, and walk up the ramp into the hovercraft.

I feel numb. This can't have happened, not really. I must be dreaming.

But Logan's blood spilled on the floor, and the guards took him away. I didn't dream that.

Tremors run beneath my feet as the door closes behind me. The hovercraft's engine has come to life. The noise it makes—a loud *whir-churn-whir*—grinds in my right ear. My left ear is starting to heal and hear some things again, but it still feels plugged up.

This ship is a bigger model than the kind I've set foot on before, with a large cargo space and even a small kitchen and a medical bay. Lieutenant Dean gives me a strange, almost sorry look as he points me up a short staircase. He must've seen what happened out in the port. I didn't know he was capable of feeling sorry for me, though. I'm sure it's an act, though I can't think of a reason why he'd pretend a thing like that. It seems a waste of time.

Up the stairs, I move through a sliding door into the main room. The passenger seats are arranged around circular metal tables, some with two seats, others with four. Cabinets and instrument panels line the empty space between them on the walls.

This is a ship meant for a military mission that could take more than one day.

My feet take me to a seat at an empty two-person table near the cockpit. There's no door to separate me from Beechy and the male copilot.

Before, knowing Beechy was here would've made me feel safer. But he isn't himself. He's barely looked at me since I first saw him back in the Core.

He is the only other person in this squadron who would side with the rebels, if he snapped out of his submission. But I don't know how much the serum is affecting him. He could be aware like me, or he could be so far gone he has no idea anything we're doing is wrong.

I want to snap him out of it. I don't want to have to figure all this out on my own.

Sam walks through the door at the back of the ship and makes for the cockpit. He must've been down in the cargo bay.

"Let's get out of here," he says.

I pull my safety strap on and snap the buckle into place. My seat jolts as Beechy lifts us off the ground. We rise higher and higher, until the people and the other ships seem small below us through the cockpit window. Lights glow on the X-shaped wings of the six fighter jets, which rise slowly to follow us. Beechy turns our ship around, 180 degrees, to face the nearest exit tunnel.

Charlie stands on the ground below. He doesn't seem scary or powerful when he looks so small, but I know better.

A mechanic walks near him with a rag in hand, and kneels to wipe a dark spot on the floor. Only once we've left the port and we're soaring through the exit tunnel do I realize he was wiping blood. Logan's blood, from when he fell after I squeezed the trigger.

I hope Logan is already in the sick bay and the nurses are fixing his leg. If he loses too much blood, or if he can't walk because of me, the guilt will consume me and make it impossible for me to go on.

Charlie might've told me to shoot him, but my hands squeezed the trigger, and no one else's.

Even the part of me affected by the serum should've known better. It should've known how important he is, how much I need him to be okay. His safety is the reason I took the serum in the first place.

Through the cockpit window, dots of light appear on the walls as we speed up inside the Pipeline. The lights streak by, reminding me of the last time I was flying in this direction, toward the mountains on the Surface. Charlie's ships were chasing me. This time, they're escorting me into battle. My enemies are going to help me capture my friends, and I can't do anything to stop them.

Charlie tricked me. He knew I would fight him again and he would need some way to stop me. I made the mistake of letting him know how much Logan means to me back in Karum, and again the other day.

Logan is my greatest weakness. Charlie will keep using him

against me, no matter what I do. He has all the cards in this game; I have nothing.

I don't want to stop fighting, but I think I have to. I have to re-administer the serum when the time comes. I have to remain mindless and follow orders. There's no other choice. Beechy is as trapped as I am; Skylar has abandoned me; the rebels will soon be captured. No one can help me.

I wish Charlie had made me shoot myself. Then I would be far away from this place, and I wouldn't feel so much guilt.

⁕

The red sky is turning gray when we reach the Surface. Dark clouds drift above the peaks. In the spaces between them, there are already a few stars visible in the heavens.

If Marden's fleet is really coming, it's out there somewhere, hopefully not far away. There's no way I can stop it, or stop Charlie from detonating the Strykers when the fleet arrives. I'd rather this would all end quickly.

If I'm lucky, the fleet will prove stronger than Charlie's weapons, and the Mardenites will wipe out our race. They will torture Charlie for keeping their god in a cage, and then they will kill him. I'm happy to die as long as he dies with me. I'm ready for it.

"Sir, where do you want us to land?" Beechy asks in the cockpit.

"Show me where the facility is, again," Sam says, moving around the pilot's chair to see the map on the dashboard. He went below to the cargo bay earlier and returned in full armor, minus his helmet.

"We're here," Beechy says, pointing to one spot on the map. "And the headquarters are right there."

I hope Sam makes a mistake and puts us down somewhere

Sandy and the others will be able to spot us on their radar. Then they'll know we're coming, and they can find somewhere to hide. Somewhere we won't be able to find them.

They can escape, even if I can't.

"Put us down there," Sam says, tapping a spot on the map. "Give the fighter pilots the coordinates."

The copilot relays the instructions into his ear-comm.

Sam turns around and addresses everyone. Seven officials fill the other passenger seats, most talking or playing cards. Lieutenant Dean has been in the cargo bay the whole flight, but the door to the staircase slides open and he appears.

"Attention, everyone," Sam says, and the talking quiets down. "We'll be making our descent in just a few minutes, landing within a mile of the rebel headquarters. You all need to be wearing safety gear and ear-comms before we touch down. There's armor in the lower deck cabinets, as well as safety suits and oxygen tanks. Any questions?"

There's silence around the ship.

"Good. Get moving."

The officials unbuckle and make for the door. As I move to follow them, a hand closes around my wrist.

"Stop," Sam says, and my feet freeze.

I want to keep walking—I want to get away from him, but I'm not supposed to fight. If I fight Sam, Sam will tell Charlie and Charlie will kill Logan.

"Turn around," Sam says.

Slowly, I turn to face him. His eyes pierce mine, cold and demanding.

"You stole something from me," he says, grabbing me by the collar of my shirt.

I'm not sure I could struggle against him, even if I wanted to. The serum is still halfway in control of me, and that means Sam is in control as always.

"What?" I ask.

"I said you stole something."

Beechy and the copilot are here, so we aren't completely alone. But Beechy is subdued, and the copilot wouldn't care if Sam did anything. I don't know how long it will take for the other officials to come back.

"What did I steal?" I ask.

"You stole my rank," he says, spitting the words like venom.

"I'm not a lieutenant."

"Not yet. But I overheard Commander Charlie and Colonel Parker talking. They're giving you rank as soon as we get back from the mission, assuming all goes well. They think you have 'big ideas' that can help them fight the Mardenites, if the first maneuver doesn't work. But I don't believe it. And I won't stand for it. You think you can cooperate all of a sudden, after everything you did, and earn everything I have—everything I've spent *years* working for?"

He needs to understand: I don't want what he has. I don't want any of it.

But all the serum will let me say is, "I'm loyal to Commander Charlie. I always will be."

Sam lets out a hard laugh. "You think I can't see right through you? You know, I should've killed you in Crust when I had a chance. I could've said it was a mistake—Charlie would've believed me. He would've thanked me for sparing him of having to deal with you and your lies."

"I'm not lying. I'm loyal to him—"

"Save it. I don't even care if it's true." A smirk tugs at his lips. "I'm going to make it a lie."

I stare at him, unsure what he's saying, almost afraid to ask. "How?"

Sam smiles wider. In a calm voice, he says, "When we return from this mission, I'm going to tell Charlie you switched sides and fought against us. I'm telling him you tried to kill me, but thankfully your aim wasn't very good. If he's kind, he'll give me permission to put a bullet through your head, instead of leaving you to rot in a cell while he and I kill your friends one by one."

I open my mouth to beg him not to do this, but no words come out.

Sam's smiles turns grim. "Of course, there's no guarantee you won't get shot tonight. Fatalities do happen in the field."

Sam might kill me tonight. Even if he doesn't, what he tells Charlie will be enough to make me lose Logan, which is worse than my own death.

It doesn't matter if I'm still one of the mindless. It doesn't matter if I follow every single one of Sam's orders. He is determined to make me lose everything.

The door slides open behind me, and he releases my shirt.

"Stop dawdling," he snaps. "Go get changed."

I manage to make my eyes narrow at him before I turn away. It almost feels like a victory—a small one, but not enough.

My feet carry me down the steps into the cargo bay, to a storage room full of cabinets. The armor inside is much too big for me, and the safety suits have sleeves too long. It doesn't matter; I won't be safe no matter what I wear.

As I pull on the suit and helmet and attach a small comm to my ear, rage builds inside me, growing stronger and stronger.

I won't let Sam do this. I won't let him kill me or take Logan away.

The only way to prevent both is to take Sam and his squadron down. It's dangerous and likely impossible, but I have nothing left to lose.

If I helped the rebels win, Sam wouldn't be able to talk. The rebels could return with me to the Core, and I could pretend to still be subdued. We could reach Charlie and kill him before he pulls the plug on Logan. It would be a shot in the dark every step of the way. Everything could fall apart, but it's the only plan I have—one that doesn't involve giving up.

As I move back up the stairs to the second level, the ship jolts, sending me back into the railing. A second jolt sends me forward, but I grab the rail to keep from falling.

The roar of the engine beneath my feet dulls to a low hum. We must've landed. A mile away from the facility, as Sam said.

His voice comes muffled through the door in front of me: "Everyone, head downstairs to retrieve weapons and unload explosives. We'll depart on the X-wings for the rebel base shortly."

Boots clunk as the officials head for the staircase where I'm standing. I turn and walk down the steps. The door at the back of the ship opens, showing me windblown trees in the clearing where we landed. The mountain valley near the river. I've been here before.

Around me, officials move to transport explosives into the underside compartments of two of the X-wings. Sam barks at me to help Lieutenant Dean carry one of the crates, so I do. It makes no sense to ignore his orders yet, not until the mission is under way and he's too distracted to notice.

But how can I fight his orders? The serum is still halfway in

control. Some steps I take feel like my own, but most feel like someone else is still pulling the strings. I need to fight harder.

The serum is powerful, but it's not invincible. It wouldn't have
to be readministered, otherwise. Charlie wouldn't have threatened
me with Logan's life to keep me from fighting it.

I'll find the loophole. I'll break free completely.

I hope it won't be too late.

# 30

Fierce wind rips at my safety suit as I settle into the third seat in the X-wing. The copper in my holster presses against my thigh.

The other jets are firing up their engines, all around the clearing. The last of the sun's light has slid behind the mountains, and the stars are bright overhead. Sam went over the mission plan, and he'll give the order for us to depart any second now.

My heart's beating so fast, I'm sure it's going to punch its way out of my chest. It might break free before I do.

"Buckle in," Skylar says to me in a clipped voice from the pilot seat. There's another pilot sitting in between us, and Lieutenant Dean sits in the fourth seat, behind me. To keep an eye on me, I'm sure.

I do as Skylar says, but inside I shoot a glare at her back. I wish Sam had put me on another ship, preferably with Beechy, since at least I used to be able to trust him. Skylar isn't subdued—her eyes are clear as day and she's acting no differently than she did when she was tied up in a cell. But she's still helping Charlie. She's still going to blow up the rebel base and capture our friends.

I almost wish I'd shot her when I had the chance.

Tremors run underneath my seat as the jet cover lowers overhead. Though it's made of glass and I can still see the trees and the other ships when it's all the way down, I feel like I'm inside another cage I can't escape. I feel like I might suffocate.

Sam's voice comes through my ear-comm: "Pilots, you're cleared for takeoff."

The X-wing he boarded sits at the other end of the clearing. Beechy is on his ship.

Beechy's supposed to reach the rebel security hub with the old comm codes, and weave some story to make Sandy and the others think we stole these ships and broke out of the lower sectors, and we're coming home. But even if the codes don't work or the rebels don't believe us, we can still break through the security barriers and get inside. Sam made sure we have multiple backup plans.

I'm going to have a hard time screwing up this mission, even if I can regain complete control of my actions.

"Skylar, lead Cameron and Landers to the northern entrance," Sam says. "Mitchell and Dallas, follow me to the entrance on the other side of the mountain. Let's get this done."

"Taking the bird out, sir," Skylar says.

I grip the arms of my seat as she pulls the control yoke back. We lift into the air, rising steadily until we're above the dark, twisted trees. Their branches and leaves blow everywhere in the wind, thrashing even more as the other X-wings rise to follow us. Two of them trail behind us, speeding toward the entrance ahead at the base of the mountain, where the river weaves into a tunnel. Sam's ship and the other two accompanying his veer away from us, to make for the entrance on the other side of the mountain.

I need to practice. I need to fight the serum. But I'm in an enclosed space and Lieutenant Dean is right behind me. There isn't much I can do that won't give me away.

Something simple is best. My knuckles are turning white from my hands clutching the arms of my chair so hard. I focus all my will on loosening my grip. Sweat beads on the back of my neck from concentration.

It takes a good ten seconds. But I manage to peel my fingers away.

I relax. But that wasn't fast enough. In battle, I won't have ten seconds to force my fingers to let go of a trigger or make them pull it. I'll have less than one.

"Attempting to contact the rebels," Beechy says into my ear-comm.

Straight ahead is the hole at the base of the mountain. Skylar dips us lower as we fly into the tunnel.

If we're in range of the comm system, we've also popped up on the KIMO facility's radar screen. Six unidentified fighter jets.

If they're smart, the rebels won't wait to see if one of our pilots will make contact—they'll board their ships, as they've been trained to do. There are more of us than them; they'll have better luck shooting us down from their ships. And they have the facility's defenses on their side. As long as Beechy isn't able to contact them, as long as they don't open the security doors for us even if he does, they'll have time to prepare before we break in. They'll have a chance at holding us off.

We'll have a chance at beating Sam.

"The comm codes aren't working," Beechy says. "They must've been changed since we left."

One good thing so far.

"Sandy wasn't supposed to change them until she heard from us," Skylar says.

"Mal could've made contact with her and told her we were captured."

"It doesn't matter—Plan B is go," Sam says. "You two, get us through the security barriers. The rebels know we're here now. We need to get inside as soon as possible, before they take to their ships."

"They're grounded," Beechy says. "Their ships have hardly any fuel left. We lost most of it before we left on the mission."

*Vrux*. That's going to be a problem.

Skylar turns her head a little, enough for me to glimpse the smug smile on her face. "Yeah, you're welcome," she says.

She leaked our fuel supply, I remember. She blamed it on Buck, but it was her all along. Now Sandy and the others in the Alliance can't defend themselves with their ships. They can't even escape this place—at least, they won't get far.

All Skylar does is smile.

I push my hand toward the gun in my holster. My fingers fight me with every inch, until I give up.

I shouldn't shoot her, anyway. Lieutenant Dean has his eyes on my back. And she's our pilot; our ship would crash.

But I will not let her get away with being a traitor.

"The first security barrier is in sight," she says, easing off our thrusters. "Cameron, Landers, slow down. There's a trigger console in the wall. We're going to have to blast it to get the doors open."

"Sounds easy enough," Cameron or Landers says. "I'm an excellent shot."

"We need to find the console first. It's not exactly easy to spot."

The security door is just ahead. The cracked letters painted on the surface form the same words as they did the last time I saw them:

KIMO CORPORATION
EST. 30 RC
WE FIGHT TO JOURNEY HOME

The people who used to work in this facility believed Marden was our true home. They believed it was right for us to steal the planet back, even though we'd abandoned it for a new one. So, they helped the old leaders of Kiel build warships and send them off to the stars, to slaughter Marden's people or enslave them.

Our leaders are always enslaving others and making war. Why can't they be satisfied?

Why can't all of it *stop*?

"Harry, take the controls for a second," Skylar says.

"Copy that," Harry, her copilot, says.

Our ship sways to the left as he takes over flight control, and I tilt with it, banging into my armrest. A hand touches my shoulder to steady me, as Harry readjusts our position before the security doors.

Lieutenant Dean's hand. He lets go so fast, I might've imagined he touched me.

A target monitor slides down from the ceiling in front of Skylar as she preps the weapons system. She must not trust the other pilots to do the shooting.

"What does the console look like?" Cameron or Landers asks.

"It blends into the wall, that's the problem," Skylar says. "But it should be somewhere to the left of the doors. We need to hit it right on target. Blasting anywhere else could lead to the shots backfiring, or the whole tunnel collapsing, depending on what we hit."

"Look for an inscription of a moon on the wall," Beechy says. "It's small, but it's not invisible."

Skylar zooms in on the tunnel wall with the targeting system, skimming the smooth metal to the left of us, close to the security doors. I can't see details well from where I'm sitting, but Skylar must be able to.

"There it is," she says, and moves her thumbs over the firing controls. She locks the guns on their target.

I hope she'll miss. I hope she'll blow up this part of the tunnel by accident.

*Beep-beep-beep-beep-beep-beep-beep—*

Skylar presses the buttons three times in concession. Thin streams of blue laser fire exit our guns, blasting the hidden trigger. By the third hit, the console cover has blown away, and there's nothing left but smoke.

The security doors zip open, revealing the passageway beyond. Usually the inner tunnels are brighter, but all the lights are off.

Either the power cut out, or the rebels are trying to slow us down. I hope it's the latter; that would mean they're preparing for the attack.

"Lieutenant Sam, we're through the first door," Skylar says. "There's still one more before we reach the flight hangar."

"We've just reached the first barrier on this side," Sam says. "Go on ahead. We'll meet you there."

"Copy that."

We speed ahead through the tunnel, the other two X-wings alongside us and a few feet behind. The lights on our ship's wings help us see the way. Skylar knows these tunnels by heart, anyway; she and I flew through them multiple times on practice runs.

We used to be on the same side.

"Make sure your weapons are prepped," she says, off-comm. Harry and Dean also hear her, but it seems like she's primarily talking to me. She's giving me a direct order, thinking I won't be able to refuse.

My hand moves automatically to the copper in my holster. My palm wraps around the cool metal.

More sweat gathers on my neck as I struggle to keep from pulling the gun out. It feels like I'm stuck in an iron mold, slamming my fists against the walls until my knuckles bleed and bruise. But I barely dent the wall.

My palm wraps around the cool metal and slides my gun out of the holster.

*No, no, no.*

If I can't even refuse one simple order, how can I beat this? How can I ever be free again?

We're almost to the flight port. Skylar will break through the final barrier without much trouble. We will enter the port and engage with the rebels. If Sam or Skylar gives me the order to shoot any of them, I might not be able to stop myself.

But I have to be able to. I have to be able to defend myself, if Sam tries to shoot me, or leaves me behind to go down with the facility.

Maybe I should try something different; I should stop fighting. When I regained some of my control after I shot Logan, it was because I had relinquished all of it. The guilt was ripping me apart; I was at my weakest.

And when I first showed signs of fighting my submission to

Charlie, we were in the cell with Skylar. I made the decision to shoot her and then managed to stop, but not because I was struggling, either. Because I'd stopped fighting, and my true emotions were leaking out into my actions.

I don't want to let my hands do as they please. I might end up hurting someone as badly as I hurt Logan, and the guilt will be a hundred times worse if I don't even try to stop myself.

But maybe it will be enough to set me free.

# 31

We reach the final set of security doors. Skylar finds the hidden trigger faster this time. She shoots twice and blasts the console apart.

When the doors zip open to reveal the flight port a short ways ahead, I'm not sure what I expect. I hope we'll find silence. I hope we'll find the place deserted, and realize the rebels moved somewhere else. Somewhere safer, where we won't be able to find them.

Instead, lasers come flying at our ship—streaks of red and blue and green that zap against our hull. They don't come from hand-held guns; they come from Davara jets. There are three in the air with rebel pilots inside, shooting at us, blocking the entrance to the flight port. It seems they have enough fuel left for this, thank the stars.

But I'm on board one of the ships they're trying to shoot down.

A fierce tremor runs through our ship as another laser hits our wing, and a small cry escapes my mouth. Skylar veers us to the right, but there isn't far to go. The tunnel is barely wide enough for all three X-wings to hover side by side. And we can't stay in one place if we're going to avoid the gunfire.

Harry sends our own stream of fire at the closest jet, but the jet is smaller and manages to jump aside.

"Sam, we're inside," Skylar says. "The rebels are shooting from the air. What are your orders?"

"Open fire," Sam says in my ear. "Get their ships down, but be careful. Commander Charlie doesn't care if we lose some of the rebels in the fight, but he wants his daughter alive."

Skylar drops us down to avoid another laser. "I don't think she's on any of these ships. But copy that. Cameron, Landers, let's push them back."

We send a barrage of fire at the ships, no longer trying to evade their attack. Our laser power is much stronger than what the rebels have, I can tell as soon as we begin. The Davara jets are powerful, but they're older models, and they won't hold up as well as ours.

*No, no, no, stop shooting,* I beg the pilots. The rebels are going to lose.

If they lose, I'm dead, and so is Logan.

A direct hit to one of the hulls sends the whole jet spinning out of control. The other two jump far back to get out of the way, leaving an opening for Skylar to fly our X-wing into the hangar.

We hit the spinning one twice more, and it crashes into a grounded flight pod. My hand hurts from clutching the barrel of my gun in panic.

Where are the other rebels? I counted three pilots in the Davaras. I know we left more than three people in the compound.

Cameron and Landers are still blasting the other two jets. Both hulls are smoking from the damage. They won't be in the air much longer.

Skylar sets us down in a clear space in the hangar, near the crashed Davara. Flames leap up from the rubble.

I hope whoever's inside is still alive. I don't know who it is—I couldn't identify the faces of any of the pilots.

"We've landed," Skylar says over comm.

Cameron and Landers are setting their ships down beside the rebel jets.

"Good," Sam says. "We're almost there."

The cover of our X-wing lifts open. Skylar, Harry, and Lieutenant Dean climb out with their guns in hand. I don't want to follow them, but I do.

I'm still gripping my copper. I might have to use it. I don't know if I should fight my orders, or if I should stick with my decision not to. I don't know which one will help me beat Sam.

I have to beat him. Everything I've fought for will be for nothing, otherwise.

The *pew pew* of laser fire reaches my ears from where Cameron and Landers put their ships down. They must be shooting the Davara pilots, or the pilots must be shooting them.

To our right, the cover of the crashed jet opens. The pilot inside staggers out, coughing and slapping the flames away.

Skylar notices and turns to him with her gun raised.

He reaches the ground, struggling to keep his footing, and removes his helmet. His shirt has a hole in his shoulder, exposing burned red skin. When he lifts his head, his eyes shoot daggers at Skylar.

She smiles at him. "Hello, Buck."

"You traitor," he yells in a hoarse voice. "I should've known you'd run straight back to Charlie, soon as you got outta this place. Soon as you realized we were gonna lose."

"How many more of you are in the facility?" she asks, ignoring him.

"More than you think. We knew you lot would show up here soon enough. We were ready for you."

I have a strong feeling he's lying.

"We were told to capture you all," Skylar says, "and bring you back to Commander Charlie for him to determine if you could be of any use to him. But he also said if you struggle too much, there's no point in bringing you back."

"Shoot me, go ahead," Buck says.

She takes two steps forward and steadies her aim at his head. Her jaw is firm; her lips are pressed together. But there's slight hesitance in her eyes.

*BOOM!*

Buck's jet explodes—the engine must've caught fire. I duck with a cry, covering my head to avoid the shrapnel.

When the dust clears, I look up. Skylar's on the ground, knocked back by the force of the explosion. Harry's helping her up. She's covered with dust, but I don't think she's badly hurt.

A strangled cry comes from behind her. As Harry helps her to her feet, I notice Buck on the ground, knocked onto his stomach from the force of the explosion. He's missing a part of his left leg, below his knee. There's a huge chunk of metal in his thigh.

Skylar is fine. Harry and Dean are too.

Buck is on the ground, knocked onto his stomach from the force of the explosion. There's a huge chunk of metal in his leg, and probably other, smaller bits in the rest of his body. He's missing a part of his left leg, below his knee. There's a huge chunk of metal in his thigh. His blood leaks onto the floor, among the ashes and debris from the explosion.

The roar of X-wing engines fills the hangar. The ships with Sam and Beechy are here.

Flames from the destroyed fighter jet lick at Buck's bloody, mangled legs. He's going to catch fire. He claws at the floor like he's trying to heave himself away from the wreckage, but it does no good.

"Help me!" The words erupt from his mouth, full of torment. "Please!"

I need to force my feet to move. Someone needs to help him, and none of the others will. Dean's staring at Buck with terror in his eyes, like he's never seen a person injured in an explosion before.

*Move, move, move!* I urge my body.

I take a slow step forward. Then another. The effort makes my forehead sweat. I'm not going to reach Buck fast enough. Sam's ship and the others are landing—someone's going to stop me.

Out of the corner of my eye, a laser beam flies at Harry from behind one of the nearby flight pods. He doesn't notice until it's too late. He stumbles with a yell, his hand moving to where the laser struck his side.

Skylar and Dean turn toward where the fire came from, raising their guns. There must be more rebels hiding behind the flight pods. I need to make sure they realize who I am and know I'm on their side, not Sam's. But first I need to save Buck. If I could pull him out of the way of the fire and bind the stump of his leg, I might be able to keep him from bleeding to death.

He's seven feet away now . . . six . . . five . . .

"Clem, duck!" Skylar shouts.

I duck automatically. A laser whizzes over my head.

Another nearly hits Dean. The rebels step out from behind the pods, all of them firing at us. I turn to face them, raising my gun against my will. Five rebels, I count. Darren, the pilot from Cady's recon mission; Fiona, my roommate; Uma, the nurse who fixed my tattoo; a male Unstable I can't remember the name of; and Sandy.

They don't recognize me, or if they do they don't care about hurting me. I move my feet so their fire won't hit me.

My arm finds an easy shot. I aim at Fiona's chest.

*No—no—no—no—no—*

My fingers squeeze the trigger, but I manage to move my arm away at the last second. The laser skims the air beside her waist. Thank the stars.

Fiona freezes, her gun still in the air, gaping at me. She must've realized who I am.

A laser flies past me, from somewhere behind me. The other officials have climbed out of their ships, armed and ready to fight.

The rebels scurry behind their pods to take cover. Skylar aims one last shot at Darren as he runs, but misses.

Sam's voice arises, magnified through his helmet. "There's no point in hiding. You're all outnumbered."

He steps into view to the right of me. Beechy stops on my left side, and the rest of the officials move to gather around us.

Cameron and Landers have one rebel in their custody, bound and gagged—a woman I recognize from Karum, who has a bloody cut on her forehead. They must've killed the pilot from the other rebel ship.

I suddenly remember—Buck. He's on the other side of Beechy, farther away from me, since I moved while I was shooting. Buck has stopping struggling. He's lying still on the ground while the flames slowly burn through his pants.

I'm too late.

"Lieutenant Dean, go with Cadets Marshall and Crowley and unload the explosives," Sam says. "Stack them around the perimeter of the hangar. The rest of you, keep your guns raised."

"Yes, sir." Dean and the other two move to follow his orders.

Sam clicks the safety of his weapon off and on, focusing his eyes on the flight pods. The rebels haven't stepped out from behind them again; they must know they can't defeat us all.

When Sam speaks, there's amusement in his voice. "Sandy, did you know Clementine and Skylar are here, as well as your husband? Beechy's become rather more obedient than I'm guessing he was the last time you saw him. Funny how a prick of a needle can change someone."

He's wrong; it doesn't change us, not completely. I'm still here, underneath this body that will hardly listen to me, that makes it impossible for me to save my friends.

There's silence in the hangar, save the dull crackle of the flames consuming Buck's jet.

Sam gives a silent signal, and eight of his officials head to the left and right sides of the hangar, where Dean and Crowley and Marshall are stacking the explosives. The eight officials slip around the pods until they're out of sight.

A laser flashes between some of the pods, coming from where the officials must be standing, followed by several more. A loud cry tells me a rebel has been wounded. A man—either Darren or the man from Karum.

Three of the officials reach the doors at the far side of the hangar.

Two of them push through the doors into the main corridor of the facility, to make sure the other rooms are empty. The third man remains standing in front of the doors, his gun cocked and ready.

We have my friends surrounded.

"We didn't come here to harm you or anyone in this facility," Sam says, taking another step forward.

Yes, you did, you liar.

"We came because you're in danger," Sam says. "I don't know if you're aware, but there's a fleet of ships from the distant planet Marden headed our way. They'll be here within a day or two. Commander Charlie has called for the transfer of all his citizens belowground to ensure their safety."

Not all his citizens. No one in the work camps will be saved; they'll be slaughtered.

Liar, liar, liar.

"All I need is for you to come quietly," Sam says, "and you can join your friends in the comforts of the Core."

More silence.

I want to shoot Sam. I can make my hands lift my gun, I'm sure of it, but I don't know if I can do it fast enough. Someone will see and shoot me first.

"Beechy, I'm telling the truth, aren't I?" Sam asks.

"He's telling the truth," Beechy says, his empty eyes narrowed slightly. "Sandy, you need to come with us. It's not safe for you here anymore."

There's a long stretch of silence.

Sandy steps out from her hiding spot, letting her gun clatter to the ground. She places both hands over her belly, as if two more inches of skin will keep her child safe, should a bullet fly her way.

She looks from Beechy to me, searching our faces for something—a sign that we're only pretending to be subdued.

*I'm fighting it,* I want to tell her. *I'm trying.*

The stoniness in her gaze tells me she doesn't want to give up. But she has no other choice, if she wants to stay alive. Using the Davara jets to shoot us down was her best plan, and that failed.

"You have us, Sam," she says. "Take us away from here, if that's what my father wants."

The other rebels slowly step out from where they're hiding. Fiona, Uma, and Darren, who leans on the man from Karum. Darren was shot in the leg. He grits his teeth in pain, but his eyes are angry.

They all drop their weapons, surrendering.

Officials move forward to pick them up. I can't see Sam's mouth under his helmet, but I'm sure he looks smug.

"Beechy, help your wife into one of the ships," he says.

Beechy slips his gun into his holster and walks forward. Sandy's cool exterior cracks as he nears her, as she takes in the fogginess in his eyes.

"Oh, Beechy," she whispers.

Out of the corner of my eye, I notice the slightest movement to the right of our group. Buck is stirring on the floor. The flames are eating at his legs, but he is still alive—barely.

His hand slips into his holster.

"It's going to be okay," Beechy says, moving behind Sandy to grasp her shoulders.

She blinks tears out of her eyes, but lets him push her ahead of him toward one of the X-wings. They pass in front of Skylar, who has shifted and is standing to the right of Sam.

Buck removes his gun and aims at Skylar, his jaw twitching in anger, his bloodshot eyes barely focusing.

I realize what's going to happen too late.

I open my mouth to yell, "Buck, no!"

But he's already squeezed the trigger. A gunshot rings out.

# 32

Time seems to slow down to an infinite moment.

Sandy, not Skylar, stumbles. Her eyes widen in shock.

She lifts the hand covering her stomach, and blood seeps through her fingers.

"No!" Beechy yells.

His wife's legs give out, but he catches hold of her. He cradles her in his arms.

"No, no, no," he says over and over, his voice breaking more with every word.

Skylar pulls her gun out and moves around the two of them to get a clear shot at Buck's head. Her hand doesn't falter this time. Buck's body twitches and falls still.

My ears ring as if Beechy is still screaming, but I'm pretty sure it's all in my head. Rage fills my body, streaming through my veins.

Skylar should've been hit, not Sandy. She's the one who betrayed us. I should've shot her back in the Core, when I had the chance.

Then Buck wouldn't have tried to hurt her, and Sandy wouldn't be lying in Beechy's arms bleeding out her stomach.

Too many of my friends have been hurt right in front of me, whether by my hands or someone else's.

Enough.

Enough.

*Enough.*

"She needs a doctor!" Beechy says, his voice husky with worry.

"I can help," Uma says, hurrying forward. But a guard grabs her arm to stop her.

"Get Sandy on a ship," Sam says, not even looking at Uma. "There's a medic back at the hovercraft. He can stabilize her until we get her to the Core."

"She's not going to the Core," Beechy says. "We have a medical bay here."

Sam marches over to him, lifting his gun. "I said put her on a ship. That's an *order.*"

I'm still gripping my own gun. I can still use it.

Sam's back is to me, protected by armor. But there's a weak place where his helmet attaches to the neckpiece of his uniform. I have the perfect shot.

"I'm not obeying your orders anymore," Beechy says.

*Now—now—do it now.*

"You will obey or I will shoot you," Sam says, venom in his voice.

Fear makes my palms sweaty. The fear that has weakened me every time I've been about to shoot someone, making me pull the trigger when I didn't want to hurt anyone, or holding me back when I needed to protect myself.

I shove the fear aside and let my anger against Skylar and Sam and Charlie and everyone who has ever hurt me or made me hurt someone else consume me instead.

I won't let anyone control me any longer. I am the only one who can decide what my hands will do.

"You won't shoot me," Beechy says. "Commander Charlie told you to return my wife and me safely to the Core, and you won't disobey a direct order. You do everything your commander tells you without questioning, and that makes you a bad leader."

Sam cocks his gun, letting out a growl of frustration. "You're wrong."

His back is to me, and he is distracted. I have to do it now.

My feet move toward Sam. I lift my gun. I squeeze the trigger.

Something hits my arm and knocks off my aim. A laser—one of the officials shot me.

The pain spreads like heat through my arm, but I ignore it as best I can. I will not let anything stop me from killing Sam.

I fix my aim and squeeze the trigger again.

The yell that comes from Sam tells me I hit him. I don't know where.

Another laser flies at me, forcing me to duck. I shield my head, wincing as I remember my arm was shot.

Sam staggers across the way. My laser seared the spot above his right boot, on the back of his leg. Not a killing shot, but better than nothing.

Relief floods through me, bubbling up into laughter. I controlled my hands. I shot him.

Beechy lets go of Sandy. He grabs Sam's arm and twists the gun out of his grip.

He is free of the serum, at last.

And so am I.

The nearest official comes at me, to secure me and take my weapon. I put myself back in the training room with Colonel Parker and remember what he taught me during our sparring lesson: *Set high, strike low.*

I switch my gun to my uninjured left hand and aim at the official's neck, as if I'm going to strike him there. He reaches for my arm, but I cut low at the last second and aim the copper at his abdomen, squeezing the trigger.

The laser doesn't penetrate his armor, but it hits him hard enough to knock the breath out of him, giving me the moment I need to fire another shot at the weaker spot between his helmet and uniform. That one draws blood. He staggers into me.

A laser skims past my left ear. The other officials are shooting at me.

I grab the first official's body and push him in front of me, using him as a shield. But I'm surrounded. I can't possibly shoot all Sam's men, or avoid their gunfire.

*This is it. I'm done for.*

*BOOM!*

A chunk of the wall to my right explodes. The door to the locker room turns to shards that fly everywhere, coating the air with dust and debris.

I duck and let go of the official. This can't be happening. The explosives should not be going off yet. Someone was supposed to set their timers so Sam and his crew would've already cleared the hangar.

Either the packages are more unstable than he expected, or someone disobeyed his orders and set the timers early. Someone who either wanted to give us rebels a chance to escape, or make sure all of us went down with the hangar.

"Abort the mission!" Sam yells.

Through the dust and the dizziness from the pain in my arm, I see him limping away from Beechy.

"Get to your ships!"

He's afraid the hangar will blow to smithereens, killing him and all his men.

No one challenges his orders. All the officials race for the X-wings. Skylar throws a worried glance at me over her shoulder as she runs. But if she cared about my safety, she wouldn't be abandoning me. She wouldn't have pledged her loyalty to Charlie.

I look around the hangar. The dust makes my vision hazy—or maybe that's the pain in my arm—and I can't tell where the other rebels are. There might still be one more undamaged Davara jet we could fly, if it has fuel, but I'm not sure if it does. Beechy said the supply was almost nothing.

"Clementine!" a voice yells.

I turn toward the voice, toward the X-wing I flew in earlier. Lieutenant Dean is calling for me. He's helping Beechy and Uma lift Sandy into the ship. It's the only X-wing left unclaimed; the other officials must've found room in the others.

I hurry over to them, securing my grip on my gun with my left hand, while my right arm screams in pain. I don't understand. Why is Dean helping us?

Out of the corner of my eye, I notice Sam climbing into his ship. He's having trouble because of the wound I gave his leg, but another official helps him up. His X-wing's engine is already running. He will make it out of here before the bombs destroy the hangar, if anyone does.

I reach the X-wing where Dean and the others are. Beechy is

already in the pilot seat, and he's helping Uma hoist a barely conscious Sandy into the seat behind him.

"Careful, careful . . . ," he says. I've never seen him look so scared.

"Get on board," Dean says to me.

*BOOM!*

Another chunk of wall explodes, this one at the back of the hangar, behind the hovercraft Beechy and I flew to the moon. The spaceship will be buried beneath the mountain soon.

"What about the other rebels?" I ask. I don't know what happened to Fiona and the others.

"They're getting on one of the pods," Uma says as she presses something against Sandy's wound—a strip of cloth she tore off her safety uniform. "We transferred most of the fuel to one of them in case of an emergency. They'll have enough to make it outside, at least."

I suppose that's the best I can hope for. Tucking my gun into its holster, I climb up into the third seat of the X-wing. But every movement of my bleeding arm makes my head dizzy, and I nearly fall. Dean catches me from behind and boosts me up.

"Thanks," I mutter.

"Don't mention it," Dean says, climbing into the seat behind me.

"Why are you helping us?" I ask.

"Commander Charlie told me not to abandon his daughter, no matter what," he says stiffly. "I need to make sure she gets back to him safely. And get you all back to him, as well."

My hope falls away. He's just following orders.

But the way he refuses to meet my eyes makes me wonder if that's really the whole reason.

To my right, the other X-wings lift into the air, making for the entrance tunnel. Beechy buckles into his seat and starts our engine.

As the jet cover lowers overhead, I look at Sandy again. Abdominal gunshot wounds are hard to treat at the best of times, and she has another human being inside her whose life has also been affected. She's going to bleed to death and lose her baby if we can't get her to a doctor.

"Hold tight," Beechy says as he lifts our ship into the air. We speed toward the hangar exit, and the rebel flight pod follows.

I cradle my injured arm against my chest so it won't bump into anything, trying to focus on anything but the pain.

Another explosive goes off to our right, and then another.

BOOM!

BOOM!

BOOM!

The walls blow to pieces behind us, burying the entrance to the room where Logan trained every morning, and the bed where I dreamed of Oliver's death, and the mess where we ate age-old food out of cans. The booming noises fade as we speed through the tunnel, flying farther and farther away. Leaving a once safe place in smoky ruins.

The X-wings with Sam and Skylar and the others are too far ahead for me to see them. Part of me wants to catch up to them and attempt to shoot them down, but that would likely be a death sentence; we're still outnumbered. And killing Sam can't be our priority anymore, not until Sandy is no longer in danger of dying.

"What's our destination?" Uma asks, voicing my next thought aloud. "Sandy needs a surgeon, as soon as possible."

"There's a medical attendant on board the hovercraft," Dean

says. "We should rendezvous with the other X-wings and return to the Core."

Beechy doesn't say anything, but he tightens his grip on the flight controls. I'm sure he's thinking the same thing I am: Returning to the hovercraft means surrendering.

Surrender and we can return to the Core, where Charlie will put Sandy into the care of his best surgeons. Surrender and we might be able to save her.

But the rest of us? We will be prisoners in the Core. When Sam gives his mission report, Charlie isn't going to be happy with me. I shot Sam. I screwed up this mission, even if I didn't do it all on my own. Charlie promised me he would kill Logan if I didn't follow orders, and he will keep his word unless I find a way to stop him.

I will find a way. Charlie did everything in his power to control me, but he couldn't. He tried to turn me into a weapon for him, a mindless person who shoots without thinking, but he failed.

He made a soldier out of me, but I will no longer obey his orders.

$*$

As we approach the end of the northern entrance tunnel, there's a crackle in the comm inside my helmet.

Skylar's voice comes through the speaker, faint and full of static: "Beechy, do you copy?"

Anger flares inside me. I wish she'd been trapped back in the facility. It's her fault Sandy was hurt; she should've been the one hit by Buck's blaster.

"Yes, I copy," Beechy says tersely. "You can tell Sam we're prepared to surrender. Make sure he's ready to receive Sandy at the medical bay."

I reach to shut off my comm, not caring to hear Skylar's answer. Or anything she has to say ever again.

But she speaks before I can find the Off switch: "We—have—a—problem."

Her voice sounds higher pitched than usual, almost panicked, which makes me pause. Her words continue, but they're completely garbled by static and impossible to decipher.

Why is the comm signal cutting out? It was plenty strong when we flew through the tunnel before.

"Skylar, can you repeat that?" Dean asks.

White noise splinters through my ear-comm. Skylar can't hear us, or if she can, we can't hear her answer.

The tunnel exit isn't far ahead of us. I can't see any of the other X-wings. All I can see are the dark figures of swaying trees at the edge of the moonlit valley.

"What's going on?" Uma asks. She doesn't have a helmet and earpiece like the rest of us.

"We're having communication problems with the other X-wings," Beechy says, fiddling with the signal dial on the ship's control panel. "This is bird four. Does anyone copy?"

The crackle of static continues. There's no response from Skylar or Sam or any of the officials aboard the other X-wings.

I run my teeth along my lower lip, gripping my armrest with a sweaty hand. Years ago, I learned in school about flight communication and electromagnetic interference. Wireless comm transmitters usually face problems only if there's a power failure on a ship—if the backup as well as the main generator stops working—or if the comm transmitter is disrupted by a major electronic device in the vicinity. Usually a transmitter from another ship, running on a different radio frequency.

But the KIMO facility's radio transmitter went up in flames. There shouldn't be any other transmitters nearby.

An odd feeling trickles over the nape of my neck, like a croacher skittering across my skin. The tunnel walls have turned to mountain stone instead of steel, and the stream of water below us flows out into the night, where the stars are bright and twinkling.

Something isn't right.

As we soar through the tunnel exit, the sky expands through the window. My eyes slowly adjust to the light of the full moon rising over the mountains. There's nothing strange about the mountains, so I look higher, toward the acid shield and the stars.

Every muscle in my body goes rigid. There are dark figures beyond the acid shield, floating in Kiel's orbit. No bigger than meteorites, but there's more than one and they're hardly moving. They can't be falling space rock.

They must be battle stations. Enemy ships speckling the canvas of stars and darkness like they've made our sky their home. I count seventeen, but there could be more. It's hard to tell when they're so far away.

But they're closer than they seem if they're close enough to interfere with our comm system.

"It's the fleet," I say, but my voice cracks so much, it sounds like someone else's. We were supposed to have two more days to prepare, two more days to stop Charlie from going through with his plan and killing thousands of innocents.

Two more days. But we have none.

Someone's shouting inside the X-wing. Dean's telling Beechy to put us down near the hovercraft before we're seen.

I'm afraid it may be too late for that. As I stare out the window, dots of dark objects stream from the underbellies of the battle stations that crossed a billion miles of the universe to reach our home. Hundreds and hundreds of smaller ships come pouring out like a legion of predators and descend into Kiel's atmosphere through the acid shield.

We thought Commander Charlie was our biggest problem. Looking out the window at the fleet invading our sky, all that is forgotten.

The Mardenites are here for war.

# ACKNOWLEDGMENTS

First and foremost, I must acknowledge Alison, my agent extraordinaire, and Eileen, my awesome editor, for all the hard work they put into helping me bring this book to life. Much gratitude is also showered upon Kathy, Michelle, Bridget, Marie, Kerry, Eliani, James, and everyone else who is part of the fantastic team at St. Martin's.

To my parents: thanks for feeding me and letting me live at home so I could make my writing a priority.

To Elisabeth: thanks for reading the messy first draft of this book.

To Julianne: thanks for your daily intrusions into my writing cave. You always make me laugh. Sorry I usually kick you out.

To Jeric: thanks for those online conversations the summer of '13. You seriously got me through drafting this book (and dealing with the other dramas of life).

To the lovely ladies of the Class of 2k14: thank you for your encouraging emails and camaraderie.

To Matthew: I owe you a million bucks for all your advice and general willingness to deal with my freak-outs. But you'll have to settle for this acknowledgment.

And finally, to Jennifer: thank you for being my constant supporter and platonic soulmate. You are the Pippin to my Merry.

Oh, and a special shout-out to the Winchester bros and the angel in a trench coat, who also kept me sane.

STAY TUNED

DON'T MISS THE NEXT INSTALLMENT IN THE

EXTRACTION SERIES

# EVOLUTION

*Available Fall 2015*